Saving Sara

A Jamie Austen Thriller

TERRY TOLER

Saving Sara

Published by: BeHoldings, LLC

Cover and interior designs: BeHoldings Publishing
For information, address support@terrytoler.com
Editor: Jeanne Leach

Our books can be purchased in bulk for promotional, educational, and business use. Please contact your bookseller or the BeHoldings Publishing Sales department at: *sales@terrytoler.com*

For booking information email: booking@terrytoler.com.
First U.S. Edition: February, 2021

ISBN: 978-1-954710-00-9

OTHER BOOKS BY TERRY TOLER

Fiction

The Longest Day
The Reformation of Mars
The Late, Great Planet Jupiter
The Great Wall of Ven-Us
Saturn: The Eden Experiment
The Mercury Protocols
Save The Girls
The Ingenue
Saving Sara
Save The Queen
No Girl Left Behind
The Launch
The Blue Rose
Body Count
Save Me Twice
Cliff Hangers: Anna
Cliff Hangers: Mr. & Mrs. Platt
Cliff Hangers: The Quarterback
Cliff Hangers: Macy
Cliff Hangers: The Book Club

Non-Fiction

How to Make More Than a Million Dollars
The Heart Attacked
Seven Years of Promise
Mission Possible
Marriage Made in Heaven
21 Days to Physical Healing
21 Days to Spiritual Fitness
21 Days to Divine Health
21 Days to a Great Marriage
21 Days to Financial Freedom
21 Days to Sharing Your Faith
21 Days to Mission Possible

7 Days to Emotional Freedom
Uncommon Finances
Uncommon Health
Uncommon Marriage
The Jesus Diet
Suddenly Free
Feeling Free

For more information on these books and other resources visit terrytoler.com.

Thank you for purchasing this novel from best-selling author Terry Toler. As an additional thank you, Terry wants to give you a free gift.

Sign up for:

Updates
New Releases
Announcements

At terrytoler.com

We'll send you a copy of *The Book Club,* a Cliff Hangers mystery, free of charge.

PRAISE FOR SAVING SARA

I think people will really like this book. Lots of globe hopping, danger, surprise, intrigue, and gunfights.

Terry Toler comes up with storylines and plot lines that I don't think have ever been done before.

Every chapter left me wanting more. I couldn't wait for the next one.

Wow! What a book. As usual, the twists and turns kept my interest at a high level. Then the ending A usual Terry Toler cliffhanger.

I couldn't believe she jumped.

This book is like a Mission Impossible movie.

The readers are in for a roller-coaster ride.

I sure love Jamie Austen! She's one of the most real make-believe people I've ever met.

Saving Sara is destined to be another best seller for Terry Toler.

5.5 million girls under the age of eighteen are victims of human sex trafficking in the world.

1

Grand Cayman Island
Caribbean Sea

Sara was missing.

No one knew it yet. Except her abductors, of course.

How she got in that predicament was mostly a blur. Two hours ago... *Was it? Maybe it was three.* She had lost all sense of time. Sometime... earlier that night, she was hanging out with her friends at the *Reef Bar* on Seven Mile Beach. Just a normal seventeen-year-old girl, about to turn eighteen in two weeks, having fun.

They were in Cayman on a senior class trip. Over eighty seniors from the Calvary Christian Academy, in Plano, Texas made the outing. Tonight would be the last night. They'd fly home tomorrow. Sara almost didn't go to the bar, but her friends Michelle and Jessica talked her into it. They'd gone to Stingray City that afternoon, and the hours in the sun had zapped her energy.

Why can't I stand up straight?

Sara wanted to lie down on the beach and fall asleep.

Why am I on the beach? Where am I?

It seemed to her like she was at Rum Point. *Why do I think that?*

Her head throbbed. She told her hands to touch her head, but they didn't respond. Her knees suddenly felt weak again, and she fell to the ground facing the ocean. Three people struggled with a boat against the waves. The night had fallen, and the moon cast an eerie shadow over the scene. Sara tried to call out to the men to help her, but she couldn't speak. She tried to stand but didn't have the strength.

What happened to me?

The bar was packed, she remembered. They danced. Boys offered to buy her drinks. Sara was too young to drink, so she ordered non-alcoholic rum runners. Loud music and lots of lights created a psychedelic array of sight and sound. She danced with two or three guys. Mostly with her girlfriends. Then her friends left her. They went and sat down at a table with two other boys they met.

She wanted to leave and go back to the hotel, so she made the decision to search for her friends to tell them. A strange sensation came over her as soon as she sat her drink down on the table. The room started to spin around in circles. So she wouldn't fall, she put her hands out to grab onto something and was relieved when she made contact with the table and steadied herself. All sense of balance left. An athlete, she played basketball, volleyball, and ran track at school. Lettered three straight years. Yet, all her strength was gone. She tried to walk but staggered like a drunk.

I'm not drunk.

She would've fallen... But... An arm steadied her.

A strong arm. A man's arm. Someone who was older than she. He had a vice grip on her forearm.

"Thank you," Sara said to him. "I don't feel well."

The man started to walk her out of the bar. She tried to resist. The grip on her forearm hurt her.

"No. I have to find my friends." She said the words but that wasn't how they sounded in her ears. Her speech was slurred. Her lips were numb.

When they came out of the bar, the bright lights of the parking lot temporarily blinded her. All she could see were the spots from the different lampposts.

She remembered a car. The back door was open, and she was shoved into the backseat.

"I can't," she resisted. "I have to go to my hotel. We leave tomorrow."

She went in and out of consciousness and didn't know how long they drove around. When the car stopped, she saw a sign for Rum Point.

That's why I thought I was at Rum Point.

Now, she laid on the beach. Sara heard music in the distance. She strained to lift her head off the sand and in the direction the sound was coming from. Off at a distance people milled around the restaurant at Rum Point. She tried to call out for help but could only manage a weak and faint whisper. They were too far away.

I'm so thirsty.

Sara willed her body to stand back up, but her muscles didn't respond. Waves of nausea came over her. With no strength left in her body, she laid her head back down on the sand. The cool breeze off the ocean provided some comfort.

One of the men from the boat walked toward her.

Good. He'll help me.

He lifted Sara to her feet. They were face to face. She recognized him from the bar. He had a black bag in his hand.

"What are you doing?" she asked him. Or at least she thought she did. When he didn't respond, she wasn't sure.

Everything suddenly went dark as he put the bag over her head.

Why was she not afraid? All emotion and fear left her like she was a zombie. She had a sense something bad was happening. Everything inside told her to scream. She tried, but it sounded more like a muted shriek like a mouse stuck in a trap.

The man led her toward the boat. She tried to put up a fight and hit him several times on his shoulder. The blows were only glancing and didn't faze him at all.

The waves beat against the side of the boat. The man lifted her over his shoulder and waded into the water. He wobbled like he was having trouble steadying himself against the waves to not drop her. She felt him lay her down in the boat. Roughly. Her elbow scraped against one of the seats. She let out a yelp.

For the first time, she started to cry.

What are you doing to me?

Then she felt a needle in her arm. A pin prick. The liquid burned as it entered her body. Seconds later, she felt herself convulse.

The engine motor revved. The mixture of gasoline, oil, and smoke from the loud engine made her cough. She felt the waves bounce the boat as it sped away from the shore.

The last thing she thought of were her parents, teachers, and friends.

They don't know where I am.

Then everything went black.

2

Grand Cayman Sandy Beach Resort

The Next Morning

The lobby of the Sandy Beach Resort was abuzz with a flurry of activity as the senior class of Calvary Christian Academy congregated by the massive, two-story, towering photo of the stingrays that took up one entire wall. Two buses waited in front of the hotel to take them to the airport and their bags were being loaded at that moment.

Hal Jolly, the Dean of Students and Activities Director, wouldn't allow himself a moment to relax until the kids were on the plane, back on US soil, and with their parents and no longer his responsibility. Other than one boy who was stung by a jellyfish and a few who didn't use enough sunblock, the trip had gone surprisingly well. Not as good as some, but better than most.

This was his fifteenth year to take the students on a senior trip. The first outside the United States. Considering how well it went, he might authorize another one.

A number of them broke curfew, which was to be expected. One couple was alone in the boy's room, which was against the rules, but a chaperone caught them before it went too far. In fact, they only seemed to be hanging out. Mr. Jolly suspected that a few of the kids went to the local bars at night when they said they were going to the beach or to shop. Most of them were over eighteen, so it wasn't illegal to drink alcohol in Cayman, although against the code of conduct for the school.

As long as no one was arrested, dead, or dying, Mr. Jolly counted his blessings. Kids would be kids. He tried to give them some leeway. They had earned it. This was their senior trip. They worked hard, earned their diplomas, and were entitled to let their hair down a little without him following them around with a judgmental thumb monitoring every little thing they did. For a student to go on the trip, he or she had to maintain an average above 3.0. Most in the senior class did, just for the privilege of going on the trip which had become a school tradition. This was their reward for a job well done, and Mr. Jolly wasn't going to ruin it for them.

Some parents wouldn't understand that sentiment and expected more from him. In his opinion, most of those kids were going off to college in a few short months, anyway. At college, they would have a lot more freedom to do whatever they wanted away from the watchful eyes of their parents. If the parents hadn't taught them the necessary values by that point, then they shouldn't expect him to, on a one-week, senior trip.

He was genuinely pleased with how well this trip had gone, and it was time to send them off with a short speech. "Listen up," Mr. Jolly said, trying to be heard above the din.

He shouted the same thing a little louder and waved his clipboard in the air to get their attention. The clipboard had a list of every student and their contact information back home along with the schedule, and a sheet for each head count. They'd do a final count on the bus and then on the plane, and that would be all. After that, the kids would be home and on their own.

A few people heard him and shushed the others in the group. Finally, one of the chaperones whistled loudly, and the area suddenly grew quiet.

"Did everyone have a good time?" Mr. Jolly shouted, as he realized that was the wrong thing to say when the group erupted in a cheer, and the loud conversations started up again.

Another loud bird whistle finally got the students' attention again and also the glares of a few people in the lobby including the manager of the hotel who stood off to the side. This time the dean would be careful not to say something that would lose their undivided attention.

"We are ready to load the buses, so be sure to go to the bathroom before we load. You won't get another chance until we get through security at the airport," he said.

He paused for a moment to let that sink in.

Then he added. "Girls are in the first bus. Boys are in the second."

A groan went through the crowd. Anything he said was going to get a response. Exasperated, Mr. Jolly raised his hands and waved them up and down to quiet the crowd.

"I think you'll survive the short bus ride to the airport in separate buses," Mr. Jolly said jokingly.

The kids laughed more than should be expected, considering the joke was from the Dean of Students. He got them quieted again. "You've had a whole week to be together, and you'll have all summer to see each other. Soon, you'll be free of me forever."

When there was no response, he moved on.

"Seriously. I want to commend each of you for the way you represented the Eagle family this week." The Eagles was the name of the team mascot.

"Thank you, Mr. Jolly," one of the student's yelled out.

"You're the best," another one shouted.

The students gave him a round of applause, which warmed his heart. As far as he could tell, he really was popular among the student body.

"Thank you," he said. "Let's go home. Everybody, make your way to the buses now."

The room erupted into an almost deafening sound as the students shuffled toward the front entrance.

"Remember," Mr. Jolly added, "Girls on the first bus. . . boys on the second."

No one listened to him, so he just looked at one of his chaperones and shrugged. Most of the monitors had already moved into position to manage the loading of the buses.

He wished the students would exit more quietly, but he couldn't do anything about it. Several people in the lobby and some in the registration line probably were breathing a sigh of relief that the kids were leaving.

A few complaints were raised from other people staying at the hotel. Not surprisingly to Mr. Jolly, more of them came from the girl's floor than the boys. His experience had been that girls got into more trouble when it came to minor offenses. The boys tended to commit the more serious violations. This group did better than most, and the violations—both minor and major—were few and far between.

The kids loaded the buses fairly quickly. Mr. Jolly got on the boys' bus and oversaw the count.

"There are thirty-seven boys on board," one of the chaperones said.

The number was correct. His clipboard had each of the regimented head counts on the sheet. As a former drill sergeant in the army, he liked to run things with military precision, even if the kids didn't always cooperate. He'd also mellowed some during the years, but he didn't slack on procedures when it came to the kids' safety.

He got off the boy's bus and walked over to the girls' bus and boarded it. One of the chaperones was already counting.

Jessica was sitting on the fourth row and had her hand raised.

"Yes, Jessica. Do you need something?" Mr. Jolly asked.

"Sara isn't on the bus," she said meekly. "She's missing. No one's seen her since last night."

A bolt of panic shot through Mr. Jolly like an electrical current.

3

"What do you mean Sara is missing?" Mr. Jolly asked as he looked around the bus. One of the students, Jessica Raleigh had just given him information that shook him to his core.

"She didn't come home last night," Michelle, a girl who sat next to Jessica said.

Mr. Jolly flipped through the papers on his clipboard. Last night's bed check showed Sara was in her room at eleven. The curfew was ten, but they extended it to eleven on the last night because the kids had been so good.

What he saw on the clipboard confused him. Mrs. Simpson conducted the bed check and signed off on the sheet, saying it was accurate. Mr. Jolly also knew Michelle was Sara's roommate. She would obviously know if Sara slept in their room last night.

A scan of the bus confirmed Sara was not on it. Further confirmation came when the chaperone said, "I only count fifty girls. There should be fifty-one. One is missing."

Michelle began to cry.

"This bed check says Sara was in her room last night at eleven," Mr. Jolly said to Michelle with urgency in his voice. "So were you. Why would Mrs. Simpson say she was there if she wasn't?"

Michelle had trouble getting the words out between the tears. Mr. Jolly couldn't understand what she said.

"Calm down, Michelle," Mr. Jolly said in a calmer tone. "Take a deep breath. I need you to tell me what happened."

"I thought Sara spent the night in Jessica's room," Michelle said. "She stayed there the night before."

Mr. Jolly knew Sara and Jessica were inseparable. They wanted to room together, but the rooms were already assigned. He didn't let them switch, thinking it would be good for the girls to form new relationships. Something he now regretted.

"Mrs. Simpson marked that she was in your room!" Mr. Jolly said, his voice raised further.

"I told Mrs. Simpson that Sara was in Jessica's room," Michelle answered. "That's what I thought. I saw Jessica this morning at breakfast, and she said Sara didn't spend the night with her. I'm sorry. I didn't know."

"Why didn't you tell me?" Mr. Jolly said with exasperation. "Never mind!"

He'd learned in the army that in a crisis, second guessing actions that couldn't be undone was unproductive. He flipped through the papers again. The bed check for Jessica's room was done by Mrs. Ballard. She only marked two in the room. The day before, she marked three and made a note that Sara was there. That confirmed what Michelle said.

"When was the last time you saw Sara?" Mr. Jolly asked the girls.

Jessica hesitated and looked at Michelle. The girls were hiding something. "Last night," Jessica said weakly.

"Be more specific," Mr. Jolly insisted. They were wasting time. He'd allowed for an extra hour on the drive to the airport to give themselves additional time just in case something came up. They didn't have to leave immediately but should soon. He wanted answers and wanted them now.

"Me, Michelle, and Sara went to the Reef Bar," Jessica said. "After dinner."

"But we didn't do anything bad," Michelle said. "I swear it. We just danced a little."

Now was not the time to confront them about going to the club without a chaperone, which was against the rules. "Did Sara come back with you?" Mr. Jolly asked.

"No," Jessica said. "She left early. We thought she came back to the hotel. I thought Sara was in her room. Michelle thought she was with me."

"Are Sara's things still in her room?" Mr. Jolly asked.

"Sara packed them before we went out last night," Michelle said, tears rolling down her cheeks. "You know how she is. She didn't want to wait until this morning. Well... She didn't pack everything. Not her bathroom stuff. I packed those for her this morning and brought her bags down with mine."

Mr. Jolly paused to think for a minute, unsure what to do next. The bus was eerily quiet. That's what he needed to do next. Ask if anyone else on the bus knew anything. Mr. Jolly shouted out, "Has anyone here seen Sara Morgan? Last night or this morning."

No one answered for several seconds. Finally, someone said, "I saw her at dinner last night."

"I know that," Mr. Jolly said. "After that. Did anyone see her? Was she at breakfast?"

Most of the people on the bus shook their heads no. Mr. Jolly got off of the bus, not wanting to waste any more time with follow-up questions.

The chaperones stood around talking. One of them saw him get off the bus and called out, "Are we ready to go, now?"

Mr. Jolly ignored the person and walked directly to the boys' bus. "Listen up," he said. When the boys didn't quiet down immediately, he shouted, "Shut up! This is important." He could fall back on his drill sergeant voice when he needed to.

"Has anyone seen Sara Morgan?" he said loudly, and with a sense of urgency, so the boys knew he meant business.

No one responded. Sara often hung out with Jason Reilley who sat toward the back. "Jason, have you seen Sara?" Mr. Jolly asked.

"I saw her yesterday at Stingray City. And last night at dinner."

"I saw her with Michelle and Jessica last night after dinner," another boy said. "They walked down the sidewalk on the beach. I don't know where they went."

"Did any of you see Sara at the Reef Bar?"

No one answered. Mr. Jolly didn't ask a follow-up question. The boys didn't know anything. He walked out of the bus and called the chaperones to huddle close to him. "We have a child missing," he said soberly. "Sara Morgan didn't come back to the hotel last night."

A murmur went up among the chaperones.

Mr. Jolly quieted them and then continued, "I need two of you to stay here with me. The rest of you get the kids to the airport and on the plane."

He handed the clipboard to Alan McKenry. "You're in charge now. Make sure everyone is accounted for. Julie, you and Ray follow me."

"I want to stay," Pat Skyler said. She was Sara's teacher and academic advisor. That sounded like a good idea. She knew Sara as well as anyone.

"Okay. Julie you go with the others. Get Sara's bags off the bus. Ray and Pat, follow me."

Once in the lobby, Mr. Jolly explained to them what had happened. "Pat. Go to the front desk and get a key to Sara's room. See if you can find her or anything that might help us know where she is."

Pat turned and walked briskly toward the front desk.

"Ray. Go find the manager. I'm calling the police."

4

The cream-and salmon-colored Royal Cayman Police Service headquarters with sea blue highlights, was as laid back on the inside as it looked on the outside. The biggest issue they had to deal with at the moment was monitoring the sea turtle nesting sites which began on May first.

Commissioner of Police, Collin Hughes, sat at his desk and worked on the Summary Interim Crime Report he had to prepare and release quarterly to the board and to the general public, which dealt with more serious issues on Cayman than turtle nests.

The preliminary report was unremarkable. One murder so far that year. An eleven-percent reduction in the number of sexual crimes. A total of ten. Nine firearm crimesfour robberies, two threats to kill, and two attempted murders, along with the one actual murder related to a domestic violence dispute.

Overall, a good report.

He smiled. A twenty-one percent decrease in acquisitive crime. This had been the emphasis of his tenure as commissioner ever since he was hired. These were petty crimes primarily against tourists. Pickpocketing, muggings, theft from hotel rooms, financial scams. He promised to clean them up in his job interview and had been successful. They had seen a decrease in those crimes every year since he was hired three years ago.

Sixty-thousand people lived on the island. More than two-million tourists traveled to Cayman every year. That's why he focused on tourist crimes. The economy wouldn't survive without tourism. Petty offenses led to more violent crimes. Violent crimes drove tourists away.

What kept him up at night was the possibility of a tourist being murdered on the island or a kidnapping or an abduction. Other islands had seen an uptick in young girls disappearing. One girl from Great Britain disappeared on a trip with her family two summers ago on a neighboring island. Her body was later found buried in a shallow grave on the Dutch side of St. Maarten. The killer was never found. That led to a call for a boycott of that island by a London newspaper.

Cayman, being a British territory, benefited in that a lot of tourists from England, Scotland, and Wales chose to travel there instead of the boycotted island. Other countries followed suit, although tourism eventually rebounded on that island. His role was to do everything within his power to prevent it from happening at Cayman and suffering a similar fate.

That's why when the call came in to dispatch that a young girl was missing from the Sandy Beach Hotel on Seven Mile Beach, he said he would take the call himself. The man on the other line said a seventeen-year-old girl didn't come back to the hotel the night before. The girl was from Texas.

His worst nightmare.

The drive to the hotel from the headquarters wasn't long but was enough time for Collin to feel his blood pressure rise. Something the doctor warned him about. He left his position as Chief Inspector of the police department in Derby, England, and moved to Grand Cayman for what he thought would be a less stressful life. A nagging feeling inside said that decision was about to be tested.

He arrived at the hotel and parked in the parking lot rather than in the drop off area at the entrance. A police vehicle in front of the hotel might spook the guests. He walked into the lobby and looked around. The ones who made the call weren't hard to miss. The stress was all over their faces.

This wasn't good. He could feel fear rise inside of him.

One member of the group saw him enter the lobby, stood, and motioned for him to come over to them. They sat in a circle in the lobby chairs. Three of them. Two men and one woman. Well dressed. The woman had a huge diamond wedding ring on her finger. One of the men had on an expensive polo shirt, shorts, and shoes with no socks. They clearly came from an affluent part of Texas.

Stay calm. Reassuring. Cooperative.

People tended to panic in these situations. Understandably. Police forces leaned toward downplaying them. Standard operating procedure was to wait forty-eight hours before doing anything. Most missing people returned in that period of time. Forty-eight hours was the most critical time. After two days, if the person hadn't returned, the outcome was usually not good.

Police investigators were roundly criticized if they waited too long to act. He wouldn't make that mistake even if standard operating procedure said to do so. If the girl returned in the forty-eight hours unharmed, then all he did was waste some of his and his department's time. They weren't doing anything else as important as this.

If she really had run into foul play, he would be on it immediately. Time was of the essence. The island was small, and they would not leave any stone unturned until they found her. A plan was already formulating in his mind to marshal his entire force and begin a search. He'd oversee the investigation personally. First, he needed information.

Starting now.

He approached them with a calm, assertive, and authoritative manner as he held out his hand and introduced himself. "My name is Collin Hughes. I'm the commissioner of the police department. My department and I are at your service. Tell me your names and what you know."

He pulled out a notebook and sat down in the fourth chair of the circle.

"My name is Hal Jolly," one of the men said, his voice cracking. "I'm the Dean of Students for a Christian school in Texas. We're here on a senior class trip. One of our girls, Sara Morgan, didn't come back to the hotel tonight. No one has seen her since last night."

He wrote down the name Sara Morgan in his notebook. "What time last night was she last seen?"

"Around ten."

Commissioner Hughes looked at his watch. The last time anyone saw her was twelve hours ago. He clasped his hands together to keep them from shaking. He only had thirty-six more hours to go.

5

He didn't have much to go on.

Commissioner Hughes sat in the lobby of the Sandy Beach Resort and interviewed the three people from the school group from Texas. He wrote down their names. Hal Jolly was the Dean of Students. Ray Lancaster was a chaperone and parent of one of the other kids, and Pat Skyler was one of Sara's teachers. She seemed to have the closest relationship with Sara and was the most distraught.

"Sara Morgan went to the Reef Bar with her friends, Michelle Baxter and Jessica Gardner," Mr. Jolly explained. "At around ten, they separated. Michelle and Jessica went to another table to talk to some other boys and left Sara alone. That's the last they saw of her."

"Were any other members of your group at the bar that night?" Commissioner Hughes asked.

"Not that I know of," Mr. Jolly said. "I asked, but no one said they were there. By that time most of the kids were back in the hotel. Curfew was at eleven, and they had to pack for the flight this morning."

At the beginning of an investigation, everyone was a suspect. The commissioner had been doing this for a long time and was a good judge of character. He felt certain he could rule out the three who sat in front of him from having anything to do with her disappearance. They also had little information. He didn't waste too much time interrogating them. The best use of his time would be to find security tapes at the hotel and at the bar.

"Do you have a picture of Sara?" the commissioner asked. It wouldn't do any good to look at tapes if he didn't know who he was looking for.

"I'll find one," Mrs. Skyler said. She took her phone out of her purse and scrolled through it.

"Can I at least get a description?"

"She's about five foot seven," Mr. Jolly said. "I'm not good at guessing a woman's weight."

Pat looked up from her phone and said, "Five ten. One fifty or so. Sara's an athlete. She's tall and thin, but strong and muscular in a feminine but athletic sort of way. I don't know if I'm making sense or not."

The woman rubbed her eyes with her free hand. Commissioner Hughes could tell she struggled to fight back the tears.

"Can you give me some more detail?" the commissioner asked. "Physical characteristics? Color of hair? Color of her eyes? Did she have any distinguishing marks? Tattoos? Birthmarks? Scars? Piercings?"

"She didn't have any tattoos," Mr. Jolly said with a nervous chuckle. "Her dad would kill her if she came home with a tattoo. No piercings either other than her ears. Piercings and tattoos aren't allowed at our school. It's a Christian school."

Commissioner Hughes nodded and waited for them to get more specific in their descriptions. When Mr. Jolly didn't say anything right away, he turned and looked at Mrs. Skyler. She would probably be able to be more specific since she knew Sara better than the others, and from his experience, women tended to be more perceptive when it came to those types of things.

When she turned her phone so it faced him, he could see for himself what Sara looked like. A picture of a young woman appeared on the screen. It looked like a school picture. A head shot from the shoulders up.

Sara had blonde hair. It looked to be naturally blond. Well styled. She had hazel eyes. Natural beauty. Fresh face. Not like a model, but like a girl next door. The type of girl that would get noticed at a bar, but not knock down gorgeous to where she would be flooded with attention.

The commissioner could see where she might get washed out in a bar setting. Not noticed by most, but pretty enough to draw the attention of a predator.

Sara also had a look of innocence. Her smile was friendly and inviting—in a trusting sort of way. He could detect a hint of insecurity in her eyes, and by the way she held her mouth. As if she didn't relish the attention. That's probably why she got separated from her friends. Her trusting nature might've gotten her in harm's way before she realized it.

"Did you see her with any strangers on this trip?" the commissioner asked.

The three looked at each other. Not in a suspicious way like they tried to hide something but in a curious manner. They each shook their heads no.

"Did you see any strangers hanging around the group at all?" he clarified the question.

"I didn't see anybody," Mr. Jolly said. "And I was looking. These kids are my responsibility. While I couldn't be with them all the time, I did keep my eye out."

"Were you in the armed services?" the commissioner asked Mr. Jolly.

"Army. Sergeant. 29th Infantry Division, and then I was at Fort Hood as a drill instructor. Until I retired and took this job."

The commissioner pretended to write, but he was really thinking. He reached in his pocket and pulled out a stick of gum. It helped calm his nerves. He offered the others a piece, but they all declined.

"Did Sara have any emotional problems?" he asked. They each shook their heads no, almost before he finished asking the question.

He fired off more questions. "Have you ever seen any erratic behavior? Did she ever seem depressed? Anxious?"

"Sara is a very well-adjusted child," Mr. Jolly said. "She's a good student. With a lot of friends."

"Any boyfriend troubles? Was she dating any of the boys on the trip?"

"I don't think Sara has ever had a serious boyfriend," Mrs. Skyler said.

"How was her homelife? Were her parents divorced? Any signs of physical abuse?"

"No! Nothing at all," Mr. Jolly said. "She comes from a good home. Her parents are active in church. They don't have any financial troubles."

"Any chance Sara ran away?" the commissioner already knew the answer but had to ask. He had to cover all the bases. These were the nuts and bolts of detective work. Ask all the right questions, even as tedious as they were. Even if he already knew the answer.

"There was one thing," Mrs. Skyler said. Then she waved her hand dismissively. "It's probably nothing."

"Tell me anyway," the commissioner said.

Mrs. Skyler lowered her voice and spoke in a slow and seemingly reluctant tone. "One day, earlier in the semester, I noticed a bruise on Sara's arm. I asked her about it. For some reason, she was mad at her dad that day but wouldn't say why."

The commissioner sat up in his chair as something in his brain fired an alert which drew his attention to what she had said. "What did she say when you asked her how she got the bruise?" the commissioner asked.

"She said she got it playing volleyball," she said pensively. "It seemed weird to me. Like an odd place to have a bruise. How do you get a bruise from playing volleyball?"

"Had you ever seen a bruise on her arm before?" the commissioner asked.

"No. And I haven't seen one since. But she seemed sad that day. Like something was wrong."

"Thank you all very much for your information. Mrs. Skyler. Please email me that picture. Also text it to my phone." He gave her the email address and number.

They all stood like the meeting was over.

"Where is the group right now?" the commissioner asked as he looked around the lobby.

"They are at the airport getting ready to board a flight back home," Mr. Jolly said.

"They can't leave the island!" the commissioner said abruptly. "We need to question them."

"I don't think that's a good idea," Mr. Jolly said hesitantly, but forcefully. "These kids need to get back home. I don't want to hinder the investigation, but I don't think any of them know anything. The fallout is going to be bad enough. If you detain the kids here on the island, there are going to be a lot of unhappy parents."

The commissioner put his hand to his chin. Mr. Jolly had a point. They needed to keep this as low-key as possible for now. Besides, he had no probable cause to detain them.

"What time does the flight leave?" he asked.

Mr. Jolly looked at his watch. "In about two hours."

Not enough time for him to go to the airport. Commissioner Hughes looked at his notes. He really wanted to talk to Michelle and Jessica. Those were two friends who were with her that night and presumably the last people to see her before she went missing. More than anything else he wanted to see the security footage from the *Reef Bar* as soon as possible.

"I'm going to send a detective, Gray Gleeson, to the airport," Commissioner Hughes said. "Make Michelle and Jessica available to talk to him. There's still time for them to make their flights. Let's do it discreetly, so we don't alarm the other kids."

"I'm on it," Mr. Jolly said as he pulled his phone out of his pocket.

"Mrs. Skyler, would you mind coming with me?" the commissioner asked.

"Not at all. I want to help anyway I can. Where are we going?"

"I want to look at the security footage at the *Reef Bar*. I think you would be helpful in identifying Sara and can also tell me what you see in her demeanor and behavior. You seem to know her as well as anyone."

"Of course, I will."

"One final thing," the commissioner said.

"What's that?" Mr. Jolly asked.

"Has anyone told the parents?"

Mr. Jolly's head and shoulders noticeably sagged. "I haven't, but I was going to do that right after I arranged for Michelle and Jessica to meet your detective."

"Thank you. Call them right away. They need to know what's going on."

6

Team Luke's MMA Gym
Dumfries, Virginia

Jamie Austen hit the heavy bag so hard with a roundhouse kick that the sound erupted through the entire gym like a thunderclap. So much so that several people in the gym stopped what they were doing and looked her way. Jamie ignored them and kept pounding the bag, alternating between strikes with her fists and elbows and kicks with the top of her foot and shins.

Luke O'Brien, the owner of the gym, walked over to her and said, "Are you pretending that bag is Alex?"

Alex Halee was her fiancé.

"No. We're good. Just trying to get a good workout in."

Luke got Jamie interested in martial arts and self-defense years ago, when she was still in high school. After she joined the CIA, Luke told Jamie she could train in his gym anytime for free. She took him up on the offer and trained there at least two or three times a month when she wasn't on a mission.

"Tension at work?" he asked.

Jamie stopped pounding on the bag, wiped sweat off of her brow and took a swig of water that sat on the bench beside her workout gear. "Not really. Everything's good. Things are getting more dangerous out there, though. I've got to keep my skills sharp."

That was true. Jamie worked as an operative in the sex-trafficking division of the CIA. She was often called upon to go into some of the seediest places around the world and rescue girls being held as sex slaves. Lately, there hadn't been a mission where there wasn't some kind of confrontation. More often than not, Jamie ended up in a life and death situation where she had to use her hand-to-hand combat skills to get out of it.

"Thanks for letting me use the gym," she said. "I love it here."

Luke looked up and scanned the area. The gym was a little over three thousand square feet. Small and compact. A big octagon stood in the center, surrounded by various stations. More than twenty MMA fighters and their trainers were in the gym at that time. Team Luke's had the reputation as one of the best gyms in the country for training MMA fighters.

"Do you want some real action?" Luke asked, as he pointed over to the octagon.

"What do you mean?" Jamie asked.

"Frankie needs a sparring partner."

He had referred to Frankie "the Assassin" Ortega. Jamie hated the man's name since she faced assassins in real life. She'd heard that Ortega was preparing for a title bout in the UFC. Bantamweight if she remembered right.

"Oh... I don't think so. He's like the tenth best fighter in the world in his division."

"Third best in the world," Luke corrected. "Come on. It's just sparring... Although, he does take things pretty seriously. That's why we can't get anyone to spar with him. The guy is a little crazy."

"I think you're all a little crazy. You'd have to be to do what you do."

"Spoken by the lady who kills terrorists for a living. You're way crazier than us. I'll referee, and I can stop the fight at any time. That's probably a good idea since your fights aren't over until someone is dead or dying."

"What are the rules of engagement?" Jamie asked, ignoring his comment.

Luke let out a laugh. "This isn't a mission. You just spar and grapple. You'll wear protective headgear. Pull your punches. Don't lock in a submission hold. And above all else don't hurt him. He's got a big payday coming in a couple of days."

"What about me? I don't want him to hurt me."

"I think you can hold your own against him. You were trained by the best."

He was referring to himself. Luke did train her, but her real training came from a man named Curly. He taught her most of what she knew. What Luke taught her gave her a good foundation to build from, but Curly took it to a lethal level. Curly had said she was as good as anyone in the world, male or female.

The offer was tempting. She often wondered how she would fare in an actual MMA fight. She also thought it'd be against a girl, not the number three male bantamweight in the world. Still, Jamie was competitive. That's why she loved this gym. The intensity in the air was what drew her there. Every fighter went all out all the time to improve his skills.

"Okay. I'll do it," she said reluctantly.

I hope I don't regret it.

***

Frankie Ortega had a crazy look on his face. His eyes were glazed like someone who'd been hit in the head too many times. He paced back and forth in his corner like a caged tiger.

Jamie didn't remember the last time she was that nervous.

She was also a little ticked off. At first, Frankie had refused to spar with her. "I ain't fightin' no girl," he said in a south Philly brogue.

She made it worse when she bantered jokingly, "Are you afraid of me?"

For a minute, she thought he was going to attack her right then and there and not wait for the bell.

This is crazy!

Luke barked out instructions and sent each of them to their corners. Then he signaled the timekeeper and motioned for them to begin. Five three-minute rounds.

Frankie charged Jamie like a bull let out of a pen. He threw a wild roundhouse "Haymaker" that Jamie easily ducked under, but the sudden pressure put her on her heels, as she parried his attacks and backed away. She needed to calm her nerves and concentrate. Frankie's footwork had him moving constantly back and forth. He had a good guard and quick head movement. It seemed like he wouldn't be easy to hit.

Everyone is easy to hit, if you're patient, Jamie heard Curly say in her head.

She was already breathing hard. If she didn't calm herself, she'd run out of steam fast even though she was in excellent physical conditioning. A deep breath and a quick exhale did the trick and the energy pulsated through her and overrode the fear.

Frankie let loose a low round kick with his right leg that sent a loud smack through the gym when it connected on her left thigh. The kick stung. That really got her attention.

"I thought we were pulling punches," Jamie said, but no one seemed to hear her. Frankie was back on the prowl and spitting out expletives that were distracting, so she didn't have time to repeat it.

Jamie could feel a welt grow on her leg. Probably bright red from the kick. She refused to limp to let him know he'd hurt her.

Frankie loaded up for another kick. This time he was aiming for her head, but Jamie was ready. She easily dodged it, then lowered her body and spun around like a breakdancer on one leg and swept Frankie's back leg out from under him, which caused him to fall to the canvas.

That felt good.

Landing flat on his back infuriated Frankie. A crowd had gathered around the octagon to watch. They laughed when Jamie sent Frankie sprawling to the ground. When he got to his feet, he didn't bother with the kicks, he just charged her with his head down. He was careless. A good fighter could take him out if he knew what he was doing.

Which she did.

If it had been a real fight, she would've let him charge in with his head down and then planted a knee right in his face. They were just

want their job, ten more girls were in line to take their places. As much as Jamie would love to make a dent in that business, she wouldn't get any help from the local authorities. They counted on the girls to attract tourists to their city and would fight as hard against her efforts as the business owners. Most of the girls would be offended by her efforts as well.

"You're on the wrong continent," Alex said, and confirmed what she already guessed. She rarely went to Europe.

"Malaysia,"

"Wrong continent."

That already eliminated three, and he would never send her to Africa. She wouldn't blend in enough to the surroundings to be an effective spy. That only left closer to home. By process of elimination, she had narrowed it down to South America.

"Columbia," Jamie said, confident she was on the right continent although hoping she had guessed the wrong place. She hated to go places where drug lords ran things. It made her job that much more dangerous.

"Warmer, but still cold," Brad said. "I'll tell you because you'll never guess."

Jamie shifted her position in her seat. She was going to Mexico or Central America. Maybe even an island in the Caribbean if she was lucky. There were so many possibilities it wasn't worth trying to guess. She was as ready for the game to be over as Brad apparently was as well.

"Brownsville, Texas," Brad said.

Jamie's mouth flew open. CIA operatives weren't allowed to conduct operations in the United States. Their responsibility was to collect foreign intelligence. Inside the US, the FBI was the authorized law enforcement agency.

Jamie asked, "What's in Brownsville?"

"A high school girl from San Antonio is missing. Maria Victoria Delgado. She goes by Vicki. They were on a senior class trip to Brownsville."

A picture of a girl appeared on the screen after Brad fired up his computer. The girl was cute. Hispanic. Brown hair. Brown eyes. Innocent smile.

"Why am I involved?" Jamie asked. She didn't have to remind Brad that she wasn't legally allowed to operate in the US.

"I'm getting to that."

Another image appeared on the screen. Grainier. It appeared to be a picture from a security camera. A girl was in the backseat of a large SUV. It looked like Vicki. The only thing Jamie could see was her head that appeared in the back window.

"This image was taken at the border into Mexico," Brad added.

Jamie nodded. She now understood why she was involved. The girl was likely taken to be sold into sex slavery in Mexico. Her stare was fixed on the girl. Jamie liked to sear the image of the girls into her mind.

Still more questions swirled. This was something the FBI could handle. It seemed strange Brad would send her after one girl.

As if he sensed Jamie's unease, Brad said, "There's more than one girl. There are four girls missing!"

8

"Four girls are missing?" Jamie asked, as she didn't understand the full picture.

"It could be a coincidence, but it seems to be coordinated," Brad said as he typed something else into his laptop. Four pictures appeared on the screen, including the picture of Vicki.

"There are four missing Hispanic girls," Brad explained. "All of them are from South Texas high schools. They were all on a class trip. One of the girls went missing inside the United States. Three were in Mexicoone in Cancun, one in Boca Del Rio, and one in Tampico. All the girls were in a bar late at night. Then they just disappeared."

Brad shoved some files in Jamie's direction. She opened one and scrolled through it. When she finished the one, she opened the other three. Brad didn't say anything while she reviewed the documents. Each contained information on a girl. Name. Picture. Description. Background information. The first thing she noticed was how little information was actually in the files.

There was little to no eyewitness information. The first thing Jamie thought of was security footage. Each bar must have some videos of the front entrances at least. If they existed, no references to them were in the files.

"Any security footage?" Jamie asked.

Brad shrugged. "There probably is, but we don't have it."

Jamie let out a huge sigh. Loud enough for Brad to know she didn't feel confident about what he'd asked her to do. In most missions, she had a fixed target. A brothel or establishment where the girls were being held. Jamie often had to do investigative work, but most of the girls and the sex rings were easy to find. Following the money trail and finding who was behind them was harder, but Jamie mostly focused on getting the girls out of their horrendous situation. This was a new type of mission for her. It seemed like someone with a lot more experience in investigations would be better suited.

If she had a way to contact Alex, she'd have him find the security footage if it existed. Alex was in the cybercrime's division of the CIA. He was one of the best in the world, if not the best, at hacking into systems. With access to the CIA and NSA systems, he could find almost anything. At least that would give her something to go on.

Cell phone records also came to mind. A cell phone let off a distinguishable ping when it came into range of a cell tower. If these girl's phones were on, they could be tracked. That could take local law enforcement in Mexico days to discover... if they even bothered. Alex could find out that information in a matter of minutes. Off the record, of course, since they weren't allowed to officially hack into those records.

The files made no mention of cell phones or security cameras. With Alex indisposed, she had no way to find those as fast as she needed them. These girls had only been gone for a couple of days and could disappear into the dark recesses of sex trafficking in almost no time.

"There's not much to go on from this," Jamie said as she closed the files. "It seems like something the local cops should handle."

Jamie wondered how much the local police even cared about finding a few missing American girls. While she cared, how effective could she be? If the local drug cartels were involved, infiltrating them to the point necessary to find the girls would be next to impossible. This seemed like a mission with little prospects of success.

"Local law enforcement is working on all these cases," Brad said. "Try to stay under their radar. Your job is to work behind the scenes and see if a larger syndicate is behind the missing girls."

From that statement, Brad had already decided she was going.

Jamie asked what seemed like the next obvious question. "Why do you want me to start at Brownsville?"

Brad answered, "That's where we have the best lead."

He scrolled back to the picture of the SUV, then said, "It's a 2017, Dodge Durango. Silver color."

"License plate?"

"Stolen."

Jamie let out a sigh. "Like I said, there's not much to go on."

"Actually, there is," Brad countered. "The SUV was stolen in Tampico. That's where one of the girls went missing."

"Come on Brad," Jamie pushed back. "Four girls are missing. We don't even know if they are related. All I have to go on is that one girl was seen in a 2017 silver Dodge SUV. There are probably thousands of them in Mexico. That's like trying to find the proverbial needle in a haystack."

"That's why I'm sending you. You're the best. If it were easy, I'd find someone else to do your job. Someone who isn't such a pain in my neck."

"I'll take that as a compliment," Jamie said with a forced grin.

"Take it however you want. I know this isn't a normal mission. But it's important. Four missing high school girls is a big deal. Some higher eyes are on this."

That meant the director of the CIA was involved. Maybe the President.

"How come we haven't heard about it on the news?" Jamie asked. "Let's get some publicity behind it, and that would open up some leads."

"These are all Hispanic girls," Brad said soberly. "They come from poorer areas. If it were a pretty, rich, white girl, the networks would be all over it."

Jamie didn't care who they were or whether they were rich or poor, white, or Hispanic. A girl was a girl to her. A righteous anger rose inside her every time she thought of just one girl being exploited. What these girls faced was horrific.

Brad was right. A pretty rich girl from a wealthy high school would get all kinds of publicity, and authorities in the states and abroad would move heaven and earth to find her. These four girls had little hope of being found. She was their best hope. Maybe even their only one.

If anyone could find them, she would have to do it.

9

Frisco, Texas

"I'm sorry to disturb you, Mr. Morgan, but Hal Jolly from Sara's school is on line three," Sean Morgan's secretary said, as she interrupted an important meeting. A half-dozen men sat in the conference room working on a business deal on the verge of falling apart at the last minute.

Sean Morgan looked at his watch.

11:03.

"I thought I wasn't supposed to pick Sara up until this afternoon," Sean said. Sara Morgan was his daughter who was on a senior trip to the Cayman Islands. A calendar entry read he was to pick her up later that afternoon, a fact his secretary confirmed.

"Four thirty. That's what I have on the calendar," she said.

"They must've arrived early," Sean replied, as he let out a deep sigh.

"Find out the gate and send a car to pick her up," Sean said. "Better yet, see if she can catch a ride with someone else. They can drop her off here."

His secretary turned and walked out the door as he returned his attention back to the disaster unfolding before him. His company, Morgan Financial Group, had made a hostile takeover bid for a manufacturing company. The owner didn't want to sell and secured a loan to buy back his own stock which raised the cost of acquisition by more than fifty million dollars. Sean already had a buyer in place to purchase the company once he secured the stock. The buyer had secured a loan based

37

upon the agreed-upon price. Fifty million less than what it would take now to purchase the company. The additional price wasn't the issue, but securing the financing was.

"Do you want to walk away from the deal?" one of his employees asked, which raised Sean's ire further.

"We have more than three-thousand-man hours on this deal!" Sean said as his voice raised to a higher crescendo than he intended. This was not their fault. These things happened in their line of work. Every deal always had problems. Sean was a master at figuring out how to solve them. The room was full of MBAs capable of finding a solution.

"I want you to figure out how to solve this problem," Sean insisted as he lowered the intensity some, but not completely, so the point could still get across. "That's what I pay you for," he added for emphasis.

"Maybe our buyer could get additional financing," one of the men said.

"He's already maxed out," another retorted.

Sean stood and looked out the window of the conference room. Thinking. Their offices were in the Star Office complex, a new facility in North Dallas, owned by the owner of the Dallas Cowboys who practiced there. His executive office was in one of the prime locations. His business had boomed since he moved there.

Sean was building a reputation as an upcoming titan of industry in the Dallas metroplex. He was from new money as it was called. Sean started the business fifteen years ago with a thousand dollars to his name. A newlywed with a daughter, the venture was risky, but Sean was a risk taker. It had paid off. The company now managed more than two billion in assets which they used to buy and sell businesses.

His personal net worth was approaching five-hundred-million dollars. That put him on the lower end of the upper end of Dallas socialites. He was proud that it came from new money. Old money was inherited. His was made the old-fashioned wayhe earned it.

The current deal would be another feather in his cap. Morgan Financial Group stood to make more than a hundred million on a three-million-dollar investment if he could get the current deal across the finish line. While he hated to tie up fifty million of his profit in pro-viding collateral for the buyer's loan, it was better than losing the deal altogether.

"Contact Fred over at Longhorn Bank and Trust and have him get to work on a loan for the difference," Sean finally said, not entirely sure that would work.

"Let's go through the specifics again," one of the men said.

"That's a good idea," Sean agreed as he sat back down. He wasn't entirely all there. His mind was on other things.

When his secretary appeared at the door again, Sean acted sur-prised. She'd been given strict instructions that he was not to be dis-turbed. The only caveat was if it was related to his wife or daughter. Then she could always bother him even if they had something that was not important. A standing rule in the office his employees followed reli-giously.

"Mr. Jolly insists on speaking to you," she said. "He said it's impor-tant."

"Excuse me, gentlemen," Sean said to the men in the room as he reached for the phone. They all began looking down and shuffling pa-pers to seemingly give him privacy which he didn't want or need.

"Hello, Hal," Sean said. "How was the trip to Cayman? I bet it was a handful going there with that many kids."

"Sean, I'm afraid that I have some disturbing news," Hal Jolly said in a sober tone.

Sean's heart did a somersault as a wave of panic rushed over him.

"Sara is missing," Hal said, sending a bolt of adrenaline like a knife shooting through his heart. Sean didn't say anything for several seconds as he tried to process the information.

"What do you mean that Sara is missing?" he finally asked.

Several of the men looked up from their papers. Sean turned his back to them.

"She didn't come back to the hotel last night. No one has seen nor heard from her. I just met with the police and filed a missing person's report."

"Missing person's report! The police? She's been gone since yesterday? Why am I just hearing about it now?" Sean demanded roughly.

"We didn't know about it until this morning."

"Don't you do bed checks every night?"

"We do, but a mistake was made. Sara stayed in Jessica's room several of the nights. The count got messed up. We thought she was in the hotel but wasn't."

Sean rubbed his eyes with his free hand. "Where are you now?"

"I'm still at the hotel in Cayman," he replied. "The rest of the kids are at the airport. I stayed behind. So did Mrs. Skyler. I intend to stay and look for Sara. I think you should come down here as soon as possible."

"Of course," Sean said as his voice cracked. He looked at his watch. He could be to Cayman in about three hours. "I'll go to the airport now."

He hung up the phone and walked out of the conference room to his secretary's desk, ignoring the men in the room. "Call the airport and tell them to get my plane ready. Also get me a car in Cayman and have it meet me at the plane. Something terrible has happened."

His hands were shaking.

"What's wrong?" she asked.

"Sara is missing. I'm going to Cayman to find her."

Sean had a pilot's license and a private plane which he would use to fly to Cayman. He could leave from the local airport, bypass security, and fly there directly.

I have to call Carolyn.

He had no idea how he was going to tell his wife the news.

10

Plano, Texas

Carolyn Morgan walked out of the *Milk & Honey Day Spa* where she got a manicure, pedicure, facial, and had her hair and makeup done. A monthly pampering ritual she normally did with her daughter Sara but had to do alone this time since Sara was in the Cayman Islands on a senior trip.

Her car was in the back, in a VIP parking space reserved just for her and other wealthy clientele. The Mercedes Benz GLE-Hybrid made the familiar beep as she hit the fob and unlocked the doors. Once she settled in and started the car, her mind rewound and played the conversations of the last few days.

A twinge of sadness returned. The same one that came over her that morning when she realized she'd better get used to going alone. In three months, Sara would start college and wouldn't be around nearly as much. They'd been coming to that same spa together since Sara was six. Now, her daughter was almost eighteen, graduating from high school, and Carolyn could feel herself losing control of her baby girl who was becoming a woman right before her very eyes.

The emotions she felt inside were mixed. Carolyn knew she was blessed to have such a good daughter. The happiness Sara had brought her over the years overran the sadness she was feeling. Other ladies didn't have it nearly so good.

The spa owner who did her hair was a good friend from church and spent the last hour complaining obsessively about the new boyfriend her daughter brought home a couple months ago. "He has earrings and tattoos!" Valerie said with exasperation.

"I can't imagine," Carolyn replied. "Sean would have a conniption fit. He'd probably get his gun and run him off."

Sean was Carolyn's husband and Sara's father. Their daughter attended a private Christian school instead of the public school for this reason. The boys at Sara's school weren't allowed to have piercings or tattoos.

"If I had a shotgun, I'd shoot him myself," Valerie said.

The two women had a good laugh from that comment before the conversation turned serious again.

"He's twenty-one years old." Valerie continued. "He's a full-grown man."

The conversation made Carolyn smile as she realized how lucky she was. Sara had been on a few dates but never had a serious boyfriend. Mostly, she hung out with her friends in groups. Sean and Carolyn had been dreading for years the day when Sara would start dating seriously and think she was in love. So far, it hadn't happened.

Carolyn drove away from the spa and fought back a tear, so she didn't smear her newly applied makeup. She tamped down the feeling, knowing she had many more experiences to share with her daughter. Sara would be home for summers. Christmases. Eventually a wedding. Grandkids. Maybe Sara would have a daughter. She could start the ritual all over again when the granddaughter was old enough.

Maybe Sara would stay in Dallas for college and still live at home. That was her hope. Carolyn had Sara's whole life planned out for her since the day she was born. Sara would go to college in Dallas at SMU, meet a boy, get married, and live close to them. That dream was shattered when, right before she left for Cayman, Sara brought up the possibility of going to Texas Tech for college.

An argument had ensued. Sean thought it was a good idea and Carolyn was adamantly against it. "Texas Tech is five hours away!" she argued.

"I think it would be good for Sara to get out on her own and away from us," Sean countered.

"Why would Sara need to be away from her mother?" Carolyn said with disdain dripping from every word.

"That's not what I meant," Sean said, softening his tone. "It's just that we've sheltered Sara."

"It's a dangerous world out there," Carolyn retorted as anger built inside her to the point of rage.

"Sara has a good head on her shoulders," Sean said, raising his own level of intensity. "We need to trust her to make her own decisions. She wants to go to Texas Tech to be near her friend, Jessica."

"She'll make new friends at SMU! You graduated from there. Don't you want her to go to your alma mater? Keep up the tradition."

"I want Sara to make her own way in life. Experience the world. Broaden her horizons. You've sheltered her too much, in my opinion," Sean said unkindly.

With that accusation, the argument became personal. It was almost verbatim to the argument they'd had a year before when Sara dropped the bombshell that she wanted to go to Europe on an exchange program. That conversation started rattling around in her head.

"Going to Europe would be a chance of a lifetime," Sean had argued.

"No way Sara's going to Europe. I'd be a nervous wreck every day."

"You need to quit worrying so much. Sara's not a kid anymore."

"I worry! That's my job. That's what a mother does. I come from a long line of worriers."

Carolyn had given Sean the cold shoulder for more than a week until he dropped it. Sara eventually decided she didn't want to leave her friends anyway, much to Carolyn's relief. Now the argument had resumed almost where it had left off the year before.

"Sara needs to live in the dorm and experience college life," Sean said. "That's part of the education you get at college."

"We'll save a lot of money if she lives at home," Carolyn blurted out.

Sean laughed, easing the tension somewhat.

Carolyn realized immediately that a money argument wouldn't win the day. She was coming across as desperate and grasping at straws. They could afford to send Sara to any college in the country. For that matter, Sara could get a scholarship anywhere with almost a full ride.

While she was mad at her husband for taking Sara's side, she tried to keep from giving him the same cold shoulder she put him through the year before. With Sara in the Cayman Islands, a truce had ensued, and the subject mostly avoided. Since Sara was coming back later today, Carolyn wondered if the fireworks might erupt again.

The clock on her console reminded her that Sara would be home in less than five hours. An alert on the same console suddenly got her attention. Her phone was still on silent but was now connected to her car's Bluetooth. Some notifications popped up on the center console computer screen.

What?

The screen showed that she had twenty-three text messages and seven voicemails.

What's going on?

She was already driving so she decided she would have to check them when she got home. Carolyn had a strict rule about being on her phone and driving. Sean, her husband, was a constant offender, and she harped at him continually. He never did it anymore around her, but who knows what he did when he wasn't with her.

Sara was much better at it, although who knew exactly what teenagers did when they were alone. At any rate, she wouldn't violate her own rule, so she ignored the messages. Carolyn was on the hospitality committee at church and someone probably started a thread that everyone was responding to. She tried to imagine what it was about but couldn't think of anything.

Her thoughts turned back to Sara. An honor student. Second in her class. Homecoming Queen. Varsity letterman in three sports. Sara wasn't perfect, but she could be a lot worse. She was probably worrying about her for no reason.

Another thought occurred to her. She'd heard of the empty nest syndrome and that many couples started having marriage problems once the kids left the house. Maybe that was what she was worried about. Having to be alone with Sean. They had a good marriage, or at least she always assumed they did, but she wondered what it would be like with only the two of them.

Carolyn decided to regain her composure and put the thoughts out of her head. She went through the gate into their community and looked in the mirror to check her hair and makeup again.

When she pulled onto her street, a chill ran through her spine. A number of cars were parked in front of her house. She recognized the cars as those of parents from Sara's school. She scanned her mind. Was there a meeting she forgot about? Did the kids get home early? Did something happen on the trip? Did something bad happen to Sara?

A jolt of fear ran through her body and her hand began shaking. She pulled around the back of the house and into the garage. Then fumbled with the keys and her purse after putting the car in park. A deep breath did nothing to calm her nerves.

It's nothing.

The mental assurance didn't bring her comfort, although it did lead her to not consider the worst. She surmised that they just wanted to talk about a graduation party or something. For the life of her, Carolyn couldn't remember any conversation about a meeting.

I hope I'm not late.

She got out of the car and walked through the backdoor closing the garage door as she entered the house. The entrance off the garage led to the laundry room and into the kitchen. There she sat her sunglasses, purse, and keys on the counter. Paulina, their housekeeper, entered the room and said the guests were in the living room waiting for her.

"It has something to do with Sara. She's in some kind of trouble," she said.

Carolyn's knees wobbled, when she heard Sara's name. She reached out for the kitchen counter to steady herself. She could tell her face was racked with worry. There was no mirror around to know if she was successful in tamping it down.

More than a dozen people were sitting in the living room, including the principal of Sara's school. Carolyn put on her best fake smile which immediately left her face when she noticed that a couple of the ladies were clutching tissues.

Everyone in the room stood when she entered. "What's going on?" Carolyn asked nervously. Her voice cracked as she said it.

"Sara is missing," Principal Green said. Several of the ladies had already started walking toward her.

"Missing?" Carolyn said, not fully comprehending what he just said.

"They think she was kidnapped in the Cayman Islands," one of the women said. "No one has heard from her since yesterday. I'm so sorry."

Carolyn's knees wobbled again. The words she heard were garbled. She opened her mouth to speak. Before she could, everything went dark as she fainted and collapsed to the floor.

11

The Reef Bar
Grand Cayman Island

Lars Fossey was the owner of the *Reef Bar*, the place where Jessica and Michelle, Sara Morgan's friends, had last seen her. Commissioner Collin Hughes and Sara's teacher, Mrs. Pat Skyler, were sitting in Fossey's office discussing the video surveillance tape. Fossey was cordial but uncooperative.

"Do you have a warrant, Commissioner?" he asked.

Commissioner Hughes bristled at the question. "I don't need a warrant if you let me view the tape voluntarily," he retorted. The commissioner tried to match the cordial tone so that the conversation didn't turn adversarial right off the bat.

"I must protect the privacy of my patrons," Fossey said in a condescending tone.

Fossey was sitting back in his chair in an almost nonchalant manner. Something that struck the commissioner as odd considering the man had just been told that a seventeen-year-old girl might've been kidnapped out of his establishment the night before. If the roles were reversed, Hughes would be in a state of panic. Fossey didn't seem the least bit concerned.

"Do your patrons have a reason to need protection?" the commissioner asked more roughly, deciding to ratchet up the pressure. "Are there things going on in your bar that I should be concerned about?"

Fossey waved his hand in the air in a dismissive manner. "That's not what I meant. It's just that we have laws in place for a reason. You need a warrant and probable cause to search the bar and to view the video surveillance camera. I'm aware of my rights."

"You don't need to lecture me on the law, Mr. Fossey!" the commissioner said, raising his voice. "I assure you that I know the laws better than you do."

"I meant no disrespect."

Commissioner Hughes decided the time had come to become adversarial. "One of those laws is that it's against the law to serve alcohol to someone under eighteen. Are you aware of that law?"

Fossey sat up in his chair and placed his elbow on the desk. "Of course." His body language expressed more concern even if the tone of his voice didn't.

"The girl missing was under eighteen," the commissioner continued. "Were you aware of that fact?"

Commissioner Hughes laid on his heavy British authoritarian accent for effect. He had dealt with bigger riff-raff in England than Lars Fossey, and if Fossey wanted a battle, he was more than willing to give him one. First, he'd appeal to his sensibilities. If he still didn't cooperate, he'd bring the full force of the law down on him. He had the ability to make his life miserable.

Fossey's demeanor turned from smug to concerned as he narrowed his eyes and clenched his jaw. He started fidgeting nervously.

"We don't serve alcohol to minors," he answered. "I can assure you of that."

"Do you have kids, Mr. Fossey?"

"I have a son."

"How old is he?"

"Twenty-two."

"Would you be concerned if he was missing?"

"Of course."

"You'd come to me, wouldn't you?"

"Yes."

"You'd want me to do everything I could to find him, wouldn't you?"

Fossey didn't verbally answer. He just shook his head yes.

The commissioner turned to Mrs. Skyler who'd been silent up to that point. "Show Mr. Fossey a picture of Sara."

Mrs. Skyler reached into her purse, pulled out her phone, and scrolled to a picture. The same one she'd shown the commissioner earlier at the hotel. She turned the phone toward Fossey and showed it to him.

The commissioner thought he saw a glimpse of recognition but couldn't be sure, so he decided to ask. "Did you see this girl in the bar last night?"

"I wasn't at the bar last night."

"Where were you?"

"Am I a suspect?"

"At this point, everyone's a suspect. Like I said, if it was your son, you'd want me to look under every rock."

Fossey let out a huge sigh. "I was with my girlfriend. She'll verify it."

"Who was running the bar?"

"My son."

"Is he here now?"

"No. He's asleep. As you can imagine, he had a late night."

"What's his name?"

"Jake."

"I'm going to need to question him. Make him available this afternoon. Wake him up if you have to."

The commissioner was losing patience. In a missing person's case, time was of the essence. He couldn't waste more time on Fossey. His attitude and demeanor were unsettling and raised several red flags. Commissioner Hughes wasn't sure if he had something to hide or he just had a distrust of the police. They'd never had any problems with the *Reef Bar* other than the usual reports of fighting, the occasional drunk, and random drug use. Nothing unusual.

The commissioner already knew everything there was to know about Fossey, including that he had a son. They'd had a few run-ins with Jake Fossey. Minor offenses, but enough so that he was on the commissioner's radar. Hughes made it his business to know what was happening on his island, especially in its most popular bar.

Fossey had come to the Caymans from Australia fifteen years before. In a short time, he'd built a small empire of dive boats, day excursions, and night dinner cruises. Along with the *Reef Bar,* which was Cayman's hottest nightclub, Fossey had become extremely wealthy in a short period of time. As far as the commissioner could tell, he'd earned his wealth legitimately.

Commissioner Hughes sat forward in his chair and leaned on the desk, so he was nearly face to face with Fossey. His tone turned deadly serious.

"Mr. Fossey, I have a missing girl," he said slowly, and with emphasis for effect. "She's from America. Your bar was the last place she was seen. If word gets out, I don't have to tell you it won't be good for your business. If you know what I mean."

"Are you threatening me, Commissioner?" Fossey asked as his eyes widened.

Commissioner Hughes had had enough of his insolence. "I wasn't. But I will now!"

Hughes took a deep and noticeable breath.

"I *will* get that warrant, Mr. Fossey, if I have to. And I'm going to come in here and turn this place upside down. In fact, it's probably going to have to be closed down for a couple weeks while we conduct our investigation. Of course, we'll have to interview all your employees. The press will be interested in knowing why we're searching your place. I'll do press conferences. I'll make sure your name is mentioned in each one of them. And that you have been uncooperative."

Fossey seemed unmoved.

"Of course, there's also the matter of your liquor license," the commissioner continued sternly. "I'm interested to know if you're serving alcohol to minors. We may have to temporarily pull that license until we can determine if you're operating within the laws of our island. I already have testimony that a seventeen-year-old girl was in your establishment last night. That's enough to get a warrant."

Hughes didn't know if any of the girls had been drinking. He had a detective at the airport questioning two of them right now. Fossey didn't know that, and the commissioner didn't mind bluffing if that's what it took. By this point, he was desperate. He could get a warrant, but it would take a few hours, costing them precious time.

The argument seemed to be working.

Fossey leaned back in his chair as he bit his lip and swallowed constantly as the commissioner spoke.

"I'll ask one more time," Hughes said. "Will you *voluntarily* show me the security tapes, or are we going to have to do this the hard way?"

Fossey raised his hands in the air in surrender. "Okay, Commissioner. I get the point. We have nothing to hide. I was just trying to assert my rights under the law. I'm sure you understand that."

The commissioner maintained his fixed stare.

Fossey stood to his feet. "Follow me."

He led them into a back room barely big enough to fit the three of them. The commissioner motioned for Mrs. Skyler to squeeze in next to him so she could see the screen. He needed her to identify Sara.

Fossey began typing on a keyboard connected to the security system. The set up was not complex, but the system was fairly new and on the high end of efficiency. That gave Hughes some confidence they would get good footage. He'd noticed when he came in that they had a camera at the front entrance. That would be the most helpful. Sara had to enter and leave out of that exit. This was his best lead. The starting point to the investigation. The perpetrator might even be on the tape. They might see the car she left in.

Anticipation built inside him as he felt the excitement of possibly finding a break in the case so quickly.

"That's strange," Fossey suddenly said.

The computer screen attached to the security system was blank.

"I'm sorry Commissioner," Fossey said. "We don't have any footage from last night."

"What happened to it?"

"It's been erased."

12

Police Headquarters

The briefing room of the Royal Cayman Islands Police Service (RCIPS) was packed full of patrol officers, detectives, investigators, and volunteer staff. Not one more person could've squeezed into the room. Some were standing out in the hallway listening through the opened door. The "Attendance is Mandatory" urgent bulletin was sent out to every member of the organization, and everyone who could be there, was.

Commissioner Collin Hughes was set to address the group. He stood at a podium at the front of the room with his prepared notes on the rostrum. A picture of Sara Morgan was projected on a screen behind him and in prominent view to the standing-room-only crowd.

When the group quieted, Hughes began speaking. This was an important time in his short tenure. Maybe even defining. He clutched the papers so no one would see his hands shaking. He prayed his voice didn't crack. Projecting strength was of utmost importance to him as their leader. A responsibility he always took seriously but times like this reminded him of how important his leadership was when it came to life and death matters.

The room didn't have a microphone, so he consciously raised his voice to project to the entire room. "At approximately 10:30 last night, a young woman from America visiting the Caymans on a high-school trip went missing. Her name is Sara Morgan." His tone was solemn but resolved.

He paused to let that sink in.

An eerie silence filled the room.

The commissioner looked behind him at Sara's picture. Emotion welled up inside of him. He had a twenty-two-year-old daughter in college back in England. Sara reminded him of his own daughter, and he could only imagine what it would feel like if Hattie were missing.

"This is the young woman," he said as he pointed at the screen. "Study her picture. Sear it into your memory. She's seventeen-years-old. Approximately five-foot ten, one hundred and fifty pounds. As you can see, she has blonde hair and hazel eyes. Athletic build."

Commissioner Hughes took a deep breath before continuing. He looked around the room to see if everyone was taking this as seriously as he wanted them to. Some were taking notes. They all seemed focused on his every word. That gave him some comfort. This was his time to rally the troops, and they already seemed unified in purpose.

He couldn't overstate the gravity of the situation. This was the biggest thing to happen on the Cayman Islands in a long time. Maybe ever. The ramifications were far reaching. This was easily the biggest case he'd encountered in his entire career.

"Sara was last seen at the *Reef Bar* with two of her friends," Hughes continued. "Detective Brighton interviewed the two girls at the airport. He has briefed me on his talk with them. From what we can gather, the three girls went to the bar, which was against the rules. They were supposed to be back at the hotel. One of the girls was under eighteen, but she insisted that none of them were drinking anything but soda."

"Where were they staying?" one of the detectives asked.

"At the Sandy Beach Resort. Last night was their last night on the island. In fact, the rest of the group has already left the island on their way back to the states."

"Do we have security footage?" a detective on the front row asked.

"Taped over."

A gasp went through the crowd of law enforcement professionals who started to murmur among themselves. They knew as well as Hughes did that the development was a major red flag in an investigation. Someone was hiding something. Figuring out what wasn't that hard. If they found who tampered with the tape, they were that much closer to solving the case.

"I have two officers at the bar," Commissioner Hughes continued. "They're guarding the entrance and the video security room. Lars Fossey is in an interrogation room here at headquarters. He claims he was with his girlfriend last night. We need to check out his alibi. Detective Jacobson will lead the interrogation and investigation of the father."

"Warrant?"

"Pending."

Hughes had erupted when he learned that the tape had been tampered with. He didn't bother getting a warrant to close the bar. He took matters into his own hands and moved quickly to mitigate any more damage to what he now considered a crime scene. A search warrant was being prepared as he spoke so they could search it thoroughly. A judge had already been put on alert that an important matter was about to come across his desk and needed to be expedited.

"Was Jake Fossey at the bar last night?" a detective asked. Jake was Fossey's son.

"Mr. Fossey said his son was running the bar," Hughes answered. "I sent an officer to his house to pick Jake up and bring him in for questioning. Detective Delancey will question the son."

"Anybody see her leave the bar?"

"Not that we know of. That's what we've got to find out. We need to question everyone who was at that bar last night. Someone saw Sara."

The commissioner liked what was happening. They weren't waiting for him to finish his remarks. The detectives, in particular, were already thinking ahead and anticipating the most obvious questions.

"I'll check and see if there are any other security cameras in the area," an investigator said. There were twelve investigators and eight detectives on the force. They were all told to drop everything to work on this case. Hughes was thankful he didn't have to tell them what to do. They were self-starters who already knew what was expected of them with little supervision. That would help him focus on the interrogations of the father and son.

"The convenience store across the street has a security camera," Josie Bwire, one of the female officers said. "I don't know if it would capture images that far away. But it might."

"Thank you, Officer Bwire," Hughes said. "Detective Steele is the lead investigator. If you have any ideas or find anything, notify her first."

The chatter in the room started to increase as the members talked among themselves. They got quiet when it became apparent that Hughes was going to begin again. His nerves had calmed somewhat.

"I am implementing Com One," Hughes said. "I want a full search of the island." Com One was a full alert. They ran drills every three months for this exact possibility. The island was broken into twelve units. A Sergeant was over his own area. He or she would be in charge of searching that area. The Detectives and investigators had free reign to go wherever the evidence took them.

"Call in all your volunteers to help with the search," the commissioner continued. "Leave no stone unturned. I don't have to tell you how urgent this matter is."

"Any chance the girl ran away?" one of the female detectives asked. "Most of the time these missing girls show up sooner rather than later. One day's not a long time to be gone. The girls on vacation sometimes meet a boy and lose track of time. Or don't want to go home."

"That's always a possibility," Hughes said but he shook his head no. He knew this was a missing person's case. "But, I doubt it. For now, we're treating this as an abduction. We can only hope she met a boy and is safe and hiding out with him. She comes from a good family and has no criminal history. The girl came to the island on a Christian school trip. Their plane has already left, and she wasn't on it. I highly doubt she disappeared on her own volition."

He looked at his notes to see if he missed anything.

"What about the media?" someone shouted from the back.

"No media. Keep this close to the vest. No leaks."

"They'll know something is up as soon as we leave this room."

"Don't tell them anything. We'll put out a press release telling them that we'll issue a statement at six tonight." Hughes said the words strongly for effect.

"Hopefully, we can find her before then," he added. He scanned the room. "Anything else?" he asked. "All vacation and days off are cancelled until further notice," Hughes said.

He expected a groan but didn't get one. That was a good sign. Everyone was engaged and ready to go to work.

"Let's find this girl before it's too late." Hughes picked up his notes and left the podium as the officers cleared a path for him to exit the room. Once he made it to the hallway, he was greeted by his assistant who had a worried look on her face. Her lips were tightened into a firm resolve and her brow was furrowed.

"Commissioner," she said. "Sara's father is here. He's waiting in your office."

His already high blood pressure which had just started to settle back down, suddenly felt like it was going to blow through the top of his bald head.

13

"Is my daughter dead?" Sara's father, Sean Morgan, asked with a solemn look on his face.

The question cut through Commissioner Hughes's heart like a searing iron. The pained look on Sean Morgan's face was that of a father in unbelievable agony. An overwhelming urge to reassure him came over the commissioner. But he decided a long time ago to always be honest with family members if at all possible.

"I don't know," the commissioner said in a calm tone. "I will tell you that I've not seen any evidence to suggest that your daughter isn't alive. At this point, I'm assuming she is and treating this as a missing person's case."

Sean nodded his head and changed positions in his chair, as he clearly tried to maintain his composure. Hughes doubted his words were reassuring but it was the best he could do. The prudent approach would be to maintain the delicate balance between professionalism and empathy.

"What are you doing to find Sara?" Mr. Morgan asked, with noticeable skepticism behind the words.

Hughes didn't mind. He'd probably feel the same way. Mr. Morgan could have no idea if he were competent or if he were even taking this seriously. He wanted to assure him on both points.

"I can assure you that my department is doing everything within our power to find your daughter. I'm optimistic that we will find her."

That wasn't entirely the truth. The commissioner had a pessimistic nature to him. He'd seen enough death over the years to have a cautious cynicism that he brought to each case. The truth: fifty-seven percent of all victims abducted by a stranger were returned home safely. That meant the odds were in their favor.

At least at this point.

However, the clock was ticking. The percentages dropped with each passing hour. At twenty-four hours, the statistics dropped to fifty percent. After forty-eight hours, they dropped to thirty. That's why he disagreed with the policy to wait forty-eight hours before beginning a search. If foul play was involved, then that would be too late more often than not.

He felt a sudden need to explain that to Mr. Morgan.

"Normal procedure is to wait forty-eight hours before beginning a search," the commissioner said in a professional but monotone voice. By Mr. Morgan's reaction, Hughes immediately realized that it came out wrong.

"Are you insane?" Mr. Morgan shouted in a fury. "You can't wait forty-eight hours. My daughter is missing. She didn't run away. If that's what you think, then you're a fool. She's not with some boy. My daughter wouldn't do that."

Commissioner Hughes raised his hand to silence the father. "You didn't let me finish my sentence," he said roughly. "What I said was that *normal* procedure is to wait forty-eight hours. I've instructed my office to start looking for Sara immediately. I hope to God that she met a boy and is hiding out with him. But I agree with you. I don't think that's the case."

Mr. Morgan sat back in his chair, the answer seemingly appeasing him for now. He was still on edge, though, and the commissioner could tell that almost anything could set him off again.

"We have detained two persons of interest for questioning." Hughes immediately regretted saying it.

"Who are they?" Mr. Morgan's eyes grew wide, and he sat forward in his chair.

"I can't say at this time."

"Let me talk to them. Give me five minutes alone with them, and I'll make them tell me where Sara is."

"At this point, we don't even know if they're involved in Sara's disappearance. Like I said, they're persons of interest."

Telling him that piece of information might bring him some reassurance. However, now the commissioner was concerned he might repeat it. Hughes leaned forward further in his chair. "That information is not to leave this office," he cautioned. "I need to know that what I tell you is confidential and between the two of us. You and I need to work together on this. That's the best chance we have of finding Sara."

"Were there any security cameras at the bar?" Sean Morgan asked.

"I can't comment on that."

"I thought you wanted to work together on this," he said with his mouth contorted in anger. His eyes were on fire like coals.

It became apparent that his anger never left and probably wouldn't until Sara was found. The anger could be a good or a bad thing. Mr. Morgan was a potential loose cannon that might be hard to control.

"We are going to work together," Hughes said, "but I can't comment on certain parts of the investigation. You have to let me do my job. I'll tell you everything I know as long as it doesn't compromise the investigation."

"We need to go to the press."

"No press."

"Why not? If we get Sara's picture out there, then we might find someone who saw something."

"The press will put too much pressure on the kidnappers."

"That's exactly what we want."

"They might panic and harm Sara. I don't want them to do something rash. Our investigators need to work behind the scenes without the press hounding them. The kidnappers will assume that we're going to wait forty-eight hours to look for Sara. I want them to think that. If we go to the press, they'll know we're not waiting. I'd just as soon operate in the shadows until the last possible minute."

"The press will eventually find out."

"I'd like to put that off as long as possible."

"I disagree. The press will put pressure on the scum who did this to release her. If the fire gets too hot, they'll want to get out of the kitchen."

"Let me handle it," the commissioner said sternly. "I will issue a press release at six tonight."

"Six is too late. I want to go to the press and offer a reward. Whatever it takes. I think we should start at a hundred thousand dollars."

The commissioner winced. That's the last thing he needed at this point. "Let's not put out a reward just yet."

"If a hundred thousand isn't enough, make it a million. I don't care. I'll give any amount of money to get Sara back."

"I understand that, but a reward is not a good idea at this point and time."

"Why not? A reward is always issued in these circumstances. A lot of people don't want to get involved. If there's money involved, they *will* come forward."

"And so will every crazy person within a hundred miles of the island. If we put out a reward, especially one that high, we'll get inundated with false leads. We'll have to follow every one of them. We're a small department with limited resources. I need my men and women following *real* leads. At least at first."

"I strongly disagree."

"Mr. Morgan, I appreciate where you're coming from. You want your daughter back. So, do I. I have a daughter about Sara's age."

Hughes made a mental note to keep calling her Sara. Make it personal. Let the father know he sees her as a real person and not a case file.

"I've been in law enforcement for more than thirty years. I know what I'm doing. You're going to have to trust me."

"What do you expect me to do, go back to my hotel and just sit around waiting for you to call? I'm not going to do that. I also am a man of considerable talent, skills, and resources. You're not going to be able to push me aside. I'm going to do everything I can to find my daughter, with or without your help."

"Good. I want you to maintain that passion. But stay in your lane. Let my team do our jobs."

"What can I do?" the father asked.

Hughes could already see the wheels spinning in the father's eyes. He wanted to ask Mr. Morgan about the bruises on Sara's arm, the ones Mrs. Skyler told him about at the hotel, but decided that now wasn't the right time. Instead, Hughes decided to stay proactive. "Get flyers printed with her... with Sara's picture on it. Organize search teams. Scour the island. Ask every person you meet if they've seen Sara. Just don't cross the line into law enforcement."

"I can do that."

"Good."

They both stood, and Sean Morgan stuck out his hand which the commissioner shook.

"One final question," Hughes said. "How would Sara try to contact you if she needed to?"

"What do you mean?"

"Who would she call? You or her mother?"

"I don't know. I haven't thought about it. Why do you ask?"

"The kidnappers might want to demand a ransom. It's possible they would call here, but more than likely they would ask Sara for a number and call you or your wife directly. What number would she give them?"

"She would definitely give them my number. I'm the one with the money."

"Do I have your permission to put a recording and a trace on your phone?" Hughes asked.

Mr. Morgan hesitated. For several seconds.

"I don't know if I'm comfortable with that," he finally said. "Why don't I just tell you if they call?"

"As you wish."

After Mr. Morgan left the office, Hughes sat back in his chair. A thought bolted into his mind.

The father is going to be a problem.

14

Somewhere in Mexico
Just south of the US border

Once Jamie crossed the border of Mexico, things got a lot more dangerous. She had entered into a region of Mexico largely controlled by the drug cartels. *The Golfo Alianza,* the "Gulf Alliance" as they were known, had been terrorizing the region for more than ten years, and things were only getting worse. It's highly possible they were the ones behind the kidnapping of the girls.

The long drive would give Jamie plenty of opportunity to think about her mission. A lot of things didn't make sense. Four high school girls on their senior trips were taken from bars on a Friday night. All on the same night. Miles from each other. Only one from inside the United States. She was last seen in a 2017 silver Dodge Durango crossing the border.

Maria Victoria Delgado.

Vicki.

She was the girl taken from Brownsville. Her picture was seared in Jamie's mind. On a mission, she liked to think about the girls a lot and what they might be going through. That way, the rage and the fury inside her was at a sufficient level to destroy whoever would do something like this to a young woman who had her whole life ahead of her.

This was what Jamie lived forthe two goals in every mission.

1. Save the girls.

2. Don't die trying.

Just driving through the region was dangerous. So much so that Jamie had gotten the big artillery out. A 357 Sig Sauer was on her hip, a Glock 23 in the glove compartment, and the big gun, a M4 Carbine submachine gun lay in the passenger seat within easy reach. Overkill perhaps, but Jamie would rather have them within reach than have to try to get them out of the trunk in case of a confrontation.

Members of the alliance were known to randomly stop cars and harass, rob, and even kill the occupants. The machine gun was because the members of the cartel were former disgruntled soldiers, kicked out for various reasons. They weren't your typical drug-running thugs. While the training wasn't as good and as thorough as Jamie received from her CIA training, those men were trained in warfare which was a whole level above typical gang or street criminals.

The "Brotherhood," as they called themselves, were known to carry the feared FX-05 machine guns. Better known as the "Fire Serpent," the nickname given to cast terror into the hearts of the populous. The serpent was more powerful than her M4 Carbine, but Jamie was counting on the fact that she was better trained.

The thought made her shudder, and she scanned the horizon for any threats. She felt bad for the people who lived in this region. Fear of them allowed the cartels to remain in control. Even the government with all its vast resources were afraid of them.

Jamie would just as soon not see any of them yet.

Having spent less than an hour in Brownsville, Texas, where Vicki had gone missing, she had just crossed the border. Her handler, Brad, told her to start there, but Jamie thought that was a waste of time. What was she supposed to do? CIA operatives weren't allowed by law to operate in the United States. She couldn't question witnesses or gather evidence. The only thing she knew to do was sit outside the nightclub and surveille it. For what reason? If you've seen one nightclub, you've seen them all. The perpetrators were long gone. They wouldn't show back up there.

If she were in a foreign country, she'd break into the nightclub after everyone was gone and look at the security tape. Or talk to the bouncers.

One of them had probably been paid to look the other way. She'd knock some heads together until she had answers. For obvious reasons, Jamie couldn't do that in the US.

She wasn't going to waste valuable time in the United States where her investigative abilities were constrained by laws. Other countries had laws too, but the bad guys didn't follow them, so she didn't always either. She'd do whatever it took within reason to save a girl.

When in Rome... so to speak.

The thought made her laugh and eased some of the tension she could feel in her shoulders.

Her best bet was to go to Mexico and start shaking some trees and see what fell out. Three girls were kidnapped in Mexico. One in Cancun. Another in Boca Del Rio and one in Tampico. For some reason, Jamie felt drawn to Tampico. That's where she'd start. Vicki was transported across the border in a 2017 silver Dodge Durango stolen from Tampico. That meant the brains of the operation were probably there.

She used the term "brains" loosely. Another thought which caused her to laugh out loud.

Her mind returned to the more serious thoughts. Even though she'd pass Cancun and Boca Del Rio on the way, those were tourist areas. The alliance didn't operate in tourist areas except to commit the occasional crime. More petty crimes. Not something as brazen as kidnapping. A sort of truce had developed between the government and the cartels. Stay away from tourist areas, and we'll let you survive. That's why visitors were warned to stay in the tourist areas. There they were safe. Venture outside of the designated safety zones, and you were taking your own life in your hands.

It all came down to money.

The almighty dollar was king everywhere. The cartels could run drugs, terrorize locals, rape women and children, all with impunity. But cost the government some tax dollars from tourists, and that crossed the line. The corruption sickened Jamie. But... she didn't run the world. If she did, the cartels would be one of the first things she'd eliminate.

A sense of frustration came over her, even though early on in the mission. She was flying in the dark with no intelligence to work with it. Missions to third-world countries usually had more intel for her to go on.

This was what she did know. Four girls were missing from high school class trips. No witnesses. No security tapes. No idea if they were in Mexico or were taken out of the country. The only thing she had to go on were the names of the bars they were taken from.

That, and the fact they were all kidnapped on the same night. That meant it was a coordinated plan. That much was obvious. Her trainer at the CIA, Curly, always said there were no coincidences in life. Go with the obvious.

It also meant an organization was behind it. A small group of conspirators couldn't have pulled off such a brazen operation. Whoever did this, knew that the FBI, CIA, Homeland Security, and the Mexican government, with pressure from the US, would all get involved in the search. They must have felt somewhat confident that they could get away with it.

They were all American girls. Another bold act by the conspirators. What was the motive?

Only two things came to mind. For ransom or to sell into sex trafficking. Ransom was too risky. There's no way they could kidnap the girls, demand a ransom, secure the money, and get away with it.

Selling them into sex trafficking didn't make sense either. The most they could get on the open market would be a few thousand dollars per girl. Most sex traffickers didn't want kidnapped American girls. They wanted poor girls from poor countries. An American girl wasn't worth the effort or the risk. Especially if the press got involved. A worldwide manhunt for an American girl would shine too much light on their organization.

The only thing that made sense was that a private party wanted the girls. An oligarch in Russia or in the Middle East. Maybe Cuba. Or a rich Cartel leader in Central or South America. Perhaps a plantation owner with more money than he knew what to do with. He'd pay a million dollars or more to have a young American girl as his private sex slave.

Jamie's imagination was running wild. The truth was that she had no idea what had happened to the girls and wouldn't until she went into the field and got her first lead.

Tampico.

That's where she'd go. It had tourist areas as well, but for the most part, it wasn't as popular as Cancun or Boca Del Rio. And the cartels were powerful in the inner part of the city, just outside the tourist areas. In the more impoverished parts of town.

That's where Jamie would begin.

342 miles.

Seven hours.

Including stops.

If I don't get shot at.

15

Jamie slowed the car.

She was making good time, but something ahead caught her eye. Two cars were stopped along the side of the road. One was a four-door, older sedan. Another car, a jet black, late-model Ford Mustang was parked behind it. Two men with machine guns were standing next to the car. A man dressed in a white dress shirt and black dress slacks was pinned up against the car and being interrogated roughly by them.

The two armed men weren't Mexican police. They were most likely Alliance members harassing one of the locals.

A debate raged in Jamie's head.

Just wait.

Stay out of their line of sight.

Until they go on their way.

That seemed like the most prudent thing to do. More than likely, they'd shake him down for some money and then let him go. Jamie should stay out of it.

That's not going to happen.

The black Mustang had an antenna on it which gave Jamie an idea. She proceeded slowly toward the cars. When she got closer, she increased her speed and passed by them. A woman was in the front seat holding a small child with a petrified look on her face. The man outside the car was bleeding from the nose.

The two armed men stared at Jamie as she passed by. She kept her eyes forward so as not to make eye contact. A small hill was ahead so she drove normal speed over the hill and out of the sight of the men. More than likely, they were just trying to scare them. From the looks of it, the couple appeared to be Mormon. Probably missionaries on their way to one of the several Mormon compounds in the area.

The mission communes provided food and health care to the local communities. Generally, they were encouraged not to venture out alone. Jamie didn't know if this couple was coming or going. Perhaps they were taking a sick child to the doctor or going to get supplies. Whatever the reason, they had gotten themselves into a jam.

Jamie should just go on down the road and stay on mission.

Not going to happen.

She did a U-turn and started driving back in the direction from which she had come. The cars were parked just over the hill. Jamie stopped her car in the middle of the road before she came into their sight so she could formulate a plan.

She hadn't acted when she drove by before because the driver's side door was on the wrong side. Had she gotten out of the car, the men would have their guns on her before she could get around to their side.

Jamie was confident she could take them out in a gunfight, but the risk of hitting the innocent civilians was too great. This way, she would be on the same side as the gunmen. That gave her an advantage. Hopefully, they wouldn't process that it was the same car. Why would anyone in their right mind turn around and come back to help the couple? Jamie was wondering that same thing.

She proceeded over the hill at normal speed so as not to draw attention to herself. The sun was behind her so they wouldn't get a good look at her or the car until she was on them. It didn't matter because the gunmen's attention was on the poor man who seemed to be pleading with them. For whatever reason, the situation had escalated. Jamie had made the right decision by coming back. They would probably still let them go, but Jamie intended to teach the two a lesson they wouldn't forget anytime soon.

She rolled down her window. The Sig handgun was out of the holster and in her right hand. Even though the gunmen had machine guns, and her M4 Carbine submachine gun was sitting on the front seat next to her, she didn't think she needed it. Two shots would be enough to take those two scumbags down. The last thing she wanted was to start spraying bullets at them. Her M4 Carbine could fire eleven-to-fifteen rounds per second.

Fortunately, the men were so preoccupied with the man, they didn't notice her right away.

"Oye!" Jamie shouted through her opened window. Based on their reaction, she startled them.

"Sigue Moviendote," one of the men said. "Keep moving," he told her.

"Suelta sus armas," Jamie said calmly but firmly. "Drop your guns."

That got their undivided attention. Jamie pointed her gun through the window at the men. A look of total confusion came over them and their eyes widened.

"Don't move or you die," Jamie said in Spanish.

They looked at Jamie then at each other, obviously not sure what to do.

She ordered, "Put your weapons on the ground."

They hesitated. Jamie moved the gun further out the window and shouted, "Now!"

They started to bend over.

"Slowly," Jamie instructed.

The men lowered the weapons and laid them on the ground. They were clearly being careful not to make a sudden movement. The picture probably didn't make sense to them. A blonde-haired American girl had a gun on them. They probably had no idea why.

"You will regret this," one of the men said.

"I already do," Jamie retorted as she opened the car door and got out, careful to keep the gun pointed directly at them at all times.

"Get in your car and go," she said to the man who was being accosted.

Jamie could hear the baby crying.

"Thank you," she heard him mumble.

When the family was safely away, Jamie kicked the two machine guns away from the men and ordered them to the shoulder of the road with their backs facing her. At that point, the prudent thing to do was get back in her car and move on down the road. However, a plan had formed in her mind. Something unconventional. Totally out of the box. Something that might fast start her investigation.

Jamie debated the options in her head. She could hear Curly, her trainer's voice. *Indecision breeds doubt. Doubt gets you killed.*

In other words, make a decision, even if it's wrong. The only thing worse than a wrong decision was indecision, according to Curly. She thought her plan was a good one.

Jamie made the two men get on their knees. She got two zip ties from her trunk and secured their hands behind their backs. Then she pulled her car to the side of the road and made the men get into the back seat. She rolled down all the windows. The summer sun was beating down on them. The temperature reading on the car registered a hundred and five degrees.

She got out of the car, pulled her phone out of her back pocket, and dialed Brad, her CIA handler.

He picked up on the first ring.

"I didn't expect to hear from you so soon," he said jokingly.

Jamie ignored the banter. "I have a question for you."

"Shoot," he said casually.

"What would you do if you had two Gulf Alliance men handcuffed in the back of your car?"

Brad didn't say anything for what seemed like a long time but was probably only ten seconds or so. "The first thing I'd do is not tell my handler about it."

Jamie couldn't help but grin. "Okay. What's the second thing you'd do?"

"Shoot them and dump their bodies in the desert."

Jamie put her hand over her phone even though it didn't cover the speaker. It was mostly for effect. The two men in the backseat of the car were listening to her side of the conversation through the opened back window.

"He said I should shoot you," Jamie said to the two men.

They immediately started squirming, trying to get the restraints off.

Jamie walked away from the car so they couldn't hear the rest of the conversation.

"Okay. That's what I'll do."

"No wait," Brad said. "I was only kidding. Don't shoot them. What are you doing Jamie and why are you holding two cartel members? That's not the mission."

"I'm stealing their car."

"Why exactly are you stealing their car?"

"It has a radio in it. I want to listen to their communications and see if they say anything about the missing girls."

"That's a good idea."

"Thank you."

"What do you want me to do?"

"I'm about fifty miles south of the border. On Highway 101. Send someone down to pick up the car and the men. I'll wait for you."

"Just throw the men in the trunk and get back on the road."

"It's too hot. The men will die. Besides, that will give me time to find out if they know anything about the kidnappings."

He didn't argue. Brad was good about that. He generally left the operations to the person in the field.

"I'm on it," Brad said.

Jamie hung up the phone, walked back to the car, turned the car on, set the air conditioning on high, and rolled the windows back up.

"Good news. I don't have to shoot you, as long as you tell me what I want to know."

The terrified look still consumed their faces.

16

Jamie knew from experience that most people were more willing to talk when they had a gun in their face.

The two lowlifes sitting in the back of her sedan were no exception. Unfortunately, they had nothing to say that would help her find the four missing girls. In fact, what they did say had thrown her entire plan out the window before she could even execute it.

"Have you heard any chatter on the radio about four missing girls?" Jamie asked them in Spanish.

"Our radio is broken. Has been for several weeks."

Jamie let out a loud groan and resisted the urge to shoot them on the spot. Without the radio, she might as well be driving her own car.

To make matters worse, it had been three hours since she'd called Brad, and his men still had not shown up for the transfer. Jamie's anger was growing hotter than the one-hundred-five-degree heat that was beating down on them. She didn't know if she was madder at the men or at herself. At one point, she considered letting them go and abandoning her plan to take their car. She quickly dismissed that point. The men would warn their bosses and they'd be after her in no time. Based on her questions, they probably already knew she was headed to Tampico.

She'd be halfway there already, if it hadn't been for this detour which Jamie was beginning to regret.

But leaving wasn't an option. Brad would be furious at her for wasting his time and CIA resources if his men showed up and she wasn't there. She had no choice but to wait.

To pass the time, she interrogated the men anyway to learn what she could about the organization. These men worked for the Northern Alliance. Tampico was part of the Southern Alliance, although right on the line between north and south, and she deduced from the men's tone and demeanor that the two gangs found themselves fighting each other over the territorial boundaries. Same organization, two different leaders. The leader of the Southern Alliance was named "El Mata." The killer.

The two men were fairly new, low-level grunts and knew little about the inner workings of the organizations. Even then, they were talkative and answered most of her questions honestly. She was trained to tell when they were lying, and when they weren't, and was mostly embellishing. The more they talked, the more brazen they became and wanted to talk. At least it passed the time. Jamie didn't bother writing anything down or trying to remember what they said, though. They would be thoroughly interrogated by professionals over the next couple weeks.

She was curious as to what prompted them to stop the Mormon couple and ramped up the questioning. This caused them to clam up. When they did finally offer some cursory explanation, with a little encouragement from her Sig, it became apparent they were harassing them to try and build a name for themselves as tough guys in the organization. Jamie got the sense that they might've actually harmed the man if she hadn't come along when she did. The woman and baby probably would've been released, but the child might've grown up without a father.

The thought made her shudder.

That's the only thing that gave Jamie some consolation. At least she had saved the young couple from harm, and these two would be locked away for the better part of the rest of their lives. Curly always said to find the victories where you could. Missions had an ebb and flow to them. A momentum. Sometimes positive, sometimes negative. How they started often had an impact on how they finished.

For that reason, she decided to look on the bright side. She had their car. It might come in handy somewhere down the road, even with a broken radio. Putting the best spin on the situation, her fortunes might turn around.

Wishful thinking.

One hour later, she was still waiting and still fuming.

***

When the CIA men finally arrived, they seemed more annoyed than Jamie. The one in charge introduced himself. "I'm Maxwell and that's TJ," he said, pointing to a burly guy who was already harassing the men in the back seat of the car. He gave Jamie a slight wave of the hand without looking over at her.

She started to make a joke about TJ Maxx but thought better of it. Maxwell did not seem in the mood. He didn't wait for Jamie to tell him her name.

"What's the situation here?" Maxwell asked tersely.

"Two scumbags were harassing a couple of Mormon missionaries. I came along and interdicted." Jamie normally didn't talk that way, but Maxwell sounded serious and professional, and it amused Jamie. So, she played along. Even deepened her voice for effect.

"Why didn't you cut them loose?" he asked roughly, clearly not amused.

"I should've made myself clearer," Jamie said sternly, giving it right back to him. "They weren't just harassing them. The man had injuries. The woman had a baby."

"I get why you *interdicted*," Maxwell said with a hint of sarcasm. "But why hold the men? Don't you have better things to do. I assume you're on a mission. You must be somebody important. The suits in the states insisted I come and help you. Doesn't seem like you needed any help. Except to know the play was to let them go."

Jamie didn't like his tone or him questioning her judgment, so she said so. "These guys are bad news. They would've killed the man. We need to take them out of the picture. Interrogate them. Find out what they know about the organization."

Maxwell rolled his eyes and started walking away from Jamie toward the car, which infuriated her. A pet peeve of hers was when people were dismissive toward her. She preferred anger and sternness over aloofness even though she could be all of the above at times.

"Turn them loose," Maxwell said to TJ.

Jamie was right behind him. "You can't let them go!" Jamie insisted. "I sat here for four hours in the hot sun waiting on you. I didn't do it for nothing."

Maxwell turned to face her with his eyes narrowed into a stern look. "And I wasted a full day on this. I drove three hours to get here, *for* nothing. Like I said, TJ cut them loose and let's get out of here."

TJ pulled a knife out of his pocket. The two men in the back seat began squirming. They didn't speak English, so they had no idea what was being discussed.

"TJ, stop," Jamie said with authority. "You can't let them go. They'll blow my cover."

"What's your mission?" Maxwell asked.

"Need to know basis."

Maxwell rolled his eyes again.

"Look," Maxwell said, moving closer so he was right in Jamie's face. "I'll hold them for twenty minutes. That'll give you a head start. That's the best I can do."

"I'm taking their car," Jamie said, trying to think of any argument that might get him to change his mind. "Or at least that was my plan."

"And why would you do that?"

"I wanted to listen to their radio and see if they say anything about the missing girls." Jamie immediately realized she had just referenced her mission.

Maxwell's eyebrows raised. "You're here looking for the girls."

"Do you know anything about them?"

"Of course. Half of my men are out looking for them."

Half his men. Maxwell was clearly a supervisor. Now she understood why he was so annoyed. This diversion had taken him off focus. Jamie agreed that he had better things to do than mess with a couple of low-level drug runners.

Jamie ignored the guilt she suddenly felt. She said, "I'm on my way to Tampico. To the bar where one of the girls went missing. I'm going to rattle some trees and see what snakes fall out. I need their car. Or at least that was my plan. Turns out the radio doesn't work."

That got TJ's attention. He had been standing over by her car. For some reason, he started walking toward the Mustang. He opened the door and got in.

Jamie turned her attention back to Maxwell who was rubbing his forehead in a rough manner. Obviously thinking about the dilemma, she had presented him with.

"I can buy you a couple of weeks," Maxwell said. "I'll take these two somewhere safe and hold them to give you time to do your thing."

"Take them to the U.S. Brad can find something to do with them."

Maxwell was shaking his head back and forth. "Won't work. Habeas Corpus. The Constitution. I'm sure you've heard of it."

This time Jamie rolled her eyes. Dismissiveness and condescension were the same thing in her book, and both made her equally mad. "Of course, I've heard of them."

Maxwell continued. "In America, they'd be entitled to an attorney. They'd be out on bail by tonight. I'd rather have them running around free down here than in the states."

Jamie almost blurted out, "Send them to Gitmo," but caught herself. That would've been embarrassing. Only the worst terrorists went there. Instead of saying anything, she just let out a sigh.

"I'll figure something out," he said. "You focus on finding the girls."

Jamie softened her tone as well. "If you can take them out of the picture for two weeks, that would be great. I just wish they would pay for what they did to that couple."

Jamie felt a sudden urge to get in the car and get out of there as quick as possible.

"They'll pay," Maxwell said.

"How?"

"I have my ways. I'll put the word out that these two are cooperating with us. They won't live twenty-four hours after we cut them loose. I wouldn't want to be them."

Images started popping into her head of what might await the two when El Mata got a hold of them. She had heard of all kinds of atrocities carried out by the Mexican Drug Cartels. Beheadings. Torture. Cutting off limbs.

Jamie changed the subject. "Anything you can tell me about the four missing girls?"

"There were actually five," Maxwell said, matter-of-factly. "Did you know that?"

"I didn't."

"Let me fill you in."

Jamie suddenly wasn't in as big a hurry to leave.

17

"Have you seen this girl?" Detective Delancey asked Jake Fossey, as he set a picture of Sara Morgan down on the table in front of him.

Fossey didn't answer right away.

The Detective and Fossey were in a small interrogation room, totally bare and antiseptic, except for one table, two chairs, and nothing on the solid white walls. Fossey sat in one of the chairs leaning back with his arms folded and one leg crossed. Detective Delancey wasn't sitting. A burly man, he towered over Fossey who seemed to be trying his best not to appear intimidated.

Commissioner Collin Hughes was watching and listening in the observation room behind a large one-way mirror. From his vantage point, he could see all three interrogation rooms which were currently filled with persons of interest in the disappearance of Sara Morgan. Lars Fossey, the owner of the Reef Bar where Sara went missing, was in the center room. Detective Jacobson was going after him hard, trying to find any cracks in his story.

Lars insisted he was home with his girlfriend watching a movie at the time Sara Morgan went missing.

His girlfriend, Cydney Birch, was in the third room, being interviewed by Roz Steele, a tough New York transplant who was capable of bringing as much pressure to bear as necessary. If Ms. Birch knew more than she was letting on, Steele would sense it and was as relentless as a bulldog attacking a piece of meat.

So far, Roz was using a "good cop" approach, trying to get her to feel comfortable. Open up. Even so, Ms. Birch was overly nervous. Commissioner Hughes didn't read too much into that. To be expected considering the gravity of the situation.

Hughes turned his attention back to the son. He was waiting impatiently for the kid's answer. Delancey was too as he paced the room like a caged tiger.

Detective Delancey was Hughes's first hire. Delancey was a detective in Miami for more than twenty years. Just a few years from retirement, he was forced out after an undercover sting revealed he and his partner were shaking down drug dealers. They would steal their drugs, throw them into the ocean, and then pocket the money. He pleaded to a misdemeanor and got probation. They never found any of the money or they could've gone after him for more serious charges. His years of otherwise impeccable service factored in, and he avoided jail time but lost his badge.

Needing a change of scenery, he moved to the Cayman Islands and set up shop as a private investigator. Bought a condo on the beach. Probably with some of the dirty money. When he came to Commissioner Hughes with information that helped him solve a cold case, Hughes offered him a job. Delancey readily admitted his problems in Miami. Hughes looked into them and hired him anyway. He reasoned that some people deserved a second chance. Also, he needed an experienced, hard-nosed detective, and Delancey fit the bill perfectly.

That's why Hughes put him on the interrogation of Fossey. He wouldn't pull any punches with the kid.

In an interrogation, normally a detective tried to build rapport and gain a suspect's trust. No time for that in this case. Sara Morgan had been missing for approximately fifteen hours, and the clock was ticking like a bomb about to explode. Every investigator knew that the longer Sara was missing, the less likely she would be found alive.

So far, Delancey hadn't scored any real points. Jake Fossey, for his age, was as cool as an eastward breeze in the wintertime. He sat back in his chair, holding the picture of Sara in front of him, with a slight smirk on his pretty-boy face. He stared at the picture for what seemed like an entire minute, which only added to the overall tension which was as thick as a morning fog. Hughes thought he saw a glimpse of recognition when Jake first looked at the picture but couldn't be sure. When Jake finally answered, Commissioner Hughes didn't get the answer expected.

"I remember that girl from the bar," Jake said. "She was there last night."

That was all the opening Delancey needed. He began firing questions as fast as a submachine gun. "Where did you see her?"

"Out on the dance floor. Hanging out at the bar. I seem to remember some other girls were with her."

"What time was that?"

"I couldn't say."

"Think about it."

"I was busy, mate," he said with a heavy Australian accent. "I had a bar to run. I don't really look at the clock." Jake's father had moved to the Caymans from Australia more than fifteen years ago, but his son had an accent even though he had grown up on the island.

The contrast couldn't have been starker. Delancey had a gruff, no nonsense, rough-around-the-edges voice and demeanor. Everything about him was big. Big bones. Big hands. Big nose that looked like it had been broken a couple times.

Jake acted like he didn't have a care in the world. Hughes knew it was an act. The kid's heart had to be doing somersaults. Especially as Delancey started ratcheting up the pressure.

"Did you see her earlier or later in the evening?" Delancey persisted.

"Definitely earlier. She wasn't there when I closed the bar."

"Did you talk to her?"

"No. I was in my office."

"How did you see her if you were in your office?" Delancey asked in his most accusatory voice.

Commissioner Hughes saw the first sign of nervousness from Jake as he changed positions. Now he sat forward and put his arms on the table, looking down, avoiding any eye contact with Delancey who was no more than ten inches from his face.

Jake answered, "Security camera. I have a monitor in my office. I saw her on the screen. Not hard to miss. She's a real looker, don't you think?"

Delancey ignored the snide comment. "Did you see her talking to anyone?"

"She was talking to a lot of people. The bar was full. What's this all about?"

Delancey hesitated for the first time. Probably not sure how much information to divulge at this point. He decided to ignore the question. Good technique. Don't ever let the suspect ask the questions.

"Was she drinking?" Delancey asked.

"Probably. But I couldn't say."

"Did you know she was underage? You know the laws about serving alcohol to minors."

Jake chuckled. "She doesn't look like a minor to me."

"She's seventeen."

"I don't remember a drink in her hand. Maybe she had a fake I.D. I don't know, mate. You'll have to ask the bartender. Like I said, I was in my office the whole night."

The kid was right. The underage alcohol angle wasn't going anywhere. Even if Sara was drinking, she was only a couple of weeks away from her eighteenth birthday. The worst that could happen to the *Reef Bar* would be a small fine.

"I intend to talk to the bartender and everyone in the bar that night," Delancey retorted, clearly not wanting to cede any point.

"Can you tell me what's going on?" Jake asked.

"The girl in the picture is missing. Your bar is the last place she was seen. I think you know more than you're telling me. What time did your dad leave the bar last night?"

That question brought a smile to Commissioner Hughes's face. Delancey knew Lars Fossey claimed to be at home the entire night. The question was designed to see if their stories meshed.

"He wasn't at the bar last night. He was at home watching a movie with Cyd."

That answer sounded scripted. Delancey must've noticed it too because he jumped all over that remark.

"If you were at the bar all night, how do you know what your Dad was doing?"

"He told me."

"When?"

"When I talked to him yesterday. He said he and Cyd were going to stay in and watch a movie."

"Did you watch it with them?"

"No! I told you I was at the bar all night."

"So, you don't really know what your dad was doing, do you?"

"He was at home. That's what he told me."

Delancey scored a minor point. It didn't move the investigation forward, but it did let Jake know that he wasn't invincible, and a made-up story wasn't fool proof. If it was made-up. The Fosseys may very well be innocent. If so, Commissioner Hughes would apologize to them later. For now, the fact that a girl was last seen at their bar and the security tape had been tampered with was enough to make them the primary lead. At this point, the only lead.

Ask about the security camera.

Delancey changed positions and walked behind Fossey. Another good technique. If anything would make a young kid nervous, it would be having someone like Delancey pacing behind your back.

"Let's talk about that security camera," Delancey said with his words dripping in accusation and sarcasm. The question brought another smile to Hughes' face. They were on the same page. Now they were getting somewhere. Commissioner Hughes felt in his gut that the tape had been tampered with. The tape had the evidence. Find out who doctored it and the case might be solved. Jake was the most likely suspect.

Commissioner Hughes moved closer to the observation window. He really wanted to hear this line of questioning and see Jake's reaction.

Before Delancey could ask a question, Roz Steele suddenly bolted from her seat in the third interrogation room and walked over to the door and into the observation area. Nearly out of breath.

"What is it Roz?" Hughes asked, trying to keep one eye on Jake's room and yet give her his attention.

"Ms. Birch just admitted to me that Mr. Fossey wasn't with her the whole night."

"What?"

"She said they watched a movie until about ten thirty and then they went to bed."

"That's what he says."

"Yeah, but she woke up around midnight to go to the bathroom. Fossey wasn't in the bed."

"Did she see where he was?"

"No. She saw a light on in the living area, and assumed he was there."

"But she didn't see him?"

"Not until later. She said he got back in bed about three in the morning. She's a light sleeper, and he woke her up."

"Is she sure about the time?"

"She looked at the clock beside the bed."

A bolt of adrenaline rushed through Commissioner Hughes like he had just been struck by lightning.

"Get in there right now," he said with urgency pointing to observation room two. "Help Jacobson question the father. Don't reveal what you know right away. Give him some rope to hang himself. Then spring this new information on him after he has set his lies in cement."

Commissioner Hughes could feel it. This was the first big break in the investigation.

18

Back in Mexico

"I didn't know a fifth girl was missing," Jamie said to Maxwell. "Where is she missing from?"

As if finding four girls in a country the size of Mexico was not enough, to make matters worse, she now had to find another girl. She hoped they were all five together at least. No guarantees of that, though.

"She's not missing," Maxwell said, as he wiped the sweat off his brow with the sleeve of his shirt. His attire was business professional—a long-sleeve white shirt, no tie, black dress pants, and black dress shoes. Not at all what an operative would wear in the field. Definitely an administrative type. Although Maxwell looked like he could hold his own in a dangerous situation. Over six foot tall and about two-ten in weight, there didn't appear to be an ounce of fat on him even though he was pushing fifty.

"You just said a fifth girl was missing," Jamie said trying to get on with the subject at hand. It seemed like Maxwell liked to play word games and make her pry the information out of him. Why? She had no clue even though she was often guilty of the same thing.

Maxwell shrugged. "I never said she was missing. I said there was a fifth girl. Same M.O. Senior trip. In a bar with her friends. Someone put something in her drink, so she doesn't remember a lot."

There was another long pause.

Jamie grew impatient. This time she shrugged her shoulders signaling for him to get on with it.

Maxwell finally continued. "When she got her bearings, she was on a beach."

"A beach?"

"That's what I said."

Jamie looked off in the distance, contemplating that new information. She noticed Maxwell doing the same thing. He kept looking both directions on the highway. Nervously. Probably worried that more Alliance members might happen upon them. Jamie had been worried about the same thing the entire time she was holding the two men. That's why she kept her machine gun next to her in the car.

She suddenly realized that she wasn't armed. Maxwell had a side arm on his belt, but she was weaponless. She calculated in her mind that it would take about twelve seconds to get to her gun which was on the floorboard of the front seat of her car now. More than enough time if a car appeared in either direction, but not if she hesitated. Fortunately, this was mostly a deserted back road, and they hadn't seen a car since Maxwell got there.

So, she turned her attention back to what he was saying and ignored the angst.

"Strange, isn't it," he said. "A beach. Of all places. Anyway. She could see a boat. They clearly intended to put her on it. The waves were rougher than usual, and the men were struggling with it. Somehow, she had enough wits about her to get away when they weren't looking. They chased her but she flagged down a passing car and got away."

"She's one lucky girl," Jamie said. "I assume she's been questioned."

Maxwell nodded his head.

Jamie lifted her t-shirt slightly and bent her head down to wipe the sweat off her face. When she looked up, she noticed Maxwell looking at her abs. not even bothering to pretend not to.

She ignored it.

A lot of questions were running through her mind. *A fifth girl? A boat? A witness?* She needed more information.

"Where did this happen?"

"South of Cancun."

That seemed strange as well since Cancun was a big tourist area. These kidnappers were brazened. Of course, she knew that already since they had the gall to snatch a girl right out of the states and drive her across the border.

"Were the men that took her part of the Gulf Alliance?"

"I think so. Yes. Definitely Mexican. They took her in an SUV. Same as the other girls."

"Why would they put her on a boat?"

"I don't know."

"Where would they take her?"

"Probably down south."

"Are there any islands close enough to take a boat to?"

"Cozumel, of course. But that's a big tourist area. No place to hide her there."

"How far is Cuba?"

"Less than a couple hundred miles. Not that much farther than Key West is from Cuba. But I wouldn't think they would take them there."

"I hope not. That's not a place I want to go to anytime soon."

"If they left the country, they probably took them to South America."

"Do you think El Mata is behind this?"

"That's as good a guess as any." Jamie paused to let that sink in and beat back the fear.

"Where's his compound?" she asked.

Maxwell laughed nervously. "Don't even think about it."

"If that's where the girls are, then that's where I'm going."

"Not even *you* are crazy enough to try to infiltrate El Mata's lair."

"I see you know of my reputation."

"I know that you don't do things by the book."

"Sometimes you have to improvise," she said, a little louder than she intended.

Maxwell matched her intensity. "You'll need a small army if you want to attack his compound. I don't even know if a small army would be enough. It's a fortress."

"I've gotten into worse places," Jamie said with a dismissive wave of her hand. "Somebody's got to get those girls back. This is what I do. Besides, I have one of their cars. I'll just drive in."

Jamie pointed at the Mustang. The door was open and all they could see of TJ was his legs hanging out the passenger-side door resting on the ground. They could also hear him fiddling with something on the inside and letting out an occasional straining groan.

"How are you going to get past the armed guards at the checkpoints?" Maxwell asked, bringing her attention back to him and the task at hand.

Before she could answer, TJ let out a yell. He was now standing next to the car holding a wire in his hand. "I fixed the radio," he said with a broad grin on his face.

Jamie practically ran to the car and looked inside. "You fixed it?"

"Yep. Faulty wire." He waved the wire in the air.

"How did you fix it without a new wire?" Maxwell asked.

TJ had a look of satisfaction on his face as his eyes beamed. "Like the lady was saying, sometimes you have to improvise."

"I love you," Jamie said as she threw her arms around TJ and lifted him off the ground in a bear hug which wasn't easy to do considering he weighed upwards of two hundred and thirty pounds of solid muscle.

"I can listen to their communications now," Jamie said enthusiastically. "See. It was worth hanging around," she said for Maxwell's benefit since he had questioned her judgment.

"I hate to put a damper on your enthusiasm," Maxwell said, "And this love fest... but seriously... " Maxwell's eyes narrowed, and his forehead furrowed as he got a stern look on his face. "You need to be careful down here. Don't mess around with the Alliance. These are dangerous men."

"I can handle myself."

"I'm sure you can. But listen to me. I've been down here for ten years. Things have only gotten worse."

"Maybe you're the problem then," Jamie said with a grin so he would know she was kidding.

"The Alliance is powerful. The Mexican government looks the other way as long as certain rules are followed. One of them is that we don't bother them as long as they leave Americans alone."

"I guess that's out the window. They kidnapped five young American girls."

"I know. Things don't make sense. Actually... we don't even know it's them. Could be anybody."

Jamie retorted confidently, "The two men in the car said before their radio went dead, they heard something big was going down in the south. I think it's them. I can feel it in my gut. Just a few minutes ago, you said it was the Alliance behind the kidnappings."

"I said I *thought* it was them. Probably. They are the only organization big enough to pull off something like this. I just don't know why they would risk stirring up trouble with us. The motive has me baffled."

"Motive is easy. Money."

"They already have a lot of money."

"Then influence. Somebody wants the girls. Doesn't sound like El Mata would take them for himself."

"Probably not."

"I'll ask him when I see him, and I'll let you know what he says."

Maxwell glared at Jamie. "Don't underestimate El Mata. Actually... don't overestimate your own abilities. You're not Wonder Woman."

"That's for sure. I'm barely an A cup." Jamie held both hands out in front of her chest in a recognizable gesture to most men.

That got a laugh from TJ and Maxwell, easing some of the tension. Jamie decided to make nice. She realized Maxwell could be of some help to her.

"I hear you," Jamie said. "I'll be careful."

In the back of her mind, she remembered what Curly always said. *Don't be careful. Careful will get you killed. Be prepared.*

Regardless, that seemed to satisfy Maxwell, so she added, "Max, can you have a man at the bar in Tampico around say... ten o'clock tonight. Someone who can speak Spanish fluently. Somebody who can sound like an Alliance member."

"Why? And don't ever call me Max."

"Need to know basis."

Maxwell twisted his lips to the side. "I think since it's my man then I need to know."

Jamie moved in closer to him and patted Maxwell on the chest. "I was just kidding. I have a plan."

"This oughta be good."

"It is," Jamie said and began to relate to him only the things he needed to know.

19

Grand Cayman

After Sean Morgan left the police station, he checked into the Sandy Beach Hotel. The same hotel where Sara and the school group had stayed. He rented a conference room and set up a mini-mobile command center. At the moment, he was the only one in there. He was busy typing away on a things-to-do-list.

His phone rang for the umpteenth time, interrupting his work. Probably his wife. He should take the call, but things at work needed his attention. More problems had arisen on the acquisition, and the deal was on the verge of falling apart. Fred, at Longhorn Bank & Trust was out of the office on vacation for two weeks. His associate was not as helpful, and it looked like the financing might be delayed.

To make matters worse, his buyer was starting to get cold feet. Only moments ago, he had said, "When a deal has too many problems, maybe it's not meant to be."

Sean wanted to throw the phone across the room. Instead, he tried to sound reassuring, "Give me a couple of days, and I'll figure something out. I've got a situation I'm working on right now, but I'll get back to you."

"You've got one week," he said.

Sean started to tell him his daughter was missing but thought better of it. He might pull out of the deal right away, if he thought Sean was going to be indefinitely detained in the Cayman Islands.

When Sean hung up, a feeling of gloom came over him. This deal was important. He wasn't sure exactly how he would work it out, but he had to think of something. Failure wasn't an option. If they lost the deal, he would stand to lose millions. An avid reader of self-help books, Sean was a strict follower of the Warren Buffett rules of investing. Rule number one: Don't lose money. Rule number two: See rule number one.

If this deal fell through... Sean shuddered at the thought.

While his firm was doing well on the surface, some might say he was over-leveraged. This deal was supposed to make him whole again and then some. Getting another deal on the table would take months. This one should've been closed already. Would have if the owner hadn't started buying back his stock.

Sean stopped what he was doing and gave himself a short pep talk. *Things are going to be okay. It will work out. I will find a way.*

He didn't get to where he was by looking backward. An optimist by nature, his natural instinct was to buckle down, look forward, and go to work. He prided himself on creativity and ingenuity, and he would bring all of his considerable skills to bear on solving this problem.

When the phone rang a second time in less than a minute, he realized he'd better take it. His wife was probably climbing the walls with worry.

"Hi honey," he said.

"What happened to our baby? Have they found her? Is she dead?" Carolyn was hysterical. "Please tell me she's not dead. She can't be. She has to be okay. Sean, tell me what's going on."

The words were intermixed with sobs. To the point that Sean could barely understand her.

Before he could answer, she said accusingly, "Why don't you answer your phone? I've been calling you for more than two hours!"

"I've been busy," Sean retorted, trying to control his anger. "I've been meeting with the investigator."

A little white lie. That meeting was a couple hours ago. Since then, he'd been dealing with work and getting checked into the hotel. Mentioning the investigator did get the focus off of him.

"What did the investigator say?" Carolyn asked with urgency in her voice. "Do they know where Sara is?"

"I'll tell you if you'll let me speak," Sean said roughly. He was trying to be sympathetic, but Carolyn needed to calm down. They were wasting valuable time. He had things to do.

The other end went silent except for labored breaths.

"I'm listening," she finally said.

"Like I said... I talked to the investigator. He wanted to wait forty-eight hours before he started looking for her. I told him in no uncertain terms that that wasn't acceptable. I lit a fire under him, and they're looking for her as we speak."

Another small white lie, but he was getting used to it when it came to Carolyn. Sometimes it was just easier to tell her what she wanted to hear. Sean paused to see if Carolyn had a comment. When she didn't, he continued. "Sara was at a bar with a couple girls. That was the last time anyone saw her."

"I know. I talked to Mr. Jolly. He filled me in on what happened." Carolyn seemed more composed.

"If you talked to Jolly, then I'll spare you the details. Stupid girl! I warned her not to go out alone."

"She wasn't alone. She was with her friends."

"Who left her alone! They were off talking to some boys."

"I know. It was stupid. You know how kids are. This was her senior trip. They just wanted to have fun."

"Don't defend her. What she did was dumb. Actually... I blame the school. If anything happened to Sara, we'll sue them for all they've got. There should've been a chaperone with them."

Sean tried to sound convincing. Carolyn would never let him sue the school. Mostly, he was bloviating for her benefit. She obviously needed reassurance. Something he wasn't always good at. He needed to backtrack. Blame wasn't the right approach at the moment.

"I'm sorry, Carolyn," he said more tenderly. "I'm just angry. As you can tell."

"What are we going to do, Sean?" Carolyn asked, as the tears started to flow again. "I can't lose my girl, she's all I have."

"I'm working on it. I've already hired a PR firm back in Dallas."

"A PR firm? Why would you do that?" she asked, as the crying abruptly stopped.

"We need publicity on this as soon as possible. We've got to get the word out right away."

"Why a firm in Dallas? Sara's in the Cayman Islands."

"We need the national press to pick this up. The lady at the PR firm said she can have this story on the local Dallas stations tonight. The networks might even pick it up. I'm going to do a press conference in front of the bar around five o'clock this evening. The footage is going to be sent back to the Dallas stations. After the press conference, the PR person is going to set up interviews with news organizations back in the states. I told you I'm on it."

"Do you think the press is a good idea? That might make the kidnappers panic and hurt Sara."

"That's what the investigator said." Sean immediately regretted revealing that information.

"I tend to agree with him."

"Well, I don't! The only hope we have of finding Sara is getting her picture out there as soon as possible. Somebody knows something. I'm going to offer a million-dollar reward for any information that leads to her safe return."

"A reward. That's a good idea."

"I'll do anything to get her back."

"Thank you, Sean," Carolyn said effusively. "That sounds like a good idea. I know Sara's not really your daughter, but I appreciate what you're doing for her."

"Sara *is* my daughter. I love her as if she were my own flesh and blood."

"I know you do. That's not what I meant."

"I'm going to do everything I can to find Sara. I promise."

"I'm coming down there," Carolyn said emphatically.

"No! I don't think that's a good idea."

"Bill is going to fly me."

Bill Duffy was a friend from church who also owned a plane and had a pilot's license.

"Honey. You should stay there. I've got things under control. There's nothing you can do here."

"I have to be there. I'll go crazy if I stay here. I have to do something. I can put up flyers. Organize searches. I can get food and drinks for the searchers. I won't get in your way. I promise. I want to be there when they find Sara."

Before Sean could object further, he heard a doorbell in the background.

Carolyn said, "I've got to go. That's probably Bill. I'll see you soon."

Then the line went dead.

20

Mexico

Three Hours Later

Jamie made good time to Tampico once she got on the road. In fact, too good. The three hours had given her time to rethink her plan, and she decided that arriving after dark was a better strategy. Especially since she was now driving one of the Alliance's cars. Fortunately, she had only seen one other car like hers, and they were far enough away that they couldn't see her.

The jet-black Ford Mustang had dark tinted windows so no one could see inside unless they were directly in front of her. That had been a constant concern while driving in the daylight. The first hour was spent contemplating what she would do if she were spotted. Outrunning them was a better strategy than outshooting them. So, she stayed on full alert and memorized the roads to her destination.

More than halfway there, she wasn't out of the woods but had allowed herself to relax some and focus on a plan for finding the girls. That wasn't going well. Every plan ended with her having to infiltrate El Mata's compound. Maxwell's words still rang true in her ears.

Don't even think about it.

But she had thought about it. For nearly three hours. Every idea had a low MSO. A *Curlyism* for Mission Success Odds. He had ingrained in her that it needed to be as close to a hundred percent as she could get it. The only way it would ever be a hundred percent safe was if she stayed home. That wasn't an option. However, she didn't have a death wish.While she was willing to take risks, if they were unnecessary, she wouldn't take them. Trying to infiltrate El Mata's lair seemed like a suicide mission. Nothing in the three hours had convinced her otherwise.

Besides, she didn't even know if the girls were there. If she found out they were, then she'd have to regroup and let Brad determine how to get them out.

That was another problem. Where were the girls? Nothing made sense. She didn't feel in her gut that the girls were at El Mata's, or if they were, they wouldn't be there long. While she was convinced that El Mata was behind the kidnappings, the boat had her perplexed. The one girl from Brownsville, Texas, Vicky, was driven across the border in a Dodge Durango stolen from Tampico.

Was she put on a boat? Were all the girls transferred to a boat and taken to the same location?

Everything about the kidnappings were all the same. All five girls were on a senior class trip. That took some intelligence to learn and coordinate. It wouldn't be that hard to do, though. Most of the schools' websites had information about senior trips. It would take some time to gather the information, but anyone with a computer could learn when and where the seventeen- and eighteen-year-old girls would be.

It also wouldn't be hard to assume that one or more of them would end up in a bar in that area. At that point, all they had to do was slip something in their drinks and get them out of the bar without being seen. Apparently, that was not as hard as it sounded since they managed to pull it off five different times. That, in and of itself, took a considerable amount of coordination. Probably with some help from the bouncers at the bars.

That thought suddenly caused Jamie to think of another. She needed to call Brad.

Before she could, her phone pinged, signaling she had a text. The sound startled her and broke the prolonged silence in the car. She had long since turned the radio off after hearing nothing but chatter and static for the first hour, which was annoying. After an hour, she hadn't learned anything important and didn't expect to.

Jamie fumbled with the phone to see who it was while struggling to drive.

Alex.

Hi Pretty, the text said.

Hey sexy, she responded.

Can u talk?

Sure. Who is this?

Very funny.

The phone rang seconds later.

"You must be home," Jamie answered warmly.

"Yep. Got back this morning. Then crashed for a few hours."

"How did it go?"

"Not bad. Although I spent most of the time chasing Pok across the middle east."

Pok was a notorious cyber criminal from North Korea. He and Alex had a running battle as to who was the best hacker in the world. It was close, but Jamie's money was on Alex.

"I shoulda killed him when I had the chance," Alex added.

Alex was on a mission to South Korea when he discovered the location of a cyber lab in North Korea that was waging war against the US. He got the not-so-bright idea to go off-mission and infiltrate the lab. Turns out, the lab was run by Pok. Alex had been ecstatic when he realized how close he was to capturing or killing the elusive Pok. He could've taken him out, but Brad, also his handler, told him to stand down.

That has been a source of consternation for Alex ever since, as Pok immediately resumed his criminal enterprise, just in different locations which Alex was now tasked with finding. Not that the mission to North Korea was a failure. It ended up being a good thing that he went there because he was able to secure nuclear codes the North Koreans had stolen from Pakistan and were planning to sell to Iran. Shutting down that cyber lab was an added bonus.

While the mission was a success, it left Alex with some regrets. Namely, that Pok was still breathing. He wouldn't rest until he rectified that fact.

Jamie realized after several seconds of silence that it was her turn to respond.

"At least you're home safe," she said. "I miss you."

"Miss you too. How about you? Things going good? Have you killed anyone yet?"

Jamie chuckled. "No. It's been a slow day at the office. I did take care of a couple of bad guys, members of the Alliance who were roughing up some missionaries. That was fun."

"I hope they got what they deserved."

"Not exactly, but they will." Jamie remembered what Maxwell had said about what would happen to the men once they put out word that they had turned on the Alliance. Maxwell told her about four men who recently had their hands cut off for taking drug money that belonged to the Alliance. El Mata was as ruthless as it comes.

Jamie continued. "I'm going to pay El Mata a visit sometime in the next few days. Wanna come?"

"Not a chance! I hope you take a couple hundred Marines with you."

"Can't do that. That would make you jealous. You wouldn't like me being with all those hunky men."

"Ha! Ha! I have nothing to worry about. You already have a hunky man."

"That's a good point. I don't want them, anyway. Marines are a little crazy. I'm glad you called, though. There's something you can do for me."

"Are you glad I called because you want me to do something for you or because you are glad to hear from me?"

"Both."

"Good answer. Let me have it then. As long as it doesn't involve firing a gun, I'm in."

"I need some security footage. From last Friday night. A bar in Tampico Mexico. A girl went missing."

"What's the bar called?"

"La Taberna."

"What am I looking for?"

"A girl from the states. She was there on a senior trip. We think someone put something in her drink or coaxed her out of the bar. I don't really know what you'll see, but you'll know it when you see it. Just look for something suspicious."

"Will do. Have you tried tracking her cell phone?"

"I was just about to ask if you could do that for me as well."

"I can, but it'll cost you extra."

"You can send Brad the bill."

Alex let out a guffaw. "Then I'll never get paid."

"Do it because you love me."

"I do love you."

"Do you love me enough to track the cell phones for four girls?"

"There are four girls missing?"

"Yep," Jamie said, letting out a huge sigh.

"I wondered why Brad sent you to Mexico to look for one girl."

"I think El Mata is behind it. The security footage won't tell me much, I suspect, but it will confirm if it were his men who took the girls. If you can track a cell phone, then I might know where they are. Hopefully, they aren't in El Mata's compound."

"Let's hope not. I'm on it. Can you give me the girl's names and cellphone information?"

"I'll text it to you. I can't thank you enough."

"Maybe you can't. But try next time you see me."

"Will do."

"Don't be careful."

"I won't."

Their traditional goodbye when one or the other was on a mission.

Jamie hung up the phone, pulled off the side of the road, and grabbed her files. She texted Alex the girl's names, cell phone numbers, and their pictures. Hopefully from that, he could find something that would help her. Knowing Alex, he was already hacking into the bar security system. When it came to a sense of urgency, Alex's was off the charts. Right up there with hers. That sometimes strained their relationship. They somehow managed to make it work, even though they were both Type A personalities.

Jamie looked down at her finger which seemed bare without her engagement ring. She never wore it on a mission. It reminded her that they had promised to talk about the wedding once Alex returned from his mission. Now that would have to wait. At some point, maybe they could sit down and actually make wedding plans. Something they both had avoided. Mostly, because they know how hard it would be to make a marriage work with their schedules and their personalities. Things were going good, and no one seemed willing to broach the subject of taking it to the next level.

So, the marriage elephant was kept outside the room and the subject avoided. Like a can kicked down the road.

Jamie suddenly remembered that she was about to call Brad. Something had popped into her head right before Alex called, and now she'd forgotten what it was.

It was important.

Alex had distracted her. Not that she was complaining, but she needed to turn her attention back to the mission.

Something about the fifth girl.

Then she remembered and dialed Brad's number.

"I heard you made the handoff," Brad said, in a matter-of-fact voice. He usually didn't answer the phone with any formal greeting. Usually, it was with a comment related to whatever mission she was on.

"I did. I met Maxwell, too. He might be of some use to me on this trip. Although, he wasn't all that happy to meet me."

"Most people you run across on a mission aren't happy to meet you. Especially the bad guys. They usually end up dead or in the hospital. That's what I love about you."

"You love me? That warms my heart. I had no idea."

"Shut up. Why did you call me?"

"I've been thinking."

"Good. That's what I'm paying you for."

"You're not paying me. Uncle Sam is."

"Whatever. He only pays you because I ask him too."

Jamie appreciated the banter. It made her feel like one of the boys. Brad didn't have many female operatives, and she got the impression that he treated her the same as all the other men under his direction. A trait she admired in him. That's just how she wanted it. To be one of the boys.

"There was a fifth girl kidnapped," Jamie blurted out.

"I know."

"And you didn't think I needed to know that information?"

"I just learned it myself. After talking to Maxwell."

He still should've called her as soon as he knew, but she decided to drop it.

"Anyway... The fifth girl got away. I think El Mata is behind the kidnappings."

"That's a reasonable assumption, but we don't assume. We go by facts."

"I know. That's why I'm on my way to Tampico. I'm going to find proof that El Mata is behind them. If not, then I'll find out who is. But I'm convinced they're all related."

"I would agree."

Jamie wished Brad would let her finish. It broke up her chain of thought. Brad always felt the need to interject his opinion after every sentence. Something that annoyed her but that she was getting used to.

Jamie continued. "I know we don't assume, but for the sake of this discussion, let's assume El Mata is behind the kidnappings. I don't think he would take the girls for himself."

She paused expecting him to say something.

When he didn't, she continued. "That means somebody hired him to kidnap five girls. A contract kidnapping. By someone with a lot of money and who wanted only American girls. Whoever it was probably paid a ton for them. This type of operation carried a lot of risk for El Mata."

"I'm with you so far."

"More than likely, that someone paid all the money up front."

"I'm not sure I understand the point."

"The point is that the contract wasn't fulfilled. El Mata only delivered four girls. The buyer can't be very happy."

"And your point is?"

"El Mata owes him another girl. I think there's going to be another kidnapping."

21

Commissioner Collin Hughes assembled all of his detectives in the conference room of the Police Headquarters for a SOTI meeting. Status of The Investigation conference. While he hated to pull them out of the field, he didn't want them working in a vacuum. An investigation was like a puzzle with many pieces. From experience, he'd learned that the pieces by themselves often don't make sense. Bring the pieces together in one room and sometimes a connection was made that broke the case wide open.

"Let's start with what we know," Commissioner Hughes said.

A large white board stood on an easel in the front center of the room, and Hughes stood next to it. Written in the center of the board was Sara Morgan's name. Hughes wrote Lars Fossey's name to the side with a line connecting him to Sara.

"Is he connected to the kidnappings?" Hughes asked.

"He owns the bar where she went missing," Roz Steele said. An obvious point that everyone already knew, but Hughes didn't mind starting with the basics and building from there. When the meeting was all said and done, they actually might not know much more than that.

"He claims he was asleep in his bed with his girlfriend," Detective Jacobson said. His main job in the investigation was to question Lars Fossey, which he did for over three hours.

"The girlfriend says he wasn't in the bed between eleven thirty and three in the morning," Roz interjected.

"That certainly fits the timeline for when she went missing," Hughes said, as he wrote the time on the board. *Ten thirty to eleven*. "Ten thirty was the last time anyone saw her at the bar. Bed check was at eleven. Sara was a conscientious girl. She would not have stayed out past curfew unless it was out of her control."

"The girlfriend says they went to bed about ten-thirty. She went right to sleep. She woke up, and he wasn't there. That doesn't mean he couldn't have left earlier. That's the first time she noticed he wasn't in the bed."

The timeline didn't make sense. It didn't seem like Lars Fossey had enough time to leave the house, drive to the bar, and kidnap a girl. This crime seemed more premeditated than that. Still, he needed to pursue that thread, even if it didn't lead anywhere. Fossey lied about being asleep in the bed. Rarely did a suspect blurt out a confession in an interrogation. They had to find an inconsistency or a lie.

When they did, that meant the suspect had something to hide. They had to find out why Fossey lied about being in the bed, before they could rule him out as a suspect, even if the timeline didn't work. Even though the lifeblood of an investigation was lies and inconsistencies in a suspect's story, it was a huge leap from lying to a girlfriend and kidnapping, possibly even murdering, a teenager.

"What did Fossey say when you confronted him?" Hughes asked. He knew the answer since he was listening from the observation room but wanted them to answer for the benefit of the others in the room. Also, to see if they got the same impression he did when he heard Fossey's answer.

"He claims she was mistaken," Roz said. "That he was in the bed the whole time."

"Do you believe him?" Hughes asked.

"No!" Roz and Jacobson answered in unison.

"Me either," Hughes said, while he wrote *No Alibi* next to Lars Fossey's name.

"I think I would know if someone was in my bed," Roz said, sending laughter through the room.

The commissioner sensed excitement building as they started talking among themselves. He needed to tamp that down without them losing their enthusiasm.

"Let's don't jump to any conclusions," Hughes said. "There could be a million reasons why Lars would lie about it."

"Commissioner Hughes is right," Jacobson said. "We don't know that he left the house. He could've been looking at porn on his computer and didn't want his girlfriend to know about it."

"There might even be another girl on the side," Roz said. "He could've been talking to her on the phone. Chatting on his computer. Maybe on a dating website. Who knows?"

"If we could get hold of his computer and cellphone, we could find out easily enough," Jacobson said.

Hughes shook his head. "We don't have enough for a search warrant. The Judge is letting us search the bar. That's all we're going to get without more evidence. We've got the bar shut down and forensics is over there going through it now. I doubt they'll find anything. But they're looking for blood or any sign of a struggle. We also have people doing a door-to-door. Hopefully, someone saw or heard something."

The bar was in the middle of a busy business district on Seven Mile Beach. While most of the businesses were closed at that time of night, there would've been a lot of tourist activity in the area around that time.

That reminded him of something. "Did we find out if the convenience store across the street has a security camera?" Hughes asked.

"It does," one of his plain clothes officers in the back answered. "But the owner won't let me look at it. Not without a warrant. He made a big deal about how he knows his rights. 'Illegal search and seizure,' he said. 'A violation of his first amendment rights.' We'll have to do this one by the book." The officer related the encounter in a mocking voice.

"Did you explain to him that a young girl is missing, and that time is of the essence," Roz asked.

"I did. But he won't budge. I did warn him to not tamper with the machine in any way. I leaned on him pretty hard, but he didn't seem to care."

"We can get a search warrant for that," Hughes said.

"I'll draw it up," Jacobson said. "I'll deliver it to him myself. First Amendment, my eye. The First Amendment is an American thing. It has to do with freedom of speech. Cayman penal code has no equivalent law. Besides, freedom of speech has nothing to do with property rights."

Jacobson was clearly angry. Commissioner Hughes would be too, except it wouldn't help matters. Ranting about things they couldn't control was a waste of time. However, he knew that type of thing was what would fan the flames of righteous indignation in his detectives. They don't like their investigations being unnecessarily obstructed, even if the shop owner was within his rights. A girl's life was more important than the shop keeper's self-righteous principles, in his opinion.

The good thing was that a tape did exist. Hopefully, it would give them a view of the entrance to the bar and they could see if Sara left with anyone.

Hughes realized that he needed to move on.

"Detective Delancey, did you find out anything from Jake Fossey, the son."

"The kid's a punk. He says he doesn't know anything about it. He was in his office the whole night, he claims. I don't believe him either. Just a gut feeling."

"What about the video security tape that was taped over?"

"He doesn't know anything about it. Or so he says. When I pressed him, he said the door is unlocked and anybody could've gone in there."

"What's the point of having a security system if it's not secure?" Commissioner Hughes said.

"Exactly. I made that point to him. He just smugly shrugged his shoulders."

Commissioner Hughes wrote Jake Fossey's name on the board but didn't put anything beside it. So far, they had nothing to go on. The board was noticeably absent of any evidence or reliable leads.

Hughes paused before finally saying, "Go ahead and cut them loose." Meaning let Fossey and his son go, for now. They were still in the interrogation rooms. Technically, he had no grounds to detain them, but so far, neither had asked for a lawyer or asked to leave, so he could keep them longer. The girlfriend had left a couple hours ago. At this point, his detectives' time would be better spent in the field.

One of the detectives in the back raised his hand. Frank Grimes. A newbie recently promoted from street work.

"Yes Frank. You don't have to raise your hand."

"I might have something. Fossey owns *Deep Sea Excursions*. They have dive trips. Dinner cruises. Things of that nature. I spoke to one of the captains. He took a group out on a night dive last night. They were doing the Wall Dive off of Rum Point."

"I've done that dive," Roz said.

Diving was something Commissioner Hughes had never done. He preferred the land over the water. Actually, he rarely even took advantage of the beaches. A workaholic, idling time was not his thing.

"The dive was over, and they were about to head back to shore," Detective Grimes continued.

"Did he give you a time?" Hughes asked.

"Around midnight."

"Okay."

"He heard a boat motor in the distance, but the boat didn't have any lights on."

"That's unusual. And dangerous. What size boat?"

"A small boat. Maybe eighteen feet. Small motor."

"Could he see anything?"

"It was cloudy, so the moon wasn't shining light on the water. However, he turned on his spotlight and shined it that way. He yelled something, but the guy just kept going."

"Which way was he headed?"

"Out to sea."

"Did he give you a description of the man?"

"Like he said, it was dark. The boat was moving away from him. It sped up when he shined the light on it."

"Good work, Frank. I'll follow up on it myself. Anything else?"

"What about the press? Delancey asked. "They're starting to get the idea that something is going on."

"I want to hold them off as long as possible. I planned on giving a statement at six, but let's see what we can find out overnight. Let's get the search warrant for the security camera. I also had the security system in the bar seized. They are going to look at that and see if footage can be salvaged. That will give forensics time to inspect the bar. We'll see if they turn up anything. Also, we'll keep up the door-to-door questioning. Hopefully, someone around the bar saw something. If we reach a bunch of dead ends, we'll turn to the public for help."

They had a game plan. There wasn't much to go on, but for now, it was all they had.

Right about that time, the door suddenly burst open. Commissioner Hughes's assistant was the one who had barged in. She seemed out of breath.

"Yes, Evelyn. What is it?"

"You've got to see this."

She walked over to the credenza under a television bracketed on the wall, took the remote in her hand, and turned the TV on.

"What's going on?"

"Sean Morgan is holding a press conference over at the *Reef Bar*."

The image of Sara's father suddenly appeared on the screen. He was standing in front of a podium. The *Reef Bar* sign was behind him. Sara Morgan's picture was blown up and framed and set on an easel to the right of the podium. Several microphones were in his face. It looked like every television station on the island was there.

Evelyn turned up the volume.

"I'm pleading with you. . . " Sean Morgan said, as he rubbed his eyes and his voice cracked. "Someone knows something. If you have any information about my missing daughter, please come forward. You can do so anonymously. I'm offering a one-million-dollar reward for any information that leads to the safe return of my daughter!"

A loud murmur went through the crowd of reporters. Everyone in the conference room turned in unison and looked at Commissioner Hughes. They turned back to the television when Sean Morgan continued.

"One million dollars!" he said with emphasis. "No questions asked. Her mother and I just want our daughter back. The number to call is 1-888-555-Sara. It goes to a voicemail. Leave your information and someone will call you back right away."

"Have you gone to the police?" a reporter asked.

"I met with the police commissioner this morning, but I haven't heard a word. Not even a phone call. That's why I've taken this action. I must find my daughter. The best way to do that is to get her picture and name out there for everyone to see. I don't have a lot of confidence that the commissioner can find her. So, I need your help."

Commissioner Hughes didn't know exactly when his mouth had flown open, but he abruptly shut it as rage erupted inside of him, sending his blood pressure skyrocketing. His gut had been right. He had a feeling the father was going to be a problem. The only thing he hadn't expected was that it would be this soon.

22

After the meeting with the detectives, Commissioner Hughes left police headquarters, furious at Sean Morgan for going against his directions and holding a press conference and offering a reward without even discussing it with him first. To make matters worse, he made it sound like he was not taking the search for his daughter seriously. The press would have a field day with that information.

While he tried to be sympathetic to victims and their families, he considered it obstruction and intended to tell him so when he spoke with him. Which he wouldn't do until he calmed down and his anger subsided somewhat.

The phone call would have to wait anyway. He was on his way to Rum Point where the dive boat captain had seen a suspicious boat headed to sea with no lights around the time that Sara went missing.

It may be a dead end, but he didn't have much else to go on at the moment.

The drive would give him a chance to settle his emotions down.

The chance of that happening went out the window when his cell phone rang. The governor of Cayman Islands, Finn Tattersall, was on the other line. This couldn't be good. More than likely, the governor had heard the press conference or the gist of it anyway and Sean Morgan's accusation that he wasn't doing enough to find his daughter.

"Hello, Governor," Hughes said. "Second time today." The commissioner had called the governor earlier in the day to apprise him of the missing person's case and to assure him he would do everything in his power to solve it as quickly as possible. While the governor wasn't his direct boss, it seemed like the appropriate thing to do.

Before the governor could respond, Hughes added, "I assume you saw the press conference."

"It's all anyone in my office is talking about. What are you going to do about the father?"

The governor's tone sounded confrontive. Hughes tried not to take it that way.

He took a deep breath and tried not to sound defensive. "The father is a loose cannon. I told him in my office that a press conference and a reward were a bad idea. He went and did it anyway without my knowledge."

"I figured as much. Still, the press is going to town with this. Eventually, I'm going to get blamed as much as you if you don't get this case solved."

"We're working on it. I'm chasing a lead right now. The father's criticism is unfair. I only learned about his daughter being missing at ten o'clock this morning. In seven hours, we've made remarkable progress, considering. The reward is going to make our job harder, not easier."

"Do you remember the case in St. Maarten?"

"I do."

"I don't have to remind you that the case went unsolved for months. Tourism took a big hit because of it. Don't let that happen here."

"I won't sir."

"Look on the bright side. Maybe the reward will generate a lead or two that might help you."

"And a thousand that won't. That's the problem. We won't know which ones are real and which are a waste of time. We're going to be inundated with calls now from every Tom, Dick, and Harry within a hundred miles of the island."

"Where did the 888-number come from?"

"I don't know. I assume Mr. Morgan set it up. We had nothing to do with it."

"At least the calls will go to him."

"The leads will end up with us. And people are already calling our office. The switchboard was lit up like the fourth of July when I left there a few minutes ago."

"Get this solved, Collin, and you won't have to worry about it. As soon as possible."

"I will, sir. Like I said, I'm working on it. I won't rest until I find her."

"Let's just hope she's still alive."

"Yes sir. We're all praying for that outcome."

***

Rum Point was on the picturesque north side of the island. It consisted of a beach, a pier, and a restaurant with a large outdoor dining area. While the area didn't have a marina, boats could be launched from any number of places, including personal residences which had sprung up at a record pace over the last ten years.

Commissioner Hughes pulled into the parking lot and went directly to the restaurant which had already started serving guests for dinner. The hope was that someone there might've seen or heard something. The restaurant had huge plate-glass windows to give patrons a breath-taking view of the ocean.

Hughes was greeted by the hostess. He didn't need to flash his badge. They knew who he was. He'd eaten the delightful food on several occasions.

"May I speak with Jackie?" he asked. Jackie was Jacques, the manager of the restaurant. Hughes didn't want to talk to anyone without first getting his permission. Or at least letting him know what he was doing.

Jackie greeted the commissioner warmly with a kiss on both cheeks, which, being from France, was his custom.

"Are you here to dine with us this evening?" Jackie asked.

"I'm afraid not," Hughes said. "I'm here on official police business."

"No doubt related to the missing girl. I have heard about that. A sad situation. How can I be of service?" Jackie spoke with a heavy accent and enunciated every word like it would be his last.

"I was hoping you could help me. I need to know if anyone saw anything suspicious last night. Around eleven o'clock." Hughes' heart sank when he suddenly remembered that they closed at ten.

Jackie answered, "There was a private party here last night. It went until about midnight. I left shortly after ten, but maybe one of the staff saw or heard something. What information would be helpful? What would be... how you say, suspicious?"

"A strange car. A boat at the pier. A man walking with a young girl."

The hostess's eyes widened into an excited look. Hughes turned his attention to her.

"Did you see something?" Hughes asked.

"I saw a man and a girl get out of a car around eleven thirty. I was working last night." She went to the window and pointed to the parking lot.

"Do you remember what kind of car it was?" Hughes pulled out a small notebook and a pencil to take notes.

"I didn't really see the car."

"What made you notice the man and the girl?"

"I think they were younger. Like my age. And it seemed strange. For one thing, it was kind of late. But... actually... that's not that unusual. A lot of young people come here late at night, to mess around. If you know what I mean."

Hughes nodded. "What seemed strange?"

"The girl was staggering. Like she was drunk."

A bolt of adrenaline shot through Hughes' heart causing it to skip a beat. A working theory in his mind was that Sara was drugged at the bar. He considered the possibility that she'd gotten drunk but had dismissed the thought. Sara didn't seem like the type to get drunk on a senior class trip when she had to be back at the hotel by eleven for a bed check. Rohypnol, or roofies as they were called, seemed like a more plausible theory.

"Which direction did they go?" Hughes asked.

"They went that way," she said, pointing south.

"Did you hear a boat?"

"No. I didn't hear a boat," she said slowly, obviously thinking. "But there was a lot of noise. The music at the party was really loud. I could barely hear people well enough to take their drink orders."

"What's your name?" Hughes asked, with his notebook raised and his pencil ready to write.

"Brittany. Although people call me Brit. Brittany Russell."

"Can I get your contact information?"

Hughes wrote down her cell phone number, address, and email address.

"You've been very helpful, Brit."

Hughes turned his attention back to Jackie who seemed pleased. "Could you ask around?" Hughes said. "See if any of your other staff saw or heard anything."

"Of course."

The commissioner pulled out two cards and handed one to Brittany and one to Jackie. "Please call me if you think of anything else."

"Do you think that might've been the girl?" Brit asked hesitantly. "The one missing?"

"I don't know. It's possible."

"If it was, does that mean I might get the reward?"

Hughes's anger toward the father returned like an out-of-control wildfire. This was one of the reasons he didn't want a reward mentioned. Now Brittany's information was suspect and tainted. He couldn't know if it could be trusted. It didn't seem like she was making it up, but now he couldn't be sure.

Either way, he was going head in the direction she pointed. South. Down the beach. He hoped it wasn't a waste of time.

***

Commissioner Hughes walked down the beach in a serpentine manner going between the shoreline and the tree line, looking for any clue that might help in the investigation. Even if he didn't find anything, he'd send someone out to do a more thorough search of the area tomorrow. The girl's information seemed credible to him as she was telling it. Had she not mentioned the reward, he would've had no reason to question it. He decided to take it as true until proven otherwise. It fit with the other eyewitness evidence of a boat traveling out to sea without lights, which would be unheard of in these parts. It seemed to the boat captain that the boat was coming from Rum Point.

After a half mile or so, he was ready to give up. Mostly because he only saw random footsteps on the beach. No evidence of two people walking where one was staggering. He stood at the shoreline staring out into the sea. The sun had just started to set, and he only had another forty minutes or so before it would be too dark to search. From his vantage point, he could see a dive boat out in the general vicinity of where last night's boat would've been anchored.

He couldn't remember if the captain of the boat said the boat was north or south of their location. Maybe he never said. Or if he did, Detective Grimes didn't mention it. If south, then it was possible that the boat came ashore further down the beach, so he kept walking. The scenario playing out in his mind was that Sara was drugged at the bar, taken to Rum Point by car, and then led down the beach to a boat, which launched from the shore. If it had been from a residence, the man wouldn't have parked in the Rum Point parking lot. He would've parked at the residence.

Hughes realized the whole thing might be nothing more than his imagination. Nevertheless, that was how he solved cases. Getting into the mind of a killer. He quickly corrected himself. He refused to think of Sara as dead. *Getting into the mind of a kidnapper.*

He continued on with a greater sense of urgency. Because he was running out of time, but also because a plausible theory had formulated in his mind, and he was anxious to see if it might be right. If so, he should find some evidence of activity in the sand. Indication of where the boat landed would be washed away by high tide. The footsteps on the beach would not be. He was puzzled by the fact that he still hadn't seen any footsteps.

A sinking feeling hit him like a ton of bricks in the pit of his stomach. Maybe the girl didn't really see two people. Or if she did, they didn't walk on the beach. The abductor had to if he loaded Sara onto a boat.

Then he remembered a walking trail. Just inside the tree line. Off the beach, but a path used by residences to walk from their neighborhoods down to Rum Point. His pace quickened, and he no longer zig zagged back and forth. Now he walked with more of a purpose. He was looking for any sign that the boy and girl came off the trail and onto the beach.

He didn't have to walk much further.

As he had hoped, two sets of footprints suddenly emerged from the bushes. One of the set of footprints was uneven, like the person was staggering. He could even see a place where the person fell to the ground. This corroborated the girl's story. A few steps forward, he found a large indentation. In the form of a body. A wave of excitement came over him.

Was this Sara?

For the moment, he would assume it was her lying on the beach.

He stopped and looked back north. The lights of Rum Point restaurant were still visible. In all likelihood, Sara probably heard the music. Did she cry out? The hostess said she couldn't hear anything with the music blaring. No way could they hear a scream from this far away. If Sara was even in a condition to scream.

Did she suffer? Was she suffering now?

He had to put those thoughts out of his mind. Hughes took out his phone and checked for a signal. Three bars. He dialed Roz's number. She answered on the first ring.

"I may have a break," Hughes said, trying to maintain his excitement.

"I'm ready to help. You know that."

"Get Detective Grimes. Also get a forensic team together, along with a dozen or so people to conduct a search. We need some big lights. Call United Rental. Have them get some heavy duty lights out here. Enough to light up a quarter of an acre."

"Where's the location?"

"Rum Point. About a mile south. On the beach."

"So, you think the boat sighting might be a clue."

123

"I think so."

"I'm on it."

"Roz... Keep this on the down low. I don't want the press getting wind of it."

"Got it. Anything else."

"Just get here as soon as you can."

Hughes hung up the phone and took a deep breath trying to slow his heartbeat. He stared out into the sea. The lights from the dive boat were still visible in the distance. Just to the north of his location. He shuddered at the thought that Sara might've been at this very location, less than twenty-four hours before. Probably scared out of her mind. Having no idea what was going on or why she was feeling so drugged.

That opened a whole new bevy of questions. What if he was right and Sara was brought there? Then put on a boat.

Where did they take her?

It suddenly occurred to him that, even if he was right, he was no closer to finding her than he was an hour ago. Before, he was looking for a missing girl on an island with a limited land mass. Now he might have the entire Caribbean Sea to search.

23

Tampico, Mexico

Jamie arrived in Tampico two hours ahead of her meeting with Maxwell's man. She found an out-of-the-way spot in an alley where she wouldn't be noticed but could see the comings and goings around the bar. The *La Taberna* was a typical Mexican bar. Not at all like nightclubs in the states. Although this one was nicer than most she'd seen in Mexico, it still had the feel of a sleazy dive bar.

Vicky should've stayed away from the place.

Now was not the time to blame the girls. She desperately had to find them. They still had their beauty and innocence. It wouldn't take long for these to be stolen away from them forever. If it hadn't already been.

Jamie allowed herself a few minutes to think about the girls and what they might be going through at that very moment. Most might think that would be counterproductive. Gloomy. Demotivating. But Jamie felt the opposite effect. Righteous indignation spurred her to action. It's what drove her. She would do anything and everything to save the girls, including risking her own life. That's who she was.

Many in the department told Jamie she was a rare breed. Killing a man took a lot of motivation and taking away everything he had in this world was no small thing to her. Even if he was a bad guy and deserved it, pulling the trigger was made easier by the fact that she knew she was doing the world a service. Everyone was better off with that person gone from the world and in God's hands to judge, which from her religious background, she knew he would do harshly.

So, she thought about each girl individually. Allowing herself to linger on their images that were seared in her mind. Each thought strengthened her resolve. Jamie could feel the adrenaline rise which always happened on a mission. She knew how to temper it so she didn't get overheated and overreact to a situation, which she had been prone to do early on in her training.

By the time she was done remembering the last girl, she was ready to go kill someone.

Not that it would be necessary tonight. She was there strictly for reconnaissance. The plan was for Maxwell's man to broadcast over the radio that a woman was in the bar asking about the missing girl from Brownsville, Texas. That's why she needed Maxwell's man. Someone who spoke Spanish fluently, who would sound like one of their men. She couldn't thank TJ enough for fixing the radio. It made her mission much easier.

Maxwell's man would tell them the girl was a private investigator. He'd say they tried to get rid of her, but she wouldn't go away. Now she was in the bar talking to patrons.

Jamie hoped the Alliance would send men to investigate. If they weren't involved in the kidnappings, they wouldn't bother. If they were, that would light a fire under them, and they would send men to confront the woman. Only they'd be looking for a girl who didn't exist.

Maxwell's man would describe her. Brown hair. Five foot six or so. Wearing a sexy red dress with a red jacket. The red jacket was the key. The temperature was ninety-five degrees, even though it was already dark. No girls would be wearing jackets on this hot night. At least not a bright red jacket and a bright red dress.

Maxwell's man wouldn't be describing Jamie. She would be inconspicuously hiding somewhere in plain sight, wearing black leggings and a long, black, nylon stretch shirt that laid loosely below her waist. Accented by a black jacket. She needed the jacket to hide her gun and carry her ID so she could get in the bar. A purse would be an inconvenience. Her hands needed to be free.

Just in case.

Her long flowing blonde hair would be in a ponytail. Jamie knew that her looks were a detriment when it came to surveillance. She was tall. Blonde hair. Slim and fit. Athletic. Everyone noticed her when she walked in a room. Many times, that worked to her advantage. Most of the time, in her line of work, memorable was bad. Brad almost didn't recommend her for the sex trafficking division for that exact reason. When Jamie was in foreign countries, especially Asian countries like Thailand, Vietnam, and Bangladesh, she stuck out like a billboard in Times Square.

Curly spent days training her on how to be inconspicuous. Or at least as unremarkable as possible. Tonight, would be one of those nights. She wanted to get in and out without anyone knowing she was there.

She'd be able to spot the Alliance men immediately when they came searching for the girl. They had a look about them. Killers had a look. Several had already come in and out of the bar. She studied them carefully. Watched how they walked. Their mannerisms. What they were wearing. Where they hid their guns. Almost all of them were armed. She could tell by the bulges in their pants. Generally, the weapon was in the middle of the back, tucked into their pants. Not a good place to carry a gun, if you wanted to get to it quickly.

And jackets. They all wore black leather jackets. That would make them easy to spot. In addition, if her plan worked, the men would arrive there with a sense of urgency and purpose. They'd scour the room for the phantom woman in the red dress and red jacket. That would tell her all she needed to know.

Jamie would leave, check into a hotel, and get some much-needed rest. She'd decided she wouldn't act until she heard from Alex. If he were successful in hacking into the bar's security system, she'd have security footage to view. He might even track the girls' cell phones to their last locations before they were turned off or destroyed.

While time was of the essence, gathering information was the prudent thing to do in this situation. Flying blind in dangerous enemy territory was never a good idea. So, she would have to wait to act which was the hardest part of her job. Harder even than being shot at, oddly enough. Jamie preferred action over inaction. Waiting would be worth it, though. No reason to run off and do something stupid with information coming that might save a lot of trouble and heartache.

Jamie looked at her watch. *Nine o'clock.* It'd be another hour before Maxwell's man showed up. She'd use that time wisely. She got out of the car and walked completely around the bar. Three exits. Two bouncers. Probably a little over seven-thousand square feet. Above the bar was what looked to be an office. A dim light was on above a lit-up sign that read *La Taberna.*

From the number of cars in the parking lot, Jamie estimated that fewer than a hundred people were in the bar. More than likely, business would pick up later in the evening. Four Alliance members were inside, unless some were already there before she arrived. Several working girls went in. That sent a pang through Jamie's heart. Every time she saw a girl selling her body to men for money, it tore her up inside. She wished she could help them. That wasn't possible, and she had to resist the urge.

That wasn't the mission.

And... those girls weren't slaves. They did it voluntarily. Maybe they were trapped by a pimp or a drug lord, but they could still move around freely and get out if they really wanted to. While those girls saddened her, what happened to the four unsuspecting girls on their senior trip, broke her heart. She purposefully told herself to focus on them. They needed her.

When she finished surveilling the building, she went back to the car and changed her plan. Going into the bar was unnecessary, she decided. From her vantage point, she had a good view of the entrance and the parking lot. If the Alliance members showed up, they would be easy to spot. That would tell her everything she needed to know without having to take any unnecessary risks. If she went inside and something went down, her cover would be blown. If they knew she was there, moving around Mexico would be much harder.

If the Alliance members came racing in, especially with a sense of urgency, that would be all the proof she needed that El Mata was involved. They wouldn't find the girl in the red jacket and no one would see her, and she would create some confusion in their ranks.

That caused her to relax some.

Jamie laid her head back and actually closed her eyes and fell asleep.

***

She instinctively woke up at quarter to ten, two minutes before she heard from Maxwell's man. He had just arrived and texted asking for her location. She gave him instructions and spotted him immediately when he came around the corner from a side street and started walking toward the bar.

The man was medium height. Dark hair. Wearing a jacket. Hands in his pockets. Unremarkable. He looked like every other Mexican man she'd seen going into the bar. That's why she chose a woman instead of a man to be the private investigator. How would she describe a Mexican man in a way that would differentiate him from everyone else?

Maxwell's man walked at a quick pace. He crossed the street and entered the alley where she was parked. Jamie unlocked the door, and he got in the passenger seat, which seconds before, was occupied by her machine gun.

She locked the car doors out of habit and sized up the man. He seemed nervous.

"What's your name?" Jamie asked, trying to build some rapport with him to calm him down.

"Roberto," he answered. "What's yours?"

"Mandy." Jamie almost never gave out her real name on a mission. Even to someone on her side. The longevity of an undercover CIA operative depended on anonymity for as long as possible. Once the enemy knew your identity, it made it harder to keep the element of surprise in play, which Jamie found was one of the most important things in spy operations. The ability to move around incognito was just as invaluable as well.

She handed Roberto a piece of paper with a script of what she wanted him to say.

He looked it over.

"All I want you to do is get on this radio and read what it says on the paper," she said. "If they ask any questions, I'll tell you what to say."

"You just want me to read this?" Roberto asked.

"Don't sound like you are reading it. Make it sound natural. You have to convince them you're one of them."

"Puedo hacer eso," he said in Spanish, obviously to show her he could do it.

"That'll work."

Jamie reached over and turned on the radio. The set erupted in static. When it adjusted to the frequency, they could hear Alliance members talking. They weren't saying anything of note, so Jamie turned her attention back to Roberto.

"Let's get this show going. From what I can tell from listening to the chatter on the radio, Jorge is the main boss. At least, he seems to be at the top of the food chain from everyone else. Start by asking for him. He was on not that long ago."

Jamie handed him the handset. Roberto took it from her hand and took a deep breath. She suddenly realized she was holding hers, so she let it out. The tension would fog up the windows if it were steam. Jamie consciously told herself to relax. For some reason, she felt anxiety.

"Jorge?" Roberto said, into the mic.

Silence on the other end.

"Say it again," Jamie instructed.

"Jorge. Are you there?" he said in Spanish. "I need to talk to you."

"Go ahead," a voice resounded through the speakers.

Jamie recognized Jorge's voice. She nodded to Roberto to start. Roberto held the paper in one hand and the mic in the other.

"I'm at *La Taberna*. There's a woman here. She's asking about the missing girl from Brownsville, Texas. What do you want me to do?"

"Who is she?"

"I don't know, man. I think she's a private eye or something."

Roberto was doing good and making it sound natural and convincing. Exactly what she wanted.

"Leave her alone. She's probably nobody."

Jamie's heart dropped a notch in her chest. Maybe they weren't involved in the kidnappings after all. On the one hand, she felt a sudden relief. She had averted a trip to El Mata's. On the other, it was back to the drawing board with no leads.

What Roberto did next, surprised her. He went off script and started talking with a greater sense of urgency.

"She's asking a lot of questions, man. Talking to customers. Showing the girl's picture around to the customers. I don't think she's going away. The lady might be bad news. She asked about the other girls as well."

Maxwell had obviously briefed Roberto on the situation. Roberto might even be involved in the investigation in some way. He seemed to have a lot of knowledge about it.

He and Jorge carried on a conversation for several minutes. Jamie listened intently for any clue that might suggest the Alliance was involved. A moment ago, she didn't think so. Now she wasn't sure.

"Can you describe the girl?" Jorge asked.

"American," Roberto said. "Wearing a red dress and red jacket. Brown hair. You can't miss her."

"Good work. Keep an eye on her, but don't approach her. I'm sending some men there now."

Jamie's heart did a somersault in her chest.

"Got it," Roberto said, and they signed off.

Roberto started to say something, but Jamie shushed him. If her hunch were right, Jorge would be back on the line immediately.

After a few seconds, the radio burst into activity. Jorge put out an urgent message asking for anyone who was in Tampico. Several answered in the affirmative.

Jorge started barking instructions. "You're looking for an American. Brown hair. Red dress. Wearing a red jacket. At *La Taberna*."

"What do you want us to do?" one of the men asked.

"Hold her until I get there," Jorge replied.

"What if she tries to leave?"

"Don't let her."

"How do we stop her?"

"Do whatever it takes!"

Jamie let out a laugh. "Won't they be surprised when they get here and can't find her?"

Roberto handed the piece of paper back to Jamie.

"Am I done?"

"Thank you, Roberto," she said. "You did good. That's all I needed."

As quickly as he had appeared, Roberto was gone. Jamie thought about leaving as well. She had the confirmation she needed. The Alliance knew about the girls and were involved. Why else would they come to the bar with orders to detain the girl? Jamie decided she wanted to stay around for the show. See how many actually showed up. Get an eye on Jorge in case she ran across him later.

She pulled out a bottle of water, took a big swig, and settled in. Less than three minutes later, she saw something that sent a chill down her spine.

A working girl.

Walking toward the bar.

Wearing a red dress.

Stilettos.

A red jacket.

Jamie's worst fear was realized when the girl walked up the steps of the bar, was greeted by the bouncer, and went inside.

Jamie pounded her fist on the steering wheel. "What do I do now?"

I have to go inside and warn her.

She fumbled with her gun. Then she checked her ID. Everything had to be in order before she rushed off to the bar. In the spur of the moment, mistakes can happen. Mistakes that can get you killed.

She opened the door and stepped out of the car.

Tires squealed.

Jamie instinctively looked to the right. Up the street. She saw a flash.

A black mustang was speeding her way. She stepped back in the alley. In the shadows, so she wouldn't be seen.

The mustang came to a screeching halt right in front of the bar.

Two members of the Alliance bolted out and practically ran inside.

A second black mustang was right behind them.

Two more men. Armed.

Their intentions obvious.

Find the girl wearing a red dress and a red jacket.

The words "Do whatever takes" were echoing in Jamie's head.

24

Grand Cayman

Carolyn Morgan landed at the Owen Roberts International Airport in Georgetown, Grand Cayman, about an hour after her husband's press conference ended. The press was tipped off, and a half dozen reporters and two news crews were there when she arrived. Sean had arranged for a car to meet her, but she had to walk through the concourse and baggage claim area of the small airport to get to it. From the time she passed through security, the press hounded her like she was a rock star.

As soon as she saw them, she slipped on a pair of Gucci designer sunglasses to hide her red, bloodshot eyes, swollen from all the crying. Carolyn quickened her pace and tried to avoid them, but they matched her step-for-step. The cameraman somehow even managed to get in front of her and was walking backward as the red light on the camera signified it was rolling.

The reporters peppered her with questions.

"What do you think happened to Sara?"

"Do you think she's alive?"

"Did she meet someone on the island?"

"Is she hiding from you?"

"Is it true that she was pregnant?"

The questions repulsed Carolyn. She wanted to answer but was afraid of her response. Her emotions were seesawing back and forth between anger and grief. Mostly, she didn't want to say the wrong thing.

Sean had told her that he was doing a press conference, and wanted to create as much publicity as possible, but she didn't expect this.

Carolyn ignored the reporters and kept walking with her head up, trying to put the best face on a difficult situation. One she had never asked for. A mother's worst nightmare. The cameraman almost crashed into the door as they got to the exit of the airport. The car was at the curb and a driver already had the door opened. Just a few more seconds and she would be free of the reporters.

For now.

Once outside, one of the reporters shouted from behind her, "What do you want to say to your daughter if she can hear this?"

Carolyn was almost to the car but wanted to answer that question. She stopped just before the opened car door and turned and faced the reporters.

"I want to say this to my daughter. Sara, if you're out there and can hear the sound of my voice, I want you to know that Momma loves you. Your dad loves you. We are doing everything in our power to find you."

Carolyn felt the tears welling up in her eyes. Her voice cracked at the end of the last sentence.

"What would you say to her kidnappers if they are listening?" the reporter asked as she shoved the microphone back in her face.

"If you took my baby, as a mom, I'm begging you to let her go. Just let her go. Sara's a good girl with her whole future ahead of her. She has a beautiful spirit. She would never hurt anyone. Please don't hurt her."

"Are the police doing enough to find her?"

Carolyn hesitated.

Sean was critical of the police and told her he was going to say as much at the press conference. That didn't seem like such a good idea. They needed everyone's help. Especially the police. She decided to evade the question.

"I don't know. I just want to find Sara. We must find her. If anyone knows anything, please call the tip line."

Sean also said he was going to set up an 800 number for people to call. He hired a firm in Dallas to field the calls, twenty-four hours a day.

Carolyn got into the back seat of the car and her driver quickly shut it. She put her right hand up to the side of her face to shield it as the reporters pressed against the windows snapping pictures, still asking questions.

The driver sped away.

Thankfully.

Is this what my life is going to be like for the next few days?

She tried hard to compose herself. Carolyn struggled with anxiety. Had been off and on medication for several years. Especially after Sara was born. The doctor said it was postpartum depression and would pass. It did, and things were better for a while. Recently, she had considered going back on them as the anxiety sometimes came back in waves.

Back in Texas, others looked at her as the calm voice of reason in a crisis. If they could see her innermost thoughts, and if she were honest, they'd see she wasn't as strong as they thought she was. This crisis was like no other. She'd never felt such pain. This would test her resolve and her faith in God.

Why did he let this happen?

Most of the plane ride down, she kept praying, pleading for God to keep Sara safe. The church had a prayer chain started and already had hundreds of people on it. She wished she could feel those prayers. Right now, her emotions were raging out of control like a California wildfire.

"God help me," she whispered under her breath.

She then thanked the driver for giving her a ride and asked, "Can you take me by the bar where my daughter went missing? The *Reef Bar.*"

"Yes. Ma'am. It's not far. It's on the way to the hotel."

In less than three minutes after exiting the airport, the driver said, "It's just ahead on the left."

"Pull in please."

The driver pulled into the parking lot, stopped the car, and Carolyn got out. She took a moment to stand there and take in the surroundings.

137

Sara was here.

She could almost feel her presence. The *Reef Bar* was what you would expect on a tropical island. Palm trees lined the entrance. It had an island feel, with pink pelicans painted on the outside walls, along with various fish and blue ocean waves. The building was more modern and newer than she expected.

The cool, refreshing breeze lifted her spirits.

Sara needs me to be strong.

Carolyn was wearing an Anne Klein single-button pant suit. Maroon colored. The sleeves stopped just above her wrist. Her blouse was rose colored. At first, she had chosen a black pant suit with a dark blue shirt. Then changed her mind. She refused to dress in funeral colors. Her daughter was alive. Even if she didn't feel the optimism, the color of her clothes could project it.

She slipped the jacket off and flung it in the back seat of the car. Faith was rising inside of her.

Sara is alive. I know it.

For some reason, being at the same place Sara had been had invigorated her spirits.

A makeshift memorial had already been started by some well-meaning islanders. A couple of people were standing in front of it. One had just laid flowers on the ground in front of a cross next to a sign that said *Come Home Soon, Sara.* Memorial was the wrong word. It looked like a memorial, but it wasn't. Sara was still alive.

She has to be.

That brought tears to Carolyn's eyes. She fought them back.

A car screeched and came to an abrupt stop inside the parking lot. A reporter and a cameraman got out. Carolyn started to get back in the car. Instead, she walked over to where the well-wishers were standing. Two women. They looked like a mother and a daughter. The girl was about Sara's age. Maybe a couple of years younger.

"Hi," Carolyn said meekly. "I'm Sara's mother."

Carolyn could hear the reporter and cameraman scurrying behind them trying to get set up. Obviously to catch the shot. It would make for good TV.

"I'm so sorry about your daughter," the mother said. "I had to come here. I hope you don't mind."

"Of course, I don't mind. It's so thoughtful."

"I can't imagine what you're going through."

"Is this your daughter?" Carolyn asked.

"Yes. This is my daughter, Elizabeth."

Carolyn held out her hand toward the girl who extended hers and they shook. More of a warm gesture as Carolyn put both hands over the teenager's hand.

"Thank you for coming here," Carolyn said. "It means a lot to me. And to my husband. It would mean a lot to Sara to know that you are thinking of her."

The reporter and cameraman set up just to the right of them. A few feet away, at an angle. Thankfully, the reporter didn't ask any questions and ruin the moment. She probably realized how poignant a moment this really was. Two mothers. Who'd never met. With a common bond. Something brought that woman there today. Carolyn didn't know a lot about business or marketing, but she knew enough to know that this shot would pull on the heartstrings of mothers throughout Cayman.

Maybe they will come and help search.

Carolyn was genuinely touched but realized she could use this to her advantage. If the police weren't going to do anything, then they needed volunteers. Sara's story needed to be what everyone was talking about.

We need all the help we can get.

God, I need your help most of all.

Carolyn suddenly found herself with her arms around the mother. Giving her a hug. The woman had tears in her eyes. Maybe that's what prompted Carolyn to try and comfort her.

I'm comforting her?

Carolyn turned to the daughter and embraced her. The hugs gave Carolyn encouragement. It warmed her heart to know that there were people who cared.

After thanking them again, she turned and walked back to the car. The reporter followed her. Not as intrusive this time. The solemnity of the chance meeting with the mother or daughter had cast a peace over Carolyn and a calm over her entire demeanor which the reporter must've sensed. Carolyn wasn't rushing to get away.

Maybe the prayers were working.

She suddenly felt stronger. When she got to the car, she turned and faced the reporter and asked, "What's your name?"

"Becky. KWAV television."

"Thank you, Becky, for being here." Carolyn reached for her purse which was in the backseat of the car. She pulled out a picture of Sara and held it up for the camera.

"This is my daughter, Sara Leigh Morgan. She's missing. I need everyone's help to find her. Please get the word out. If you know anything, call the number for the tip line."

Carolyn was kicking herself for not knowing the number. She never thought to ask. She'd rectify that as soon as she got to the hotel.

"I'm sure the news organization has the number and can put it on the screen."

As quick as the anxiety had left, anger had taken its place. The sudden urge to scream something to the kidnappers. A threat of what she would do to them if they harmed one hair on Sara's head. Pictures of a momma bear protecting her cubs came to mind. She resisted the urge and took a deep breath so she wouldn't say something she regretted. No use antagonizing the kidnappers. They held all the cards. Instead, she tried to maintain the same conciliatory tone.

"To those of you who took Sara, please let her go. Sara. If you're listening, honey, I will not rest until I find you."

Carolyn got in the car, shut the door, and instructed the driver to take her to the hotel.

25

Tampico

Jamie paced in the alley across from *La Taberna* like a caged panther in a zoo, mulling her options. Which were only two, she decided. Go inside or wait out there and see what happens.

Unknowingly, she had put a young woman's life in danger.

"Why was she wearing a jacket and why did it have to be red?" Jamie said aloud to herself. Her plan seemed like a good idea at the time. Now Jamie was beating herself up for not accounting for every possibility, no matter how remote.

Four armed men from the Gulfo Alliance were in the bar looking for the girl. Jamie's first urge was to follow them in. But that wasn't a good idea. A confrontation in the bar would only make things worse. Other innocent lives would be put in danger. More than likely, the Alliance men would think the same thing. Not that they were concerned about innocent lives, but they wouldn't harm the girl in front of all those witnesses in a tourist spot. Besides, Jamie distinctly remembered Jorge ordering them to hold the girl until he got there.

Hopefully, they would talk to the girl, realize she was nothing more than a prostitute and would leave without causing an incident.

Hopefully.

If so, they'd come out of the bar soon and leave. Jamie kept a close eye on the door, hoping that was what happened. If they were in an "act first, ask questions later" frame of mind, they'd drag the girl out of the bar and hold her outside. Either way, she'd know soon.

She let out a big exhale of nervous energy.

After thinking it over further, she decided the best course of action was to maintain her position and wait. The Sig was in her jacket along with an ID, and she was ready to act when and if something happened.

After nearly ten minutes of waiting, Jamie was confused. The men hadn't come out. *What did that mean?*

Were they questioning the girl inside?

Were they holding her waiting for Jorge to arrive?

Did they decide she wasn't a threat and sat down to have a beer?

The only way to know was to go inside and see for herself. She hesitated. The mission was what stopped her. She remembered the reason she was in Mexico to begin with. To find the four missing girls. She had evidence, albeit circumstantial, that the Alliance was involved in the kidnappings in some way. Jorge's reaction confirmed it in her mind. In addition, he knew about the four missing girls, and as far as Jamie knew, that wasn't something that had been widely publicized.

Maybe she needed to leave. She got what she came there for.

Not going to happen.

Just don't do anything rash.

She could imagine a scenario where saving the girl could jeopardize the mission. While she wouldn't abandon the girl in the red jacket, she wasn't going to take any unnecessary risks. The bar had security cameras. She'd just as soon keep her face off of them. Jamie made the decision that she wouldn't go inside under any circumstances. If the girl were in trouble, people inside could help her.

Another consideration was that everything seemed normal in the bar. The bouncers hadn't moved. No patrons had come running out. The two Alliance cars were still parked in front. Nothing had happened to indicate a commotion inside.

Jamie leaned back on the hood of the mustang and continued to wait.

Then she remembered.

A rear exit.

A bolt of fear ran through her like she had been tasered.

This was why she did reconnaissance. Three exits. One in the front. An emergency exit on the side, which was in plain view. No one had come in or out of it in the last hour. But. . . an entrance for the employees and deliveries was in the back.

What if they took the girl out the back entrance? She'd never know. What if she went around back and they came out front while she was back there? For the first time in a while on a mission, Jamie was racked with indecision.

I have to know.

Jamie vaulted off the hood of the car and started running on her side of the street, still in the shadows. She crossed the street and walked in the space between the bar and the establishment next door. As she neared the rear of the building, she heard shouting. In Spanish.

A man's voice. Then a girl. Clearly under duress.

Jamie winced.

She pulled her weapon out of the inner flap of her jacket and placed her back flat against the corner of the building, holding the gun in front of her slightly out and up. The way Curly had trained her. She tried to picture in her mind where the men and the girl would be in relation to her. From their voices, they seemed to be about halfway. Which made sense. Just outside the back entrance. They probably had the girl up against the wall and had surrounded her.

That gave her an advantage. They were probably totally focused on the girl, and their only concern was the parking lot. Jamie dared to take a quick glance around the corner. They couldn't see her. Too dark. One lone light illuminated their position. The men and the girl were right where she expected them to be.

The problem was that the situation had escalated. The woman was against the wall like she expected. One of the men had one hand around her throat and another holding a gun pointed right at her head. With his superior height and weight, she was helpless against the wall.

The other three men were standing a few feet away. In sort of a circle. One had his back to Jamie, and the other two were facing Jamie's direction. Not an ideal configuration for what she was contemplating, but she could easily take the men down if it came to that.

The thought made her want to let out an exasperated sigh but didn't. She was close enough to hear them, so they could hear her as well.

Where is Jorge?

Even though it would make it five against one, Jamie wished he would arrive and calm the situation. The one guy with his hand on her neck was clearly out of control. Jamie could hear the girl moaning and gasping for breath. The sounds of the girl suffering caused Jamie to want to end it right then and there.

Wait, Jamie.

If Jamie confronted the men, someone was going to get shot, and it wasn't going to be her. Jamie resisted every urge to act.

When the girl let out a muted scream, Jamie instinctively moved. Not in a dash, but like a panther sneaking up on its prey. Past the point of no return. The man with his hand on the girl's throat was shouting now.

"Who do you work for? Why are you asking about the missing girls?"

The girl was crying while gasping for breath.

"I don't know what you mean," she said, having to force out the words.

"If you don't tell me, I'm going to kill you."

He was spitting the words like fire coming out of a dragon's mouth.

Jamie had seen enough.

***

The order in which the men had to die was based on natural selection. A term Jamie had stolen from Darwin, and jokingly incorporated into descriptions of her gunfights. In the heat of the battle, a natural order of things took over. Random order. A contradiction in terms—order based on chance, but also necessity.

The man with his hand on the girl's throat was the most immediate threat. Two taps of her Sig, and the man's temple exploded, and he fell to the ground in a heap. The gunshots created an eerie echo that made it sound like they came from the parking lot. Behind them. The two men facing Jamie instinctively looked in that direction even though they clearly saw the flash from Jamie's gun which was in front of them.

Their minds couldn't comprehend that quickly the contradiction between what their eyes saw and what their ears heard. By the time their brains recognized that the threat was in front of and not behind them, their time was up. This was where random order of natural selection kicked in.

The two men facing Jamie would die next. They posed the next biggest threat.

Which one would be first? The most skilled. Another irony.

He was the quickest to raise his weapon and prepare to fire. Before he could, Jamie unloaded two more shots to the center of his chest. He never got a shot off. The one a little slower on the trigger got to live approximately three seconds longer than his compadre.

His gun was down lower than his friends and his finger wasn't on the trigger. In addition, his eyes looked down and to the left. At his dead friend. A mistake.

Keep your focus on the immediate threat. Curly's words were drilled into her mind.

Which was what Jamie had the discipline to do. She didn't take one look at the girl other than to make sure she wasn't in the line of fire. Jamie would find out her well-being after the men were no longer a threat.

Had the second guy simply laid down his weapon, he might've lived. Instead, he clumsily tried to raise his weapon and fire. Instead, he hit the ground, dead on contact, before the weapon was even raised to where it could be fired.

The third guy was the least threatening and was the last threat to deal with because his back was to Jamie. Natural Selection. Random order. Why was he fortunate enough to be the one standing with his back to Jamie? Had he been on the other side, facing her, he would be dead and one of his buddies would be the one who was still alive.

Jamie didn't intend to kill this one. She wanted to question him. Now that the situation had turned into a mess of her own creating, she might as well make the best of it and learn what she could. Maybe he knew something about the missing girls.

She ordered him to drop his weapon and get on his knees. When he didn't immediately obey, Jamie said, "Do you want to die? I said drop your weapon! Get on your knees! Now!"

His best option would've been to drop his weapon and surrender.

She gave him a quick kick to the back of his knee, and he crumbled to the ground. Disarming him took almost no time. He lay on his back facing up. Jamie's foot was in his chest and her weapon pointed at him. His hands were up in a position of surrender. She searched him and relieved him of a knife in his pocket. Then ordered him on his knees with his hands behind his head.

Now she could check on the girl.

She was slumped to the ground by the wall, clutching her throat. Her eyes were glossed over, almost like she was in shock. The man's red finger marks were visible on her neck.

"Are you okay?" Jamie asked.

The girl tried to speak but her voice was raspy.

"I don't know," Jamie thinks she said.

"I'm sorry," Jamie said. "It's my fault. You need to get out of here. See a doctor if you need to. You'll be alright."

The girl stood like she was going to leave.

Then Jamie realized the problem.

"Wait," Jamie said to the girl. "You can't go."

"Why not?"

"It's not safe."

"I want to get out of here."

"You can't."

Jamie pointed the gun at her.

"You have to come with me."

26

The Sandy Beach Hotel
Grand Cayman Island

When Carolyn Morgan arrived at the Sandy Beach Hotel, she went straight to the conference room where her husband had set up a command center to lead the search for Sara. When she walked in, everyone in the room stopped what they were doing, and for a few seconds they were frozen in place as if time stood still for a few seconds.

Present in the room was her husband Sean, Hal Jolly, the Dean of Students for Calvary Christian Academy, and Pat Skyler, one of Sara's teachers and Carolyn's good friend from church.

A television crew was also in the room, with a camera pointed at two chairs with a backdrop, creating a makeshift set. A cameraman and a lady were there as well. Sean was sitting at the conference table with notepads, papers, and his laptop setting in front of him.

Sean looked up from the conference table and their eyes met. She looked at him and all the peace and strength she felt earlier at the bar was gone. Her waterworks returned with a vengeance. He rose to greet her, and she almost collapsed in his arms. He kept trying to reassure her that everything was going to be okay. She wanted to speak, but if she did, the words would be muffled by the sobs which she was trying to hide from the others. While she knew Sean's words were meant to be comforting, she wouldn't believe him until Sara was safely back in her arms.

Pat stood behind Sean waiting for her turn to greet Carolyn. Tears were running down her cheeks also as she wrapped her arms around Carolyn's neck, letting Carolyn hold it as long as she wanted. Seeing her friend and having a familiar face to draw solace from gave her comfort. Pat loved Sara and the feeling was mutual. Of all the teachers in the school, Sara had commented many times that Pat was her favorite.

Mr. Jolly handed the two ladies a box of tissues. He then held out his hand toward Carolyn, but she ignored it, brushed past it, and took Mr. Jolly in her arms, squeezing him tightly.

His lips were twisted, and his eyes drooped in what appeared to Carolyn to be a look of guilt. "I'm so sorry," he said over and over again. "I should've done more to prevent this. I'm so sorry."

"It's not your fault," Carolyn said, to reassure her friend.

She ignored the stern look Sean gave her. He said on the phone that he blamed Hal and the school. They should've had more safeguards in place to prevent this from happening. The fact that Sara was missing for more than twelve hours before anyone discovered her gone was totally unacceptable as far as Sean was concerned.

Carolyn didn't disagree with that sentiment. It's inexcusable that the bed check didn't discover Sara missing. If they had been able to report her missing at eleven that night, they might've found her by now. Giving the kidnappers a twelve-hour head start was a huge mistake. Maybe a tragic error.

Still, these people were her friends. They loved Sara. Sean mentioned the possibility of suing the school for negligence. That's not something Carolyn would ever consider. Seeing the look on Mr. Jolly's face and the pain in Pat's eyes told her they were suffering almost as much as she was. Blame was counterproductive right now. The only important thing was everyone working together to get Sara back.

Sean handed Carolyn a room key. "We're in the best suite in the hotel. Top floor. Compliments of the hotel. You need to go and get freshened up. In thirty minutes, we're going to start interviews. I have more than a dozen lined up. Here and in America."

"I don't know if I can do it," Carolyn said as fear rose inside of her.

"You can and you will," Sean retorted. Not in a mean way. But confidently.

Carolyn pushed the tears away from her eyes and off her cheeks. Roughly. "Look at me. I'm a basket case. There's no way I can go on TV and hold it together."

"That's what we want," the lady reporter chimed in. "Your raw emotion. People need to see what this is doing to you. I know it'll be hard, but you need to get this story out there. Sara's name and image needs to be on people's minds. Nothing pulls on heartstrings like a mother's plea for her missing child."

"That's how we're going to get Sara back," Sean said. "We're going to blast Sara's name and image out there as quickly as possible."

Carolyn bit her lip to fight back the tears.

Sean put both hands on Carolyn's shoulders. "I need you to be strong. For Sara's sake."

"I'll try," Carolyn said.

What choice do I have?

***

They conducted one interview after another. The first was for the local station. Sean had arranged for them to have exclusive coverage. The lady in the room asked the questions and broadcast it live to the studio. They also recorded footage to send to affiliates with a more in-depth interview. They would use their camera and station to broadcast back to the states. Carolyn had noticed the huge satellite dish outside the hotel when she drove up. Along with a dozen or so reporters who were on the outside of the hotel in a holding area.

That's why the reporter and cameraman were in the room. Filming real-time as events unfolded. Carolyn asked Sean if that was really necessary. He insisted that the footage could become a documentary at some point. Perhaps used for a missing person's episode of a television show if Sara wasn't found right away.

"I'm just trying to think of everything I can," Sean said.

Sean had signed an agreement with the station giving him certain rights. The footage could not be used by the station without his permission and without compensation. The live interviews could, of course, but the candid shots were part of the agreement.

At first, Carolyn felt uncomfortable having cameras in the room. It was almost like they were filming a reality TV show.

The reporter, Lola Miller, had said, "Just pretend we're not here. You'll get used to it."

Carolyn reluctantly agreed. Marketing was Sean's forte. In a way, that's what Sara needed right now. Marketing. Sean was approaching it like a business deal. Keeping emotions out of it. Carolyn understood. At least one of them was thinking clearly. It wasn't her. She was just trying to put one foot in front of the other and keep the pain at bay long enough to function.

Something impossible to do with one emotional interview after another. Just as one finished, she had to turn around and feel the gut-wrenching, stomach-churning feelings all over again. Carolyn wondered if at some point the emotions would be spent, and she wouldn't cry anymore. It didn't happen. Every interview brought her face to face with the reality of her daughter's plight, and the emotions spewed out like lava from a volcano.

Raw. Hot. Searing. Painful emotions.

She wouldn't wish them on her worst enemy. Not that she had any. Most people loved her. Most people loved Sara too. Lola said Carolyn was doing good. That she was a sympathetic figure. The interviews would help.

Carolyn tried to put the focus on Sara. Describe her daughter for the people watching. Sara won the Miss Congeniality award in the senior high school yearbook. Along with Homecoming Queen and Most likely to become the First Woman President of the United States. A straight "A" student. Had plans to go to college in the fall. Active in church. Sara had a bright future ahead of her.

Focusing on her thoughts became Carolyn's primary concern. Those were the memories of Sara that brought her happiness. Thoughts of what Sara might be going through at that very moment weren't allowed into her conscious mind. It took all her strength to battle them. The Bible said to take thoughts captive. That's what she was trying to do. Put those negative thoughts in prison. Unfortunately, even that thought brought her mind back to the prison Sara was in at that moment.

Fortunately, the interviews kept her mind occupied. The major networks hadn't picked up the story, but all the cable stations had. They did three interviews with local Dallas stations, six with the cable news networks, and three with various Christian affiliate stations. Sean had definitely done a good job putting together so many opportunities in such a short time.

Lola Miller said she was pleased. She even gave Carolyn a consoling hug.

Carolyn could tell she was moved by the story even though she was clearly trying to maintain her professionalism. She left to go get the hotel to refill the coffee pot. They were expecting a long night.

She was exhausted. Emotionally drained of all her strength. It was after ten. She wanted to stay awake and see if there were any developments, but she also wanted to crash in bed. Get away from the intrusiveness of everyone watching her suffer on camera.

Sean thought it was a good idea for her to go back to the room. "I'll let you know if there's any news."

As Carolyn was starting to leave, Lola Miller ran back into the room. Out of breath.

"Look at the television," she said with urgency. The set was in the corner of the room, set to Lola's station.

A sense of panic seized Carolyn as a rush of adrenaline went through her like a B-12 shot.

"What's happening?" Carolyn asked.

"Something at Rum Point," Lola answered. "There's a big police presence. Our camera crews just arrived."

The cameraman was already at his camera and was filming. Carolyn could see the red dot. He kept panning back and forth between Lola,

Sean, the television, and her. They were gathered closely around the television.

"Will somebody tell me what's happening?" Carolyn shouted. "Did they find Sara?"

Sean seemed amazingly calm. "Let's don't jump to any conclusions. It could be anything."

Pat stood next to Carolyn and put her arm around her.

Breaths were hard to come by. Carolyn could feel a panic attack coming over her. She fought the urge to begin sobbing. Fighting them off took all of her strength.

The reporter at the scene began speaking. Carolyn didn't catch her name. A light from the camera barely illuminated her figure and cast an eerie shadow over the scene. The light wasn't bright enough to see what was happening behind her.

"I'm at Rum Point, where the police have cordoned off the area. We're not allowed close enough to see what's going on, but all the activity is about a mile down the beach to the south. I can tell you that the commissioner is here. As are several investigators. I saw a forensic team arrive just a few minutes ago. Large lights are being set up. Huge lights. It looks like we're going to be here for a while."

The station went to a double screen. A newscaster back in the station asked, "Is this related to the Sara Morgan disappearance?"

"We believe it is but have not confirmed it."

Carolyn let out a moan.

"Why are investigators focusing on Rum Point?"

The reporter answered. "I don't know what has led them to this area. They must've gotten a tip. As you know, Rum Point is a big tourist area. There's a lot of foot traffic here. Perhaps someone found something suspicious."

"Oh my!" Carolyn cried out.

"Tell our viewers what the scene is like there. What do you see?"

"As I said, I see a lot of activity down the beach. We aren't close enough to see what they are doing. The restaurant is already closed. I can see a crowd of people beginning to gather. Wait just a second."

The reporter started walking and the cameraman followed. "I can see Commissioner Hughes walking this way. Let's see if he'll talk to me."

A man suddenly appeared on the screen and was standing next to the reporter. Carolyn didn't recognize him, but Sean said he was the commissioner which Carolyn had already assumed was the case.

"Commissioner. Can you tell us what's happening?"

"We got a lead earlier today that led us to this beach. Our team of investigators are on the scene. I have no further comment at this time."

"Is it related to the abduction of Sara Morgan?"

"Yes."

"Did you find a body?" the reporter asked.

Carolyn's knees buckled. She would have fallen if Pat weren't holding her up.

27

"Did you find a body?" the reporter shouted the question to the commissioner of police, Collin Hughes as he was walking away.

He suddenly stopped and turned back around. Carolyn dreaded the possible answer that might come out of his mouth.

"I want to answer that," Commissioner Hughes said. "We have *not* found a body. I repeat. We have not found Sara. So far, I've uncovered no evidence to suggest that Sara Morgan is not alive. As far as I'm concerned, we're still treating this as a missing person case."

Carolyn let out a huge sigh of relief. It seemed as though everyone exhaled at the same time. Probably all holding their breaths just as she'd been doing.

"You said you found something that's related to Sara's disappearance. Can you tell us what that is?"

"Like I said before, I have no comment. This is an ongoing investigation. I want to assure the public that I'm doing everything in my power to find Sara."

Carolyn instantly liked the commissioner. He spoke in a British accent. She was drawn to police dramas on television. Several originated from England and Ireland, so she heard that accent a lot.

But there was more to it than an accent. Carolyn considered herself a good judge of character. The commissioner seemed like an honest and decent man. He came across as sincere. The fact that he was optimistic about finding Sara encouraged her. And he mentioned a lead. She had no idea what the lead was, but it sounded promising. Enough to put a lot of resources behind it. That's no small thing, considering how many people were at the scene working this late in the evening.

She decided not to go back to the room. If those people were willing to stay up late working on behalf of her daughter, so would she. No way she was going to bed until she learned what the commissioner had found. She'd stay up all night if she had to.

Before anyone could comment on the new developments, Sean's phone rang.

"It's Commissioner Hughes," Sean said, after looking at the caller ID on his phone. "Hello Commissioner. Can I put you on hold for a second?"

Sean pushed the hold button and then asked everyone to leave except Carolyn. When the room was empty, he put the commissioner on speaker.

"Sorry about that. There were some reporters in the room. I didn't want them to hear our conversation."

"That's a good idea." Carolyn recognized the voice on the phone as the same one on the television.

"My wife, Carolyn, is here with me," Sean added.

"Hello, Mrs. Morgan. It's my pleasure to meet you."

"I wish it was under better circumstances," Carolyn replied.

"I do as well. I wanted to let you know what was going on at Rum Point. I assume you must've heard the news since a reporter is already there asking you questions."

"We saw you talking to the reporter," Sean responded. "What have you found?"

"This is part of why I didn't want the press involved so soon. It's better if we can conduct our investigation in private, away from the press. I'm sorry, you had to hear it on the news."

"Why didn't you tell me you had a lead at Rum Point?" Sean asked, roughly. "You could've called."

Carolyn saw Sean ball his fist and tense his shoulders in anger. She wasn't sure what he was so angry about. The fact they had a lead, and that the commissioner was personally calling them, was a good thing from her perspective.

She was even more surprised when the commissioner responded angrily.

"Why didn't you tell me that you were going to hold a press conference and offer a million-dollar reward?" the commissioner retorted. "I told you that was a bad idea. Our phones have been ringing off the hook. I don't have the manpower to keep up with all the calls."

"The press conference and reward were a good idea," Sean said defensively. "I've gotten more than a thousand tips on our hotline. We're going through them now."

"That's the problem. You have to go through all of them to find one that might be real."

"The more tips the better," Sean said, raising the intensity of the conversation even further. "Someone saw something. The reward will make them come forward."

"I disagree. A good person will come forward even if there is no reward. With a reward, anybody will say anything to get the money."

Sean started to say something, but the commissioner cut him off. "Let me give you a good example. We got a call today from someone who says Sara's body was dumped in Malportas Pond."

Carolyn's heart skipped a beat as hope was sucked out of her like a vacuum cleaner sucks up dirt on a carpet.

"Do you believe them?" Carolyn had to ask.

"No Ma'am. I don't. But I have to follow up on it. That means I have to send a dive team to search the pond. An investigator will have to be on the scene. It takes valuable resources from the real leads."

"I can see that," Carolyn said.

Sean clenched his jaw and glared at her.

She didn't want to appear to be taking the commissioner's side, but he had a good point. Actually, Carolyn could see both sides. What she didn't understand is why they were arguing about it.

Sean didn't let it drop. "With all due respect, that's your job. To follow up on leads."

"The problem is that it diverts our attention and resources from *real* leads. Leads generated from an investigation."

"How do you know the lead about the pond is not real?" Sean said.

This time Carolyn glared at Sean. She didn't want to consider that possibility.

"There are only a few lakes and ponds on the entire island. Of course, someone is going to call and give us that tip. Just in case it turns out to be accurate. Then that person would be entitled to a million dollars. We'll get dozens of tips. With the same type of information. They're nothing more than someone hoping to get lucky by guessing where and how the kidnappers disposed of the body."

"Sara is still alive," Carolyn said. "You won't find a body." If she kept saying that enough times, maybe she could make herself believe it.

"I'm hoping for the best as well," the commissioner said.

"I intend to follow up on all of our tips," Sean added.

"Can we just agree to disagree?" Carolyn asked, adding her own emphasis to the question showing her frustration with the whole conversation. "What's done is done. I don't see what good it does to rehash it at this point. We can 'Monday morning quarterback' this after we get Sara back. What's the lead you're pursuing at Rum Point, Commissioner, if you're able to say?"

She wanted the two men to stop their petty spat and get on to the facts at hand. She was dying to know what the commissioner had found.

"I can't comment on it at this time, but I can tell you that it's definitely a lead worth pursuing."

Sean exploded. "Come on Commissioner. Don't play coy with me. Why can't you tell us what you found? You can't keep us in the dark. I'm Sara's father. I have a right to know what's going on."

"How can I trust you not to go to the media?"

"You can trust us," Carolyn said. "I promise you, that whatever you tell us, we'll keep confidential. I know my husband. He just wants to help. We can keep a secret."

"That goes without saying," Sean said.

The other end was silent for several seconds. "I got a tip that a suspicious boat was seen motoring away from Rum Point last night. About the same time that Sara disappeared."

Sean seemed stunned as his eyes widened and mouth gaped open.

"Did they identify who was driving the boat?" Sean asked.

"Did they see Sara?" Carolyn said.

"No to both of those questions. That's all I can say at this point. I think I found where the boat came ashore on the beach. I have no idea if it's related to Sara's disappearance, but it's a lead I want to follow up on."

"When we met earlier today, you said you had a possible suspect. Have you ruled him out?" Sean asked.

Carolyn wished Sean hadn't changed the subject. She wanted more information about the boat.

"There are two people of interest. Again, don't tell the press that. I haven't ruled them in or out. We're still pursuing an investigation. Everything's on the table at this point."

"I appreciate everything you're doing. I really do," Carolyn said. "I'm praying for you and your team."

"Thank you. We need all the prayers we can get."

"Is there anything else?" Sean asked.

"Yes. Can the two of you come to my office in the morning and provide a DNA sample?"

"Are we suspects?" Sean said angrily.

"No. I want to have your DNA on file. That way... if we find any evidence, we can compare your DNA with the sample to see if it's a match. That will tell us if the evidence came from Sara's DNA."

"Commissioner Hughes, my husband is not Sara's biological father. I didn't know if you knew that. But I can give you a DNA sample. I'm definitely her mother," Carolyn said chuckling and feeling the tension release some. "Labor took sixteen hours. Believe me, I know for a fact she has my DNA."

"That would be perfect. Come by police headquarters at nine o'clock. We can meet in person. Perhaps I'll have more news then."

"That will give me time to go through my leads," Sean interjected. "I'll turn them over to you, if it's not too much trouble for your people to follow up on." The words were dripping with sarcasm.

Carolyn swatted Sean's arm like she was correcting a child. The way he was treating the commissioner was uncalled for. She'd never seen this side of him before.

No sooner had Sean hung up the phone then he said to Carolyn, "You could've been more supportive of me."

Carolyn took his hand. Sean pulled it back and walked away from her. "It seemed like you were taking his side."

"I'm not taking anybody's side," Carolyn responded. "I want to get our daughter back. He's trying to help. Why are you mad at me?"

"I'm trying to get our daughter back as well! I'm doing more than he is. I've been working as hard as I can to get Sara back. Do you know how hard it was to get all those interviews set up?"

Carolyn walked over to Sean and put her hand on his arm. He had his back to her. Tears were welling up in her eyes. "I know how hard you're working, honey. Why are you so upset?"

He pulled away again. This time it made her angry. She took a deep breath. Everyone deals with a crisis differently. She had to give him grace. There was no book on how to deal with a missing child. Sean was dealing with the stress in his own way. In times like this, Carolyn cried. Sean obviously got defensive and angry when under this much pressure.

That was surprising to her. Sean usually handled stress well. But that was related to business. This was different. What she did know was that arguing about it would not be helpful. She measured her words.

"I agree with you. I think you did the right thing. By having the press conference. And the reward. I know your heart. You want to get Sara back as badly as I do. I don't want to alienate the commissioner though. We need his help. You can't do everything."

"I don't trust him."

"I think he's a good man."

"There you go again. Taking his side."

"I'm not... taking his side," Carolyn said, trying to keep from responding impulsively. This was not like one of their fights back home, and she was determined not to let it escalate into one. "But... I'm being realistic," she said calmly. "He's the commissioner. He wields a lot of power. I think you should be nicer to him."

Before Sean could answer her, his phone rang again. He walked over to the conference table where he had set it down.

"This is Sean Morgan."

Carolyn came and stood next to him. "Is it the commissioner?"

Sean moved a few steps away and waved his arm signaling he wanted her to be quiet.

"I understand," Sean said. He was nodding his head up and down.

"I will do that. But it'll take some time."

More silence as Sean was listening to the person on the other end. Carolyn's curiosity was piqued, and she hated that she couldn't hear the other end of the conversation. Who would be calling at this hour?

Abruptly, Sean hung up the phone.

"Who was that?" Carolyn asked.

"The kidnappers!"

Carolyn let out a muted scream. "What did they say?" Her heart would've jumped out of her chest if it could've.

"They have Sara," Sean said soberly. "They said she's alive."

"Oh! Thank God."

"They want money."

"How much?"

"Twenty million dollars."

"We don't have that kind of money."

"We have to get it. He gave me three days." Sean sat down at the conference table and stared off into space. "They said if we don't pay it, they'll kill Sara."

Carolyn didn't know what to say.

28

Tampico

Jamie realized she had a mess on her hands. Four missing girls. Three dead Mexicans. And the girl in the red jacket. She might be the most pressing problem. She was now linked to the killings. When the bodies were discovered, all leads in the investigation would point to her. Not Jamie. The only thing that could tie Jamie to the killings was the girl.

That's why she couldn't let her leave. Not only was the girl's life in danger, but she could blow Jamie's cover. All hell was going to break loose in southern Mexico as soon as El Mata learned that three of his men were dead and one other was missing. Six were dead and unaccounted for if you counted the two up north. The local police would also be involved. There'd be an investigation. Witnesses in the bar would be questioned. The girl was the last person seen with the men. She wouldn't have a chance. They'd find her and pick her up within twenty-four hours.

Jamie had to find a way to protect her while at the same time completing her mission. While she now knew El Mata was involved, she was no closer to finding the missing girls. The best course of action would be to go to a safehouse and regroup. She intended to do her own interrogation of the remaining Alliance member. If he knew anything, she had ways to make him talk.

First, she'd let out some frustration. She kicked the Alliance member in the ribs and ordered him to his feet.

"Move all that trash up against the side of that wall." Jamie pointed at the dead bodies. She wanted them moved and hidden from obvious view. The longer it took for them to be found, the more time Jamie had to come up with a plan.

He didn't seem to understand what she meant.

"Drag your dead friends over to that wall, or you're going to be dead as well." She pointed the gun at him to make her point.

He got up carefully, his hands in the air, and he did as he was told. Jamie watched him carefully, keeping the gun on him at all times while also watching the girl in case she decided to run.

"Get their wallets and give them to me."

When they were discovered, she wanted the men to have no IDs on them. She took the cash out of the wallets and handed it to the girl.

"What's your name?" Jamie asked.

"Anna," she whispered.

Maybe she could build some trust with the girl by the gesture. She slipped the ID's into the pocket of her jacket and threw the wallets on the ground next to the bodies.

"Let's go," Jamie said to the man. He didn't seem inclined to put up a fight.

"You're coming as well," she said to Anna, taking her by the arm. Jamie hated to treat her roughly but wanted her to know that she meant business. Anna pulled her arm away in defiance but didn't try to run away. Instead, she asked, "Where are we going?"

"I honestly don't know, but I'll tell you when I do," Jamie said almost jokingly, so she kept the tension as low as possible.

Jamie told the guy to walk in front of her and not to try anything foolish. They started walking around the side of the building in the same direction Jamie had come.

Just as they got to the corner of the building, she turned and fired a shot at the lone light on the side of the building, shattering the glass and throwing them into complete darkness. She wasn't worried about the people inside hearing the gunshot. The music was blaring all the way outside to their location. The light off would make it harder to see the bodies. They'd probably think it was a burned-out bulb.

The Mexican must've thought Jamie was firing at him because he hit the ground. She let out a laugh and helped him back to his feet. The chuckle did her good, as she inhaled much-needed air and exhaled deeply through her lungs. Jamie tended to grit her teeth and hold her breath in a confrontation.

When they got to the street, Jamie made them remain in the shadows until the coast was clear. No cars were coming so they crossed the street to the alley where Jamie's car was still parked. They went around to the back of the car and Jamie ordered the man to his knees.

"I think I'll call you Tex," Jamie said to him. She liked to name her combatants. The name had to be something she could easily remember. Tex-Mex was one of her favorite foods. The man was Mexican. Tex was the first thing that popped in her mind. So, Tex it was.

He simply looked up at her with his eyes wide open, terrified. He cringed and ducked his head every time she got near him. Jamie opened the trunk of the car and pulled out some zip ties. She secured his hands behind his back and told him to stay on his knees and not make a move.

"Anna. You probably wonder what's going on. I can't tell you. What I can tell you is that you're in grave danger, and that I'm going to see that you are protected. I'm sorry you're involved in this, but there's nothing I can do about it."

"I should be thanking you. You saved my life back there."

Jamie wasn't about to tell her that the only reason she was in that predicament was because of her. "We're not out of the woods yet," Jamie said. "I've got to get you to a safe place."

Jamie wanted to get out of there as quickly as possible, but she was also curious about Jorge. If the Alliance was involved in the kidnapping of the girls, he would probably know about it. She needed confirmation. Tex might have some information, but Jorge would know more.

Was it worth the risk?

At this point, no one knew she was there. The bodies hadn't been found and wouldn't be for a while, and the hiding place had served her well up to this point. If need be, she could make a quick exit. She also had the firepower to fight her way out if necessary. She decided to wait. To make the most of the time, she started questioning Tex.

"What do you know about four missing girls?" she asked him roughly. He was still on his knees behind the car.

"I don't know anything about any missing girls," Tex said.

Jamie hit him on the side of the head with the palm of her hand. So hard, he fell to the ground, obviously stunned. When he staggered back to his knees, she pointed the gun at his head.

"You should look away," Jamie said to Anna. "This isn't going to be pretty."

The man closed his eyes and squinted hard, like he was expecting the worst.

Jamie said, "I'm going to ask one more time. You need to know that I'm not a patient person. I don't like to ask the same question twice. If you don't answer truthfully, I'm going to send you to hell with the rest of your buddies. Now... what do you know about the four missing girls? Think carefully before you answer. Your life may depend on it."

"I don't know anything about *four* missing girls."

Jamie didn't react right away because he seemed to be telling the truth, and the way he ended the sentence meant he had more to say.

"I know of one girl," he added nervously.

"Tell me about her."

"We came to the bar." He jerked his head in the direction of La Taberna. "Jorge was there. He told us which girl to take."

"What day was this?" She wanted to see if he knew information that would collaborate his story.

"Last Friday night."

The Tampico girl went missing last Friday night. Jamie's heartbeat sped up.

"What happened?"

"Jorge slipped something in her drink. Some guys started talking to her friends, and we got her alone."

"Where did you take her?"

"To the beach. A boat was waiting. We loaded her on it and then left. That's all I know. I swear."

Jamie believed him. It also matched the story of the girl in Cancun who got away. It also confirmed that Jorge was involved. That meant she wasn't leaving until he got there. She needed to figure out a way to talk to him.

Where is he?

Jamie had an idea. She pulled Tex to his feet, took his arm, and led him over to the passenger side of the car. After opening it, she helped Tex into the seat. Jamie knelt next to him with the door still open. She reached across his body for the radio handset.

"I want you to tell Jorge that you have the girl."

Jamie still had the gun in her off hand. "Don't try anything funny or you're dead. Nod your head if you understand."

Tex nodded his head in an exaggerated manner so she'd know he understood.

"Go ahead," Jamie said.

"Jorge. Are you there?" Tex said into the microphone.

"I'm here."

"This is Miguel. I've got the girl. What do you want me to do with her?" Jamie nodded in approval.

"Hang tight. I'm almost there."

"Copy that."

Jamie took the handset from him and put it back in the cradle.

"You did good," Jamie said, patting him on the cheek.

She helped him out of the car and moved him to the sidewalk in front of the car. Still in the shadows but closer to the bar.

"Now we wait."

***

They didn't have to wait long. Jorge raced down the street in a late model Dodge Durango. Jamie remembered that the girl from Brownsville was taken in a similar vehicle. She made a mental note to ask Jorge about that—if and when she got the chance.

Jorge exited the vehicle and looked around. He had parked behind the two black mustangs. From the bulge in his clothes, his gun was in the front and to the side, in a holster.

"Call out to him and tell him you're over here," Jamie said to Tex. "And don't say anything to warn him or you're a dead man."

Jamie was confident that Jorge could make out the image of a man and a girl but couldn't see them clearly enough to see that Tex's hands were restrained behind his back.

Tex let out a whistle getting Jorge's attention. "Over here," he said.

Jorge looked their way.

"I've got the girl," Tex said.

Jorge started walking their way with a purpose. He wasn't a big man, but he would strike fear in the heart of anyone he was coming for. Rough face. Mean looking eyes. The eyes of a stone cold killer. The other men she had confronted behind the bar didn't have that look. She didn't see this often. Most of the time, men like that were in the middle east. Terrorists had that look. Hardened fighters in Afghanistan had that same demeanor. Jorge was obviously the kind of man who would cut your heart out and not lose a minute's sleep over it.

While Jamie wasn't evil like him, if she had to kill him, she wouldn't lose a minute's sleep either. Before that happened, she hoped to extract information from him in whatever means necessary.

Jamie stiffened. This wouldn't be easy. Jorge wouldn't go quietly. Taking him prisoner by gunpoint and interrogating him there in front of the bar suddenly didn't seem like such a good idea.

A different plan came to mind.

When Jorge got within ten feet, Jamie kicked Tex's leg out from under him, and he tumbled to the ground.

Just the distraction she needed.

Like a cat, she bridged the gap between her and Jorge within seconds while shifting the gun to her left hand. His eyes widened like saucers at the sudden movement which was the last thing he would be expecting. Curly always said that, next to ability, surprise was the most important element of a street fight.

The simplest thing to do would've been to show him the gun and disarm him with it. Jamie dismissed that option. Jorge was a dangerous man. She needed to put him to sleep. Questioning would come later. If she just held a gun on him, Jorge would have many opportunities to surprise her with an attack. He could have other weapons on him. From experience, she knew men like Jorge wouldn't surrender voluntarily. She wouldn't. Better to have a confrontation now. Under her terms.

Jamie came in hard and fast. Jorge instinctively recognized the attack and reached for the gun with his right hand. Exactly what Jamie was expecting and hoping he'd do. She came in slightly to the left of him. When he turned back to the left, Jamie planted her right foot hard and turned her hips to the left. She lifted her right hand and brought it down with a crushing tomahawk chop that connected on the side of Jorge's neck. She followed through with the blow so her body followed him to the ground as he collapsed in a heap, unconscious.

Anna let out a scream. She had the presence of mind not to let it all out and give away their position.

Satisfied he was out, Jamie relieved Jorge of his gun then searched for any knives or other weapons. Another gun and two knives were on him. As she suspected, Jorge was armed for a fight. She made the right call attacking him. There's no way he would've surrendered peacefully.

Jamie dragged Jorge to the back of the car. She restrained his hands with zip ties and then lifted him up and into the trunk.

"Get in," she said to Tex roughly pointing to the place where she had put Jorge.

He hesitated.

Jamie shoved him toward the open trunk lid. Tex reluctantly crawled in. She didn't blame him. She wouldn't want to be stuck in that hot trunk with Jorge either. Fortunately, all her clothes and travel supplies were in the backseat. Another stroke of good luck.

Things in this mission were looking up.

The amount of intel she'd gathered in such a short time was remarkable. She knew about the boat. Jorge was one of the masterminds of the plot to kidnap the girls. At least the Tampico girl. He probably had intel on the other girls as well. Hopefully, he would know where the boat was going.

Jamie slammed the trunk closed and told Anna to get in the car. Once inside, Jamie took out her phone and called Maxwell. It went straight to voicemail.

She desperately needed to talk to him. The best course of action was to go to a safehouse. Jamie also needed a different car. No way she was going to travel around Alliance territory in one of the Alliance cars anymore. They didn't know who she was. That was to her advantage. She wanted to maintain it.

Maxwell could pick up the two prisoners at the safehouse. He could even handle the interrogation of Jorge and his man after she was done with them.

If she could get in touch with him. Maxwell might even be able to make the dead bodies disappear before dawn.

She dialed his number again. No answer. *Why won't he answer the phone?*

Brad would never leave her hanging like that. He was available to her twenty-four hours a day, seven days a week. If she got Brad's voicemail, which was rare, he'd get back with her within minutes. Usually seconds.

Anna's phone rang, startling both of them.

"Can I answer it?" she asked.

"Sure. But don't say anything about what happened." Anna nodded like she understood.

"This is Anna."

After a brief silence she said, "Yes. I'm all right."

"Okay." It sounded like the conversation was winding down.

"She's right here," she said.

Anna handed Jamie the phone.

"Maxwell wants to talk to you."

Jamie's mouth flew open to the point it felt like it was going to hit the floor.

29

"Are you spying on me?" Jamie asked Maxwell angrily.

"Not spying. Just keeping an eye on you to make sure you don't do something stupid."

Having one adrenaline rush after another in such a short period of time had given Jamie a short fuse. At first, she blamed herself for putting Anna in harm's way. Now she blamed Maxwell and intended to let him know it. He obviously sent Anna into that bar to observe what she was doing and report back to him. The bone-headed move almost got his girl killed and forced Jamie to kill three men.

"Just so you know, you almost got her killed."

"What happened?" he asked.

"Four of El Mata's goons had Anna cornered behind the bar. She would've been killed if I hadn't come along." Jamie wasn't about to tell him why she was in that predicament. Maybe he'd piece it together if he talked to Roberto, but more than likely not. Neither of them would have any way of knowing that Anna was wearing a red jacket and red dress. A set of unfortunate circumstances and dots they would not likely connect. Even if they did, Maxwell should've let Jamie know that Anna was going to be there.

"I'm afraid to ask what happened to the four men," Maxwell responded.

"Let's just say that hell is a lot busier tonight processing some new arrivals."

"You killed four of El Mata's men!"

"Not four. Just three. One's in my trunk. Two actually. I captured one of their leaders, Jorge, for good measure. You can thank me later."

"Let me get this straight. You killed three men. Captured another. And you have El Mata's third in command in the trunk of your car."

"You're welcome."

"I wasn't thanking you. Are you trying to start a war between Mexico and the United States?"

"I'm trying to find four missing girls," Jamie said sharply. "Turns out El Mata is behind the kidnappings. I have proof now. Jorge is the one who orchestrated the kidnapping of the girl in Tampico. One of them told me they put her on a boat. Same scenario as the girl who got away up in Cancun. I need to interrogate Jorge and find out what else he knows."

"You need to let him go before El Mata finds out and all hell breaks loose around here."

"That's not going to happen."

"Bring him to me and we'll interrogate him."

"I will when I'm done with him."

"I'm ordering you to bring him to me." Maxwell's tone had escalated considerably.

Jamie was willing to match it.

"You order me? I don't work for you. I work for Brad. He's the only one who tells me what I can and cannot do. I'm going to interrogate Jorge and find out what he knows and get on with my investigation. What you do with him afterward is your business."

"I'm the highest ranking official in this jurisdiction. I say what happens. Not Brad. Not anyone else in the US, except my boss. So, I repeat, bring him to me."

"I'd like to see you try and make me!" Jamie said as she hung up the phone.

Anna looked stunned.

Her mouth was agape and her eyes so wide her painted-on eyebrows were high on her forehead. She'd probably never seen anyone talk to Maxwell that way. Jamie handed her back the phone.

Jamie couldn't stand the suits for that reason. They were paper pushers who sat behind a desk and second guessed everything the operatives did in the field. Then tried to order them around like they knew best. Brad wasn't that way. He had his bureaucratic moments for sure. But most of the time, he had her back.

More than likely, Maxwell was calling Brad now. She was certain Brad would tell him to go jump in the nearest lake and let his operative do her job. The thought caused her to let out a laugh.

Anna sat in the passenger seat staring straight ahead. Apparently afraid to open her mouth and interject anything.

Jamie had been hoping for some help from Maxwell. She needed a car and a place to interrogate the prisoners. The plan in her mind was to go to the safehouse and hunker down there for the night. Interrogate the witnesses. Get something to eat. Sleep for a few hours. That wasn't going to work. Maxwell would know where the safehouse was and send men there. While she could defy him over the phone, even with all the bravado, she wouldn't get in a physical confrontation with fellow CIA members. If they wanted to take the men away, she wouldn't stop them.

The better idea was to ditch Anna and go into hiding for a while. Not so easy to do when she was driving an Alliance car. At least Anna would be safe which was reassuring to her. She didn't need Jamie's protection. The only thing linking her to the killings was the security footage and some possible eyewitness testimony. That was Maxwell's problem. He sent her in there, so he could deal with the fallout.

Jamie took a deep breath to calm her nerves. As frustrated as she was, taking it out on Anna would be unfair. This wasn't her fault. So, she softened her tone when she finally addressed her.

"Where's your car, Anna? I'm going to take you there."

"Just around the corner," she said, her voice still raspy. Her neck had heavy bruising. She'd be hoarse for several days. *At least she's alive.*

Jamie started the car. "You need to lay low for a while. Things are going to get hot around here over the next few days. I want you to be safe."

As Jamie pulled out of the alley, a banging noise could be heard coming from the trunk. Jorge was obviously awake.

"Shut up," Jamie shouted. "Or I'll come back there and shoot you."

The banging stopped. That made her realize though that they could hear her talking. She lowered her voice and said to Anna, "I'm going to do what I can to get the security footage out of the bar. That way there's nothing to tie you to the scene."

"How are you going to do that?"

"I'll figure out something."

Alex hadn't gotten back to her. He must've had trouble accessing the system at the bar. If he had, she'd have him delete it. If she didn't hear from him, she'd break in after the bar closed and steal it. It might be a good idea to hide the bodies better as well. Buy her some extra time.

"That's my car over there," Anna said pointing to a late model sedan. It had government car written all over it. Maybe it wasn't such a good plan to have Maxwell get her a car. Besides, she'd steal a car before she'd ask him for any more help. She was stubborn that way.

Jamie pulled alongside Anna's car. She didn't get out right away which made Jamie nervous as she looked around in both directions. The angst wouldn't leave until she got to a more secure place.

Jamie saw that tears had formed in Anna's eyes.

"Thank you," she said to Jamie. "You saved my life. You were amazing."

"I'm glad you're okay," Jamie said, flashing her a smile.

The girl reached across the console and hugged Jamie's neck, taking her by surprise. She hugged her back. Then Anna opened the door and got out. Before she shut it, she said, "You be careful out there."

"I will," Jamie said, not wanting to tell her what Curly said about being careful. "You be safe."

"I hope you find the girls," Anna said.

As soon as the car door was shut, Jamie sped away.

***

When she was safely away, Jamie stopped the car on a side road in a cluster of trees. She needed sustenance. Her throat was as parched as a shriveled-up plant in an unattended garden. In the back seat, were snacks and bottled waters. She gulped down two so fast she almost started choking. She ravaged two power bars and then drank half of a third bottled water. Her throat felt refreshed, and the food gave her a sudden burst of energy.

The quiet place off the road gave her a chance to sit and think. Driving around increased her chances of running into hostiles and put her on high alert. Plan A had been asking Maxwell for help. Since that was out of the question, she needed to figure out plan B.

She wasn't too far along in the process when her cell phone rang. *Brad.*

"I can explain," were her first words.

"No need. Maxwell filled me in." Jamie didn't want Brad to only hear Maxwell's side.

"El Mata is behind the kidnappings," Jamie blurted. Curly always said to give the suits positive news right up front if you had any. If the news was good enough, she might not ever get around to telling him the bad news. Linking the Alliance to the kidnappings this quickly was as close to good news as she could give him short of saying she knew where the girls were.

"There's a fifth girl missing," Brad said.

"I knew it! Where?"

"Cayman Islands."

"No way."

"Same scenario. Young girl on a senior class trip. Kidnapped out of a bar. It's all over the news up here. I spoke to the police commissioner. He has evidence the girl was taken off the island on a boat."

Jamie could hardly contain her excitement. Very few things on a mission were more thrilling than when pieces started to fit together.

"One of the men I captured said he took the girl from Tampico down to the beach and loaded her on a boat. It's like the girl in Cancun. Same thing."

Brad already knew that, but Jamie reminded him of it anyway. If nothing else, for emphasis, confirmation that they were on the right track. Brad expected results from her. Sometimes impossible results. Giving him this much information this quickly was going to make him happy.

"Yep," was all he said. Compliments were few and far between when it came to Brad. She could count on one hand how many she'd received in four years. When they came, they felt good. No criticism from him was as good as a compliment. At least, that was how she had come to rationalize it.

Then an uneasy feeling came over her. "Wait a minute," she interjected. "That doesn't make sense. Does El Mata have a presence in the Cayman Islands?"

"That's a good question. One I want you to answer for me. I need you to go to Cancun as soon as possible and get on the first flight to Cayman."

That was not a good Plan B in her mind. Jamie had to push back.

"Brad, I'm making good progress here. I've got El Mata's number three man in my trunk. He may know where they took the girls. I can make him talk."

"Go to the safehouse," Brad said in his 'don't question me' voice. "Drop the men off. Get to the airport. Maxwell will interrogate them."

Jamie bristled at hearing Maxwell's name. The thought of seeing his smug face again caused her to ball her fist. She couldn't guarantee that she'd be able to control her temper if he started his power play with her again at the safehouse.

The anger of the previous conversation returned with a vengeance. She had to plead her case.

"Brad... Let me work the leads in Mexico. Four girls are missing from here. Only one in Cayman. The one is important, but I think I'd be more productive following this thread than starting from scratch on the island."

A thread was a term Curly had taught her to describe a series of connected leads.

"The commissioner says he's got a possible suspect," Brad retorted, "but he's not talking. I want you to go down there and do the same thing you did in Mexico. Rattle some trees. See what snakes fall out."

"What's the rush? Can't you give me another day or two? I can always go to Cayman in a couple of days."

"Not possible."

"Why not?"

"There's a hurricane headed that way. You have two, maybe three days tops before it hits. After that, the whole island might be underwater."

Of all the arguments Jamie was anticipating, that was the one she least expected.

30

The next morning

Jamie dropped Jorge and his minion off at the safehouse and drove through the night to get to Cancun. Unfortunately, Maxwell was at the drop, but she avoided a confrontation. She wanted to take one crack at questioning Jorge, and Maxwell reluctantly agreed.

Turns out, Jorge was too out of it to answer any of her questions coherently anyway. The blow to his neck had obviously caused a concussion. Eventually, he'd recover, and Maxwell assured Jamie they would interrogate him vigorously. If Jorge gave them any actionable information, Maxwell said he'd call her himself.

Jamie sat in the gate area waiting to board her flight. Brad had arranged a private plane to take her to Cayman so she'd get there quicker and could get in and out of customs easier. The name on her boarding pass and passport was Mandy Nobles. That was better than most assumed names she got on missions. The last one she drew was Maud Felt, a German name. How was she supposed to speak and act German? That pushed the limits of her acting abilities. The only good thing about it was that Maud Felt meant "mighty warrior" in German. For that reason, she embraced the character and drew on it during a couple dangerous situations she found herself in.

Her name, Jamie, was from the Hebrew meaning "he who supplants." She had to look up the definition of supplant, being unfamiliar with the term. It meant one who displaced or replaced someone else.

Overthrows. Unseats. Deposes. Topples. That name was to her liking as well. First of all, it was biblical. With her religious background, she embraced the spiritual meaning. In her job, she saw herself as someone who uprooted the bad guys and supplanted them. If she could, she'd "supplant" every despot and evil dictator in the world. While she couldn't, her name made her feel like she could take on the world.

"You're going to board in about fifteen minutes," the gate agent told her.

"Thank you. How long will the flight be?" Jamie asked.

"About an hour and twenty minutes."

If they left on time, she'd get there with time to spare.

She was surprised she hadn't heard from Alex. Not that it really mattered. At this point, looking at the security footage was of no use to her. She already knew what had happened to the girls. Picturing it in her mind was easy enough to do. At least in Tampico. Jorge slipped a drug in the girl's drink. When she lost her bearings, they took her from the bar. Jamie was sure that was what the footage would show. Since she already knew the identity of the two people involved, the security camera wouldn't tell her anything she didn't already know.

What she really wanted to learn was if Alex had had any luck tracking down the last location of the girl's cell phones. While she didn't expect the bad guys to be stupid enough to leave them on, stranger things had happened. Most cases were solved because the perpetrator made a mistake. The perfect crime had never been committed. Finding that mistake was her job. If the kidnappers made it easier for her, then all the better.

Since she'd be boarding soon, and out of touch for a few hours, she decided to call Alex. The curiosity was getting the best of her. She glanced at her watch. *Quarter to six*. Alex was an early riser and probably awake. Maybe even working on her problem at that very moment.

Unless he stayed up all night. Working on it. Then she might wake him up.

Too late. The number was already dialed.

"Hey gorgeous," he answered sleepily.

"Hey sexy," she replied.

"I don't look sexy at the moment," Alex said. "I'm still in bed. I probably look pretty rough. Late night last night."

Jamie laughed. "You think you look bad. You should see me. I've been up all night. I'm at the airport."

"Are you coming home?"

"No. Brad is sending me to the Cayman Islands."

"I wish I was going to an island to lay out in the sun."

"I don't think I'll be doing any suntanning. I didn't even bring a bathing suit. It's strictly business. There's another missing girl. She's seventeen. Her name is Sara. She's from Dallas."

"Oh..." he said. More of a groan than anything else, letting her know how badly he felt about that new development.

"At least you won't have time to meet any good-looking island men," Alex said.

"I didn't say that," Jamie kidded. "There might be time to take in the scenery." She was enjoying the conversation and was glad she called. This banter made her feel human. Like a real person. With a real life. Instead of a killer who had gunned down three men the night before.

"You can look but you can't touch," Alex said playfully.

"I don't even look."

"Yeah right. Don't lie to me. If you see a good-looking guy walking down the beach, don't tell me you won't take a look."

"I doubt I'll even see a beach. Are you saying you never look at a pretty girl in a bikini?"

"That's different. I'm a guy. We're supposed to look."

"Alex Halee! That's the most sexist thing I've ever heard you say. If I were there right now, I'd slap you."

"I'm just kidding. Is this what you woke me up for? To tell me you're going to the Cayman Islands to look at guys."

"I'm not going to..." Jamie decided the remark didn't deserve a response. "No. I called to tell you I don't need the security footage anymore."

"That's nice to know, since I spent half the night working on it." If he was trying to make her feel guilty, she did.

"Sorry about that. I got the intel I needed last night."

"Not much there anyway. The bar in Tampico had the best footage. I could see a couple guys taking your girl out of the bar. The bar in Cancun didn't have any footage I could use. The other one was too dark to see anything. I didn't look at the one in Brownsville, Texas. You know. I didn't feel like breaking any federal laws. I like not being in prison."

"I wouldn't want you to go to prison on my account. Visiting you would be a pain."

"Nice to know you'd visit me."

"Of course. Depends on how long you were in for, but I'd visit for a while. Anyway... thanks for the effort. Could you do me another favor?"

"What's that?"

"Go into the Tampico bar security system and delete the footage from last night. All of it."

"I can do that."

"You don't want to know why?"

"Nah! Need to know basis. Right."

"Right. Thanks. You're the best. By the way, any luck on finding the cell phones?"

"Yeah. I mean no. I'm working on it." By the tone in his voice, Alex perked up noticeably. This was what he loved to do. Hack into difficult systems. Cell phone networks were almost as difficult as banks.

He continued. "That's really why I was up half the night. I tracked all four phones up until the time the girls were taken. In Mexico and the one in the US. Then the phones went off the grid. I kind of expected that. Once they were taken, the first thing the perps would do is turn off the girl's phones."

"I figured. It was worth a shot at least."

"Actually, what was strange is that they weren't turned off. They went out of cell tower range. I got a few pings from out in the water just off the land."

"I have intel that the girls were put on a boat."

"That would make sense then. But where would they take them? I quit tracking once they were over water."

"Maybe to a nearby island. Or south, to Central America. Maybe South America. Could you go into those networks and see if the girl's phones show up on their systems once they got into range? Maybe we'll get lucky."

"That's a lot of networks. It'll take me awhile to hack into them."

"Start with the closest islands and work southward."

"What's the closest island?"

"Cuba. But I doubt they would take them there."

"Cuba is a nightmare to hack into. But I can do it."

"Don't even bother. I doubt El Mata would be selling American girls to a Cuban oligarch."

"Okay. I'll focus on surrounding islands and south. Should I check the Cayman Islands?"

"No. Supposedly, Sara was taken from the island in a boat as well. Why would she be taken off the island and the other girls brought there?"

"Roger that. I'll get back with you."

"Thanks. I love you."

"Don't be careful."

Jamie hung up in better spirits than when she started the call.

***

Grand Cayman

"You have to tell Commissioner Hughes about the ransom," Carolyn said to her husband Sean.

They were in their hotel room at the Sandy Beach hotel and had been arguing about the subject for nearly an hour. The conversation had gotten heated on several occasions.

Sean was adamantly opposed to going to the police.

"The person on the phone said no police. If we involve the cops, they said Sara will die. I can't take that risk."

"How do we even know they're the real kidnappers?" Carolyn retorted. "Commissioner Hughes said we would get a lot of fake leads."

"They have my cell phone number. Where would they have gotten it from? Sara must've given it to them."

"That's true. I hadn't thought of that." Carolyn's spirits suddenly buoyed. Those words caused a jolt of excitement to run through her. That might be proof that Sara was alive.

Still, a lot of questions remained.

"I just don't want to make a mistake."

Sean replied. "You have to trust me. I know what I'm doing. If we tell the police, they'll want to have cops at the exchange. If the kidnappers get one whiff that somethings up, they might hurt Sara. I have to go alone."

"What about the risk to you? Are you just going to walk up to the exchange with twenty million dollars in a suitcase?" Carolyn had seen many movies that depicted an exchange like what Sean was talking about. Some of them did not end well.

"No. The money will be wired. Once they have confirmation that the money is in their account, then they'll release Sara."

Sean put on his jacket.

Carolyn sat on the bed. She'd gone back and forth between sitting in a chair and standing and pacing and sitting on the bed.

"What if they don't? What if you wire the money and they don't release her? Can you really trust them?"

"What other choice do we have? It's the only way to get Sara back. You heard the commissioner. He has no clue where Sara is. He's got a couple of persons of interest, but they aren't talking. Sara could be anywhere. This is the only way."

"I have a bad feeling about this. I still think we should tell the police."

"Carolyn, I forbid you. Don't tell them! Not if you want to see your daughter alive again."

"*Our* daughter you mean." That remark made her stand.

"Of course. Our daughter. You know what I meant."

"Where are you going to get the money?" she asked as she moved closer to him and helped him adjust his tie. She brushed some lint off his coat.

"I've got it taken care of."

"Sean. Look at me." Carolyn stood right in front of him. He turned his head away. Sean often did that when they were fighting. Avoiding intimacy. Carolyn put her hand gently on his cheek and moved his face so he was looking directly at her.

"You have to talk to me. No secrets. You can't do this alone. We should make these decisions together."

"I told you I have it taken care of."

"How?" she backed away a few steps.

Sean hesitated. Like he was hiding something.

"Sean. Where are you getting the money?" she asked sternly.

Sean sat down on the bed.

She sat down next to him.

"Okay. A couple of years ago, I took out a K & R insurance policy."

"What's that?"

"A kidnap and ransom policy."

"Why did you do that?"

"The board of my company thought it'd be a good idea. You know. As the business grows, I'm traveling a lot. Someone could kidnap me and hold me for ransom. The policy protects the firm from any financial losses it might suffer."

"Okay. I didn't know that. I understand why you have a policy. But how does that help Sara?"

"The policy covers family members as well. You and Sara are covered."

"Why would we be covered?"

"Because someone might kidnap you to extort money from me and my company. In this case, Sara."

"Is the kidnapping related to your business in some way?"

"I don't think so."

"How much is the policy for?" Sean looked away again. That annoyed her.

"Twenty million dollars is the maximum payout. I've already talked to a claim's adjuster. I sent them the police report and everything."

"So, they're going to pay out the money?"

He turned his back to her. Sean was standing in front of the mirror, adjusting his tie, even though she had just fixed it. Now it was messed up again.

"No. I have to borrow it. Once I pay the ransom, then I can put in a claim. They'll process the claim and reimburse me for the loss. So, you see... I have everything covered."

"I hope so."

"We have to go now."

They walked out the door and took the elevator down to the lobby. Neither of them said a word. They got in the car and drove to the station.

Carolyn still had a bad feeling about it.

***

Jamie's flight arrived ahead of schedule. The pilot said the winds were at their back, pushing them forward.

When they landed, she turned on her phone. When it found service, she heard the familiar ping, signifying she had messages. Texts from Alex.

I've got news.

I found cell phones.

Call me.

A cross between euphoria and fear came over her. Happy he found them, but nervous to finally know where the girls were. Or where they might be. Jamie immediately dialed his number.

"You found a phone?" she said as soon as he answered.

"All four of them."

"Really?"

The plane was taxiing to the gate, so it was noisy. She thought she heard him right. He had found all four phones.

"The signal only pinged once," Alex said.

"They probably reached their destination. And then turned them off." Jamie was dying to know where they were.

"My thoughts exactly."

"Where are they?"

"Cuba."

"You're kidding," she said as a wave of unbelief came over her. Deep down, she knew he wasn't kidding. Her worst nightmare. The only thing worse than going into El Mata's lair, was going into Cuba.

31

Jamie helped herself to a pastry and a cup of hot tea after arriving early for the nine o'clock meeting with the commissioner of police. As it turned out, the meeting was not just with him, but his entire team. Also present was an FBI agent from Dallas who was now on the case. She didn't catch his name.

Three detectives along with the commissioner were the only local law enforcement represented. Jacobson, DeLancey, and Steele. Once everyone had been introduced, the commissioner began.

"It's been thirty-six hours since Sara Morgan went missing from the *Reef Bar*. During that time, we've made significant progress in the investigation. I appreciate Roy Jones from the FBI being with us today and Mandy Nobles from the CIA."

Technically, Jamie was still on a covert operation even though she was cooperating with the local authorities. So, she continued to use the name on her passport, Mandy Nobles. It wouldn't take long to get used to being addressed by that name.

"We'll take all the help we can get," the commissioner continued in his heavy British accent. "In my operation, we check our egos at the door. There is no us versus you. We will cooperate with the FBI and CIA any way we can. And we expect the same courtesy. My detectives have been instructed to tell you everything they know about the investigation and will inform you of new developments. We appreciate you repaying the favor."

Jamie felt a twinge of guilt. She had no intention of telling them about Cuba. Her philosophy was need-to-know basis. She'd tell them when she thought they needed to know that information. Right now, she didn't even know what she was going to do with it and wouldn't until she talked to Brad. She assumed she'd be on the next plane to Havana.

At the same time, she appreciated the sentiment and wanted to be helpful to them in any way she could. Her ego was checked at the door as the commissioner had said. Jamie was pretty much a no-nonsense kind of a gal anyway. Never one for politics. She just wanted to be left alone to do her job. A self-starter, that usually meant working alone. CIA operatives never got credit for arrests or good outcomes anyway. That came with the territory of covert operations. Recognition was not why they did what they did.

Jamie stifled back a yawn. She was going on little sleep and hoped the commissioner got to the good stuff soon.

A screen was set up behind him. A laptop was connected to a viewer that could project documents, pictures, and videos onto it. A picture suddenly popped up. Jamie leaned forward in her chair. A beach. The beach was empty. Good for Alex. No men with their shirts off were anywhere in sight. The thought of the early morning banter brought a smile to her face.

"This is a picture of the beach at Rum Point," Commissioner Hughes said.

Jamie was immediately struck by how beautiful it was as she took another sip of her tea and devoured the last of the roll.

The image changed to a close up of the beach. She couldn't see the water from that angle.

"You can see the indentation in the sand. I believe Sara Morgan's body may have made that indentation."

It took some imagination, but Jamie could see how it could be perceived to be the outline of a body. Did that mean they thought she was dead?

"Why do you think she was brought to that location?" the FBI agent asked.

"I have reason to believe Sara was loaded onto a boat. A dive captain reported that on the night in question, he saw a suspicious boat heading out to sea with its lights off. The time was about an hour after Sara presumably left the bar."

Jamie wondered if they had security footage of Sara while she was in the bar or while she was leaving it. She made a mental note to ask Alex to look into it.

"Do you believe her to be deceased?" the FBI agent asked.

"I don't. If you look closely at the indentation, it's not uniform. It looks to me like the body moved." Commissioner Hughes zoomed in on one spot.

"Couldn't the body have been moved by the kidnapper?"

"I'm getting to that." Another picture appeared on the screen.

Commissioner Hughes pointed to a spot in the sand. "Right here you can see two sets of footprints walking from the indentation toward the shore. Presumably toward the boat."

Jamie decided she could be helpful at this point.

"I just arrived from Mexico where I'm investigating the disappearance of four girls under similar circumstances. Two suspects are in custody. They've confirmed that one girl was taken from a bar in Tampico Mexico and loaded onto a boat. Alive, I might add."

"That's good information," the commissioner said. "That's confirmation to me that we may be on the right track. Today, I have teams out on the sea searching an area five miles out from the island. In addition, Sara Morgan's mother is coming in this morning and providing a DNA sample. We collected some DNA from the scene. At some point, we'll know if the DNA we found is Sara's. Unfortunately, our lab is notoriously slow. It may take a few days. Could the FBI lab in the states turn it around faster?"

"I don't think so," Roy Jones, the FBI agent from Dallas said. "It would take a day just to get the sample there."

"Do you have any suspects?" Jamie asked. DNA samples and the like bored her until they had actual results. She liked dealing with people. Confronting suspects. Interrogating them. Shooting them if need be.

"We have two people of interest. One is the owner of the bar. Lars Fossey. He has an alibi, but it's shaky. He says he was in bed asleep. His girlfriend says she woke up later, and he wasn't in the bed."

Jamie always perked up when she heard that a suspect lied about his alibi. She hoped she'd get a chance to confront Lars Fossey. A notepad sat in front of her, but she wasn't taking notes. Jamie had a perfect recall for these types of things. Curly made her do hours of memorization exercises. If she wanted to remember it, she did.

"You said you have a second suspect," the FBI man chimed in. "Who is he?"

"The owner's son, Jake Fossey," the commissioner said. "Now would be a good time to turn the floor over to our lead investigator, Roz Steele."

Jamie loved that name. It reminded her of Remington Steele. She wished they would give her a name like that on a mission. Maybe she could suggest it. If the woman was anything like her name, she was one tough character—not to be messed with.

"Jake is 22 years old," Roz began in a New York accent and modulation. "He was working at the bar that night. Although he says he was in his office the whole time. Detective DeLancey interviewed him for several hours." Roz pointed to a middle-aged gentleman who sat right across from Jamie. He smiled at her and she returned it.

"Jake said he never left the bar. That he was there all night," Detective DeLancey said. "That's not true."

Jamie couldn't wait to hear why it wasn't true.

Roz fiddled with the laptop and a video appeared on the screen.

"This is from a security camera at a convenience store across from the bar. Notice the time stamp in the corner. Ten thirty-two p.m. Watch carefully. I'll describe what you're seeing. Two people can be seen leaving the bar at that exact time."

Roz was standing now by the screen. She had a laser pointer in her hand. "Right there," she said. "We believe that's Jake Fossey and perhaps Sara Morgan leaving the bar."

"You can't see their faces," the FBI agent said. "Why do you believe it's them?"

"Keep watching," Roz said.

Seconds later, a car entered the screen. A high end four door luxury car. It looked like a Porsche. If you blinked, you'd miss it.

"There!" Roz said. "That car. It belongs to Jake Fossey."

"So, he did lie when he said he was at the bar the entire time," Detective DeLancey interjected. "It felt like he was lying when I was interrogating him. Now I have the proof."

Jamie stood up and walked over to the screen. "Can you rewind it and stop it when the car comes into view?"

The video rewound and then started forward. Roz froze it the moment the car appeared in the frame. Jamie leaned in and stared at the image.

"I don't see the girl," Roy Jones said.

"She could be lying down in the seat of the car or be in the back seat," Jamie responded. "Our girls in Mexico were drugged. Sara might've been as well. Probably was, actually. I don't think you would see her. Unless she went with him voluntarily."

"The main thing is that he lied," Commissioner Hughes said. "Not only that, but the security tapes at the bar were taped over. That's highly suspicious."

Jamie made a mental note to cancel the previous mental note to have Alex look for security footage. "Have you asked him about it?" Jamie asked.

"We just got the video earlier this morning," Roz answered. "We're having him picked up for questioning and brought back here as we speak. It'll be interesting to see how he wiggles out of this."

"Can I be there?" Jamie asked Roz.

"Commissioner?" Roz said, handing the question off to him.

"You can be in the observation room."

A knock on the door interrupted the meeting before Jamie could respond. A woman opened the door part way and addressed the commissioner.

"Jake Fossey is in the interrogation room."

The commissioner stood. "Let's go see what he has to say for himself."

"If he doesn't talk, can I waterboard him?" Jamie asked, as the whole group burst into laughter.

"That would be illegal in the Cayman Islands," the commissioner said, clearly trying to hide a smile.

That never stopped me before. She could feel the excitement. Jamie was like a human lie detector. She had an uncanny ability to know when someone was lying.

Give me ten minutes alone with him. I'll make him talk.

***

Jamie and the others filed into the observation room. The commissioner and Roz went into the interrogation room where Fossey sat at a table with another man in a suit. Detective Delancey wheeled a television into the room with the laptop attached to it. Presumably to show him the security tape.

Jamie assumed the younger man was Jake Fossey. Sandy blonde hair. He wore shorts and a tank top. Flip flops.

The commissioner shook hands with the suit. Jamie assumed he was Jake's attorney.

"Mr. Fossey, thank you for coming in today," the commissioner said. "We have a few follow up questions from yesterday. Can we get you anything? Water, tea, soda?"

The commissioner had a good manner about him. He had a way of disarming a person. Make him feel comfortable. Jamie's interrogation style was like a bull in a china shop. Intimidation. Fear. Threats. Physical pain if necessary.

"I'd like to begin by clarifying one thing you said yesterday," Commissioner Hughes said. "You said that you were at the bar the entire night. That you never left it. Is that correct?"

Jamie liked that he was getting right to the point.

Fossey didn't answer.

"Mr. Fossey? Were you at the bar the entire night? You never left?"

Jake looked at his attorney.

His attorney spoke, "I've instructed my client not to answer any more questions. Do you intend to charge him with a crime today?"

"No sir. We just want to ask Jake some questions."

"In that case then, this interview is over. Let's go, Jake."

The two got up and left the room.

32

A stunned silence filled both rooms as the excitement of a possible breakthrough in the case walked out the door with Jake Fossey and his attorney when they abruptly left the interrogation room, refusing to answer any questions.

Commissioner Hughes stood from his chair, walked into the observation room with Roz following him. Slowly. His head down, and his eyes were narrowed in a look of confusion. Either stunned or defeated. Jamie wasn't sure which. Probably both.

"Waterboarding doesn't sound too bad now, does it?" Jamie said, getting a few light chuckles.

"This is a setback for sure," Commissioner Hughes said. "Let's take a fifteen-minute break and meet back in the conference room so we can regroup. At least we know who our primary suspects are."

A break was a good idea. Jamie needed to call Brad. Before the meeting, Alex had filled her in on the location of the girls in Cuba. When she called Brad to let him know, he was in a meeting. His secretary offered to interrupt him, but Jamie didn't feel like that was necessary. He should be out of his meeting by now.

"What you got for me?" Brad said when he answered the phone.

"A bunch of dead ends here. The primary suspect has lawyered up. It doesn't matter anyway. Sara Morgan isn't here."

"Tell me what you know."

"She's in Cuba."

The phone went dead silent. Jamie almost expected that reaction. Cuba was one place they were reluctant to operate in. The close proximity to the United States and the strained relations that went back decades meant that every operation had to be covert. Getting cooperation from the Cuban government was next to impossible.

In spite of a travel ban, getting people in and out was not the problem. Most countries, including Canada, allowed travel to and from Cuba. An operative could easily go in under an assumed name and a foreign passport. The problem was staying there for any length of time undetected.

"And you know this how?" Brad asked.

"Well, I don't know it for sure." Alex had only tracked the cell phones of the four girls. Jamie was assuming the kidnappings of four girls taken from Mexico and Sara Morgan were related.

"But. . . I highly suspect that's where she is," Jamie quickly clarified.

"Don't make me yell at you this early in the morning," Brad said without trying to hide his frustration. He didn't like his operatives making assumptions without some proof.

"Here me out. It'll make sense after I explain it to you."

"I can't wait."

He wasn't kidding with her. Most of the time, Jamie could tell when Brad was trying to be funny. This wasn't one of those times. She needed to get right to the point.

"The four missing girls in Mexico were put on a boat."

"I already know that."

Brad didn't like to be given information more than once. Jamie liked to explain things from A to Z. If only for her benefit. It helped to organize the thread in her mind.

"Alex tracked their cellphones to a location in Cuba."

"I'm listening."

She also knew that information would get his attention. There was no logical explanation for the girl's cellphones being in Cuba unless that's where they were taken.

"Alex found the exact location. It's a house owned by a Cuban oligarch."

"I wish you had said anyplace other than Cuba," Brad said soberly. "You know that complicates things."

"These are American girls! Kidnapped. I think we can get permission to do about anything we want."

Brad didn't respond. Jamie could see his face in her mind. Brad was in his cubbyhole of an office. No windows and no pictures on the wall. Just his desk, credenza, and two chairs. Papers, if there were any, would be carefully stacked and organized. Not a paperclip would be out of place. The wheels in his brilliant mind would be churning as Brad was already forming a plan on how he was going to sell this to his bosses. Something he was a master at. Above all else, Brad was an analyst. One of the best in the business. He was probably already two steps ahead of her.

Jamie continued after giving him a few more seconds. "I just got out of a meeting with the police commissioner in Cayman. Sara Morgan was almost definitely taken off the island by a boat."

"Almost definitely?"

After she said it, Jamie realized how strange that must've sounded. "You know what I mean. I know what happened, I just can't prove it beyond a reasonable doubt."

"This isn't a courtroom. All you have to do is convince me."

"Sara was drugged at the bar. I saw security footage of the bar owner's son, driving away from the bar at the same time Sara went missing. He claimed he never left the bar. Of course, he didn't know about the security footage that blew his alibi out of the water."

"That's suspicious."

"Yes, it is. Not conclusive but suspicious."

Jamie didn't wait for another response. "His father may also be involved. His alibi didn't hold up either. An eyewitness saw a man and a woman walking down the beach at Rum Point. The woman was staggering like she was drunk."

These were all presumptions. Jamie didn't know any of these as facts even though she was presenting them as such. This was like a courtroom and she was presenting her opening statement. She had to put her best evidence forward to get past summary judgment. Brad being the prosecutor, judge, and jury.

Most investigations were not open and shut. Brad knew that well. A CIA operative in the field usually had to piece together a series of assumptions into a logical scenario. That's what she was doing. Curly always said, *Go with what makes the most sense until it doesn't.*

"I'm with you so far." Brad seemed to agree with her.

"An eyewitness saw a boat leaving the Rum Point area headed out to sea. Its lights were off. The driver was acting suspicious."

"And you think the boat was taking Sara to Cuba?"

"Where else would they be taking her? The same scenario that happened in Mexico happened to Sara Morgan. Class trip. In a bar. The girl is drugged. Loaded on a boat. The girls in Mexico were taken to Cuba. Why would the destination for Sara be different?"

"I can think of a lot of reasons."

So could Jamie. "Regardless, I need to go to Cuba. Today if possible. We have confirmation that four of the girls are there. It makes sense that Sara is there as well. Even if she's not, I can rescue the four girls which was the original mission anyway."

"What about the hurricane?"

"What about it?"

"I've seen the weather. It's a monster storm. It's supposed to go right over Cuba. You don't have much time. I can get you in, but how are you going to get out of Cuba with the girls before it hits?"

"I'll figure something out. I always do."

"Not even you can beat a hurricane."

"All the more reason for me to go to Cuba now. Even if I have to hunker down there. I certainly don't want to be on this island when it hits. If it's as bad as you say, it might be weeks before Cuba is open for travel again."

"I'm sold. I just have to sell my boss. I can't authorize you to go to Cuba on my own. My neck doesn't stick out that far."

"When you talk to your boss, tell him that the owner of the bar in Cayman also owns a bunch of boats. Dive boats. Dinner boats and the like. They may have been used to transport all the girls."

"I'm on it."

Jamie was only giving Brad that information for added confirmation of her theory. The boy and his father were insignificant to her. Commissioner Hughes and the FBI could handle the law enforcement investigation. Jamie had one job. Find and rescue the girls. Proving who did it was not in her purview of responsibilities. If she found proof, then all the better.

"I'll go back to the hotel and pack my bags and wait for your call," she said.

The line went dead. Brad didn't greet you when he answered the phone or sign off with any kind of goodbye.

Jamie's adrenaline rose inside of her like the needle on a gas tank being filled up with gas. Danger had that effect on her. The thought of going to Cuba was exhilarating. It made her almost giddy. Her intention had been to go back to the hotel, get something to eat and grab a couple hours sleep.

Curly always said, *Sleep and eat when you can. You never know when you might get another opportunity.*

A good breakfast was going to happen, but she didn't think she'd be able to sleep. She was too excited. Cuba was one place she'd never been before.

***

Jamie went back to the conference room to let the commissioner know she had to leave unexpectedly and wished them luck in their investigation. She left the police station and went back to her hotel. After she packed, she went down to the restaurant to take in the buffet. After eating twice as much as she should've, she decided to go back to the room. She might be able to take a nap after all.

As she exited the restaurant and was heading for the elevators, a huge commotion erupted from the lobby. Lots of noise and chatter. Something was going on. As tired as she felt, her curiosity would not let her go back to the room without checking it out.

201

The lobby was filled with people. Hundreds. Men and women. Even children. A lot of teenagers. Several tables were set up along a side wall, under a large mural of a stingray. Jamie walked over to the table. A picture of Sara Morgan was in a frame and on an easel behind the table. That raised her curiosity even further.

"What's going on?" Jamie asked a perky woman standing behind the table with a name tag on. *Pat Skyler.* On the table were flyers, posters, and signs. All with pictures of Sara with big bold letters across the top that said MISSING. It became immediately apparent that this was where they were organizing volunteers for a search.

"Are you here to help with the search for Sara?" Pat asked, confirming what Jamie already knew.

"I'm sorry, no. But I wish you luck."

The lady had no idea that Jamie was right in the center of the search for Sara. In fact, Sara's safe return rested squarely on Jamie's shoulders. She suddenly felt a twinge of guilt. All of these efforts, though admirable, were a waste of time. Sara was in Cuba. Of course, these well-meaning people had no way of knowing that.

Jamie wasn't going to tell them. They needed hope. To feel like they were doing something. The rush of people who had come out willing to help find a stranger warmed her heart. That motivated her more, if that was even possible. She wasn't just going to Cuba and risking her life for Sara, but for all these people as well. Everyone was earning a stake in Sara's safe return.

"Are Sara's parents here?" Jamie asked.

The lady pointed to a woman across the room. "That's Sara's mother. She's in charge."

Jamie remembered from the investigation file that the mother's name was Carolyn. "Thank you," Jamie said as she started walking that way.

Jamie was immediately impressed with Carolyn Morgan. Even from a distance. She had the look of a woman on a mission. Jamie had that look most of the time. In a way, Carolyn was on a mission to find her daughter. She appeared confident. Strong. Organized. Clearly, by the number of people in the room and the attention to detail, they had put together an amazing operation in a short period of time.

When she got closer, Jamie could see the dark circles under her eyes from crying. She could only imagine what Carolyn was going through behind the makeup that couldn't hide all the pain from someone as perceptive as she. Yet, the woman was rising to the occasion. Answering questions. Shouting out instructions. All the while, greeting and thanking the well-wishers who were in line to speak to her.

She almost hated to interrupt her but needed to.

"I'm sorry," Jamie said, touching Carolyn on the arm. "Can I speak to you for a minute?"

Carolyn pointed to the table Jamie had just come from. "That's the signup table. You can register there. Thank you so much for coming out."

Jamie leaned in closer so the others couldn't hear. "It's important Carolyn. I'm with the CIA. I'm going to find your daughter."

33

"Let's go somewhere we can talk," Carolyn said to Jamie.

She took Jamie's arm and led her out of the lobby and down a hall into a conference room. Normally, Jamie didn't like it when people put their hands on her, but she let it go.

"This is my husband, Sean," Carolyn said as they entered the room.

Sean barely acknowledged her. The keyboard on his computer was filling the room with clicking noises as he was furiously typing something on it.

"So, who are you exactly?" Carolyn asked.

"My name is Mandy Nobles and I'm with the CIA. I've been sent here to find your daughter."

That got Sean's attention. He stopped typing, stood to his feet, and walked to their location which was just inside the door.

"Why would the CIA be involved?" he said as he closed the door. "We have things under control."

"Honey, we can use all the help we can get," Carolyn said, the tension between them obvious.

The two couldn't possibly know that Jamie was their best bet to find Sara alive. If things went right, she might have Sara back to them in less than twenty-four hours. Six hours to catch a flight to Cuba. A couple of hours to drive to the house where the girls were being held. Overnight surveillance of the building. An early morning raid.

Maybe a shoot-out. Probably not. The oligarch would feel safe in his own country. The only muscle would be personal security. Once Jamie saw the physical location, she might be able to devise a plan to get the girls out without anyone noticing. Alex was probably already looking at the location on Google Earth. Brad had ordered satellite pictures. They'd have some ideas as well. Brad might even let her bring Alex along.

The trickiest part would be getting the girls out of the country. Brad would have to figure that out. There were a lot of details left to be decided.

"Like I said, we don't need any help," Sean said. He turned and walked back to the seat in front of the computer.

Jamie was taken aback by his rudeness. Considering she was risking her life for his daughter. "Actually, you do need me," Jamie said in a congenial but firm tone. "More than you know. I have several promising leads in fact."

Sean stopped before he got to his seat and turned back around so he was facing her. "What kind of leads?"

"I'm not at liberty to say. But I'll know more in the next forty-eight hours."

"Yeah, I've heard that before. I have my own leads I'm following up on."

"About that," Jamie said. "I understand you set up a tip line. You need to turn those tips over to the authorities. Let the professionals do the investigation. You have no idea who you might be dealing with."

"I can handle it," Sean muttered and sat back down in front of his computer.

Jamie walked over to him with purpose. "These are dangerous people who took your daughter."

Sean ignored her. His lips were pursed into a sneer.

Jamie looked at Carolyn who seemed as exasperated as Jamie as she shrugged her shoulders.

Jamie took a piece of paper and pen off the conference table. She wrote a phone number on it. "I'm writing down my phone number. If you run into any trouble or need anything, call me at this number."

Jamie handed the paper to Sean. He made no effort to take it.

"Have I done something to offend you, sir?" Jamie asked.

"I'm working and you're bothering me."

Anger flashed through her body like a charcoal grill that just had lighter fluid thrown on it.

Of all the nerve. Jamie bit her lip to keep from saying something she regretted.

"Fine," she said tersely. "Don't take my help."

Jamie turned around in an exaggerated huff and walked out the door. Carolyn followed her.

"Please wait," she said. Jamie stopped to turn and face her. "I apologize for my husband's behavior. He's under a lot of stress."

Jamie softened her tone. "I understand. I really do. But you need to talk some sense into him. I'm not kidding when I said to let the professionals handle the investigation."

"What are we supposed to do? Just sit around and wait?" Carolyn's voice cracked as she said it.

Jamie moved in closer to her. "No. Keep doing what you're doing. Organize searches. Do interviews on television and radio. But don't pursue any leads. That might put you and your husband's lives in danger. Not to mention Sara. You can make it worse for her."

"I just want to find my daughter," Carolyn said as tears began rolling down her cheek.

"I know you do. So do I. But you need to trust me. I'm good at what I do. I promise you I'm going to find your daughter. I'll put myself in harm's way if I have to."

"I appreciate it. This is the hardest part. The waiting."

"What did your husband mean by he has some leads he's working? Anything you can share with me?"

Carolyn hesitated. Jamie could tell she wanted to tell her something but was restrained for some reason. "We got a ransom demand," she finally blurted out like she had a secret she had been dying to tell someone.

"Did you tell the police?"

"My husband said we shouldn't."

"That's not wise."

"That's what I said to him. We actually got several ransom demands. Three or four on the tip lines. It's very disturbing. They say they're going to kill Sara if we don't pay them money."

"That's because you put out a million-dollar reward. That was stupid. You shouldn't have done that. Every crazy person that hears about the reward is going to call the tip line."

"That's what the commissioner said."

"You should've listened to him."

"One of the men demanding a ransom called Sean's cellphone. How would the kidnappers know the number unless Sara told them?"

"Your husband is a successful businessman. I bet his cellphone number is on his business card. Or on the company website. Maybe the company letterhead. He might've given it out on one of his social media accounts."

Jamie could see some of the hope leave Carolyn's face like air escaping from a balloon. She was obviously heartened by the thought of getting Sara back by paying a ransom. Jamie didn't doubt they were even thinking about paying it. She hoped they didn't do something stupid. If she got the chance, she'd tell Commissioner Hughes, just so he was aware of what they might be thinking.

"I hadn't thought about that," Carolyn said.

"With a two-hundred-dollar handheld device, I can capture your husband's cellphone number if I'm within a few hundred feet of him," Jamie explained.

"I had no idea."

"That's why I said to let the professionals handle it. I'm doing everything humanly possible to get your daughter back to you safely."

"I appreciate that."

The piece of paper with Jamie's phone number was still in her hand. She handed it to Carolyn. "Call me any time, day or night. If I don't answer, leave me a voicemail. I'm going to find your daughter. I promise. Like I said, I may have something promising for you in the next day or two."

Jamie hated making those kinds of promises, but she felt so bad for the mother. They gave each other a hug and Jamie went up to her room. More motivated than before. If that was possible. Seeing Carolyn had given her a name and a face to spur her on. Sean had given her a different emotion. She wanted to find Sara just to wipe that smug, arrogant, look off his face.

***

Jamie wasn't back in the room longer than ten minutes when Brad called her.

"Hi Brad," Jamie said excitedly. "Tell me the plan."

"No plan. The mission is a no-go."

"What?" She couldn't believe the words coming across her phone. She was so sure they would approve it that she hadn't really considered the possibility that they wouldn't.

"Not enough time."

"I can go there today."

"They won't let me send you there through normal channels without an identity built. We don't have that for Mandy Nobles."

An identity was a full internet profile. When Jamie arrived at customs with the name Mandy Nobles on her passport, the Cuban authorities would check her out thoroughly including looking at social media accounts, work history, even public records. Mexico and Cayman wouldn't bother. They weren't a closed communist country where the government controlled everything.

"How long would it take for you to get me an identity?" She already knew the answer.

"A couple of weeks."

"Let me go in covertly."

"How do you propose to do that?"

"I don't know. But we can think of something."

"I'm out of ideas."

"I could take a boat."

"They have a defense sonar system around the entire island. You wouldn't get within a mile of it."

"The girls were taken there in a boat."

"By a powerful man in Cuba who knew how to get the authorities to look the other way. I'm telling you Jamie, there's no way you can get in there without getting caught. I don't want you to spend the rest of your life in a Cuban prison. I'd rather do things right or not do them at all."

"There has to be a way."

"There's not. Come back home and we'll regroup. In a month or so, we can have a plan together to get you in there. The girls aren't likely going anywhere."

"A month is a lifetime to those girls when they're living in slavery. There's no telling what disgusting things have already happened to them."

"I know. I'm as frustrated as you are. But I agree with the decision. It's too dangerous. If you had a way to get in undetected, I would go out on a limb for you. As it is, the best thing to do is to regroup. Your flight leaves for DC in two hours. You're flying commercial. I'll send you the boarding pass on your phone."

This time Jamie hung up without saying goodbye. Totally disheartened. To make matters worse, she had practically promised Sara's mother that she would have her back home within forty-eight hours.

Jamie was so mad she was almost crying. Not at Brad. He was right. Cuba was complicated for this very reason. The risk was too great. She'd never get through security. If she did, she had no way to get the girls out.

To make matters worse, the hurricane was bearing down on the area and forecasters predicted a direct hit on Cuba.

Jamie gathered her things and left the hotel room.

As she was walking through the lobby, she heard her name. Not her name, but Mandy's.

"Mandy," the familiar voice said.

Jamie looked over at the mother who was standing across the room.

Carolyn blew Jamie a kiss.

As if she couldn't feel any worse.

34

Jamie sat in the gate area waiting to board her flight home, moping. Feeling sorry for herself. Not so much for herself, but for the girls. She didn't remember ever feeling this low. The mission had started with such success. Within thirty-six hours, she'd found the location of the five girls. Except for the glitch with the girl in the red dress and red jacket, everything had gone as well as could be expected. Even the incident with Anna was a positive. Three bad guys were dead. Two were in custody. Add in the two who were harassing the Mormon missionaries, things couldn't have gone better for the early stages of an operation.

Until the whole thing got blown up like a submarine hit by a torpedo.

Jamie tried to look on the bright side and keep from sinking to the bottom of the figurative abyss. The mission wasn't over. It was just delayed. What was the saying? Justice delayed is justice denied. That applied to her situation as well. Mission delayed is justice denied. At least for the girls. As bad as Jamie felt, the girls, no doubt, felt worse.

She got up from her chair and put on her backpack and decided to walk the concourse. A brisk walk would burn out some of the frustration. Besides... her plane was delayed which meant she was going to get into DC even later than planned. Alex was set to meet her at the airport. The only consolation. At least she'd get to see him sooner than expected.

After the walk, Jamie felt better physically, but not mentally. She'd need to take a few days back home to work out some of the frustration.

Maybe she'd go back to the gym and spar with Frankie. She'd heard he won his match and was the new bantamweight champion. That caused her a momentary respite from the depression. She tapped out the number one bantamweight in the world! And she had gone easy on him.

The way she felt right now, who knows what she might do if they got back into the ring together. That thought made her laugh. She wouldn't mind getting in the ring with a number of people at that moment. El Mata being at the top of the list. Maxwell. And Sara's father!

What was his problem?

Before she could think about that further, the gate agent announced that they were boarding. Sara put the backpack over her shoulder and got in line. The boarding pass on her phone said she was in the back of the plane. Brad didn't even have the courtesy to get her a first-class ticket. Not that she expected one. It had only happened a few times in her career and only when she was traveling with someone important or the mission called for her to have an identity with a certain socioeconomic status. She liked those missions.

Actually, she liked all missions. Even this one. Except for the feeling that she had somehow failed Sara and her mother. Curly told her not to get emotionally involved in an operation. He said the emotions would eat her alive. She couldn't help it. That might be one piece of advice she wouldn't follow from her mentor. Curly had many great qualities. Being in touch with his emotions was not one of them. He was a stone-cold emotionless man. He probably hadn't felt anything in years. She didn't want to end up like that.

So, she would embrace the depression and be glad she still felt something.

Being in the back, Jamie was one of the first to board after first class, children, frequent flyers, and people who needed special assistance. She boarded, settled into her seat, and closed her eyes. At least she could get some sleep. Her eyes hadn't been closed longer than a couple of hours over the last two days. She drifted off almost immediately.

A loud noise woke her.

The ground felt like it was shaking.

It startled her.

For a few seconds she didn't remember where she was. It took a few seconds to shake off the fog.

A roaring sound was coming from outside the aircraft. Unlike anything she'd ever heard before.

It jolted her awake. Jamie looked out the window. A huge plane had landed on the runway next to theirs. A military plane. Configured unlike any she'd ever seen before. One monstrous, powerful plane. As a contradiction, it had a Sesame Street character painted on the side. Gonzo, if she remembered her characters correctly.

A flight attendant walked by.

"What's that?" Jamie asked.

The flight attendant bent over and looked out the window.

"That's a hurricane hunter."

"What's a hurricane hunter?"

"They fly into the hurricane and get measurements, gauge the strength, that kind of thing. I wouldn't want that job. That plane was here yesterday as well. The crew got off and ate lunch while the plane was being refueled and checked for damage. I had a chance to meet them and get a picture taken with them."

"Who would be stupid enough to fly into a hurricane on purpose?" Jamie asked.

The flight attendant was shutting the overhead compartments.

"Somebody with a lot of courage."

That resonated with Jamie. Most people would think she was crazy to do what she did.

An idea suddenly popped into her head.

She bolted out of her seat. The flight attendant saw her standing and said, "I'm sorry, miss. You need to take your seat. We'll be taking off soon."

Jamie grabbed her backpack and flung it over her shoulder. "Is the door still open?" Jamie asked, as she pushed her way past her.

"Yes. But it's closing soon."

"I've got to get off this plane," she said as she rushed down the aisle.

Jamie hoped she wasn't making an impulsive and big mistake. Because of the hurricane, this was the last flight she could take off the island. There were more flights tomorrow, but they were all booked. If she didn't leave now, she'd have to ride out the hurricane.

Didn't matter. She had to know.

The flight attendant was doing her announcements at the front of the plane. Fortunately, the door was still open. Jamie bolted through it without giving it a second thought. She ran down the jetway and through the closed door into the concourse.

Where is the hurricane plane?

She went from one side of the concourse to the other looking at both sides of the terminal. The airport was small. It had to be nearby. But where? Finally, she spotted it. The big bird had come to a stop just off the first gate. The door was still closed. She found the best vantage point to view it.

Several tourists had gathered around the window as well. Jamie pulled out her phone and searched *hurricane hunter plane*.

The picture came right up. It looked like a bloated duck. Grey colored. Four turbo prop engines. It reminded her of a tank with wings. Which made sense. A plane flown into a hurricane with wind speed upwards of a hundred-fifty miles an hour would have to be strong enough to withstand such stress.

The door opened.

Five people came out and down the stairs. Four men and one woman. They were wearing solid green flight uniforms. Jamie recognized them as Air Force. Her father was an astronaut, so she was familiar with all things Air Force. NASA wasn't part of the military branch, but they cooperated in a lot of ways. She remembered reading that Owen Roberts for whom the airport was named, was a wing commander in the Royal Air Force in World War II. Everywhere anyone looked in the airport, they could see something related to the Air Force and aviation.

Jamie's anticipation meter went through the roof. The plan that had formed in her mind was crazy. It probably wouldn't work. But... she had done crazier things in her career.

No she hadn't.

The five started walking toward the entrance to the concourse. Jamie left her position and set out to find them. Owen Roberts International Airport wasn't big. It only had nine gates. They'd deplaned near Gate One.

When they didn't immediately appear where she expected them to be, a sense of panic pulsed through her. What if they ate lunch in an employee area away from the passengers?

Jamie paced around in a circle trying to think of what to do. If she had her CIA credentials, she could flash them and get into that area. They were to never carry those on a covert operation in case they were discovered. Talking her way through airport security was not likely. Going through the secured door and setting off an alarm wasn't a good idea either.

Then she remembered a food court at the main entrance. Maybe they were there. That meant going outside security. It didn't matter. Jamie could see her plane taxiing toward the runway for takeoff. She wasn't taking a flight anytime soon.

Already at the exit, she practically ran through it to the food court area. Again, not far away. The airport only had a duty-free store and some sandwich shops. She spotted them in one of the fast-food restaurants standing at the counter, ordering. A sense of relief came over her.

Jamie waited patiently for them to take their seats. When they did, she walked right up to them.

"Do you mind if I sit with you?" Jamie asked.

The guy's eyes lit up. "Sure," one of them said. The woman rolled her eyes. Not so much in disgust, but in a "typical men" kind of look.

Jamie had no idea what she looked like. She felt like death warmed over. Hopefully, she didn't look as bad as she felt. Apparently, she looked good enough to get the men's attention because they each had a smile on their faces. Jamie was good at getting men to like her, but she needed to develop a rapport beyond her looks for them to take her seriously.

They were going to think she was a lunatic when she got to the purpose of the intrusion.

"My dad's a pilot," Jamie blurted out. Maybe that was a good starting point to the discussion.

"Oh really," one of the men said. "So, you're an Air Force brat."

"You might say that," Jamie responded. Actually, she didn't know her dad growing up. All her life, she thought he was dead. When she was seventeen, her mother died. On her deathbed, she told Jamie she had a father—Adam Lang, an astronaut. She'd only met him once, and that was by video. Then he went on a long mission to outer space to the ends of the universe. He'd been gone for several years now. She'd never see him again. A long story she wasn't going to get into now, but she couldn't help but feel the twinge of sadness. She thought about her dad almost every day.

"Are you in the military too?" the man asked, bringing Jamie back to reality.

"No. I'm with the CIA." She wouldn't normally divulge that information to complete strangers, but she needed to earn some credibility, and fast.

"What do you do for the CIA?"

"Kill bad guys mostly. Actually, I work in the sex-trafficking division. I rescue girls who are in slavery."

Jamie could see their collective interest pique as their eyes widened and curiosity was taking over their demeanor. They each were at various stages of eating their sandwiches, so this was a good time for her to talk without being interrupted.

Before she could, one of the men asked with his mouth full, "What brings you to Cayman?"

"I'm on a mission."

A couple of them who didn't have food in their mouths, noticeably laughed.

"Is sex trafficking a big problem in the Cayman Islands?" one of the men asked. By the number of stripes on his uniform, he seemed to be the one in charge.

"It's a big problem everywhere," Jamie said, almost like she had a chip on her shoulder. Most people had no idea how pervasive it was.

"Have you heard about the missing girl?" Jamie said. "Sara Morgan?"

The woman jumped in for the first time, "I saw that on the news. A teenage girl was in the Caymans on a class trip. She was kidnapped. A scary deal. I saw her mother and father on TV. So sad."

"I was hoping you might be able to help me get her back."

A few more chuckles.

"How could we possibly help?"

"I need you to fly me somewhere."

"Whoa!" the leader said. "I have no idea what you're talking about. Whatever it is, only authorized personnel can be on our plane."

"How do we know you're really in the CIA?" the woman asked. "No offense intended, but we get a lot of people who come up to us with all kinds of stories. This isn't the first time someone asked to ride with us. Do you have some ID?"

"I don't carry ID when I'm on a covert mission."

The woman looked around the restaurant which was starting to fill up with people. "You don't look covert to me."

"Undercover then," Jamie said, a little snidely. *It's complicated.* They were devouring their meals. Jamie didn't have a lot of time.

The one guy, maybe the pilot because he had wings on his lapel, said, "I guess there's no way to prove you're CIA then is there?"

"I could throw you down on the floor and choke you out in less than a minute," Jamie retorted. "Would that prove it to you?"

His buddies started razzing him.

"I'd pay money to see that!" one of them said.

"That won't prove you're CIA, my little sister could tap him out."

Jamie leaned in so she was closer to them and lowered her voice. "I'm serious. I really need your help. A girl's life is at stake."

"We can't help you. Our boss would never even consider it," the leader said.

Jamie took out her phone. "How about I call the President of the United States? Let's ask him. I believe *he* is your Commander and Chief and outranks your boss."

All five stopped eating at once and stared at Jamie in disbelief. Like they weren't sure she was for real. The truth was, she was bluffing. While she did have a direct line to the President's office, it would go to an operator first. The odds were slim to none that she could actually get through to him. Besides, Brad would kill her if she made such a call. Still, it had the desired effect. For the first time, they seemed to be taking her seriously.

"What did you have in mind?" the leader asked.

"I want you to fly me into the eye of the hurricane, and I'm going to parachute out of the plane and into Cuba."

35

Jamie didn't have to wait long for their reactions after she told them she wanted to parachute into Cuba through the eye of the hurricane.

"You can't be serious," the woman said.

"Dead serious," Jamie retorted. "What's the phrase? I'm serious as a heart attack."

"Can't be done," the woman said, and then took a big bite of her hamburger.

"I think it can," the leader replied.

He held out his hand to Jamie. "I'm Josh," he said.

Jamie shook it and replied, "I'm Mandy Nobles."

"Doubting Thomas over there is Monica." Josh pointed to the woman who said it couldn't be done.

"That's A-Rad." He referred to the man on his left.

A-Rad reached out and shook Jamie's hand. "Pleased to meet you," he said in a southern drawl."

"His real name is Andrew," Josh explained. "But he's a crazy radical. So, we call him A-Rad."

He motioned at the man sitting across from him. "That right there is Stormy. He's the weather expert on the plane. He can tell you anything you need to know about hurricanes."

Stormy gave Jamie a joking salute. She thought he looked like a nerdy weather geek.

"And I'm Maverick," the fifth one chimed in.

"He's the best pilot I've ever met," Josh added.

"So, you're named after the Tom Cruise character in Top Gun?" Jamie asked.

"Nope. That's the name my momma and daddy gave me."

They all had a southern accent. Jamie read that the hurricane trackers were based out of Mississippi.

"As I was saying... " Josh said. "It can be done. The conditions inside the eye are no different than jumping out of a plane on a beautiful sunny day."

"Not exactly," Monica said. "The hurricane is constantly moving and shifting. Don't forget it wobbles. The timing of the jump has to be perfect."

"If we go down to 10,000 feet, Miss Mandy here will only be in the air for two to three minutes," Josh said. "We fly to one end of the eye and that'll give her time until the other end catches up to her. Stormy how wide is the eye?"

"About eighteen miles based on the last reading. It fluctuates between fifteen and twenty."

"That gives her enough time to get on the ground and find shelter."

"We don't even know if the hurricane is going to hit Cuba," Monica argued.

"What's its latest track?" Josh asked Stormy.

Stormy took a napkin and spread it out on the table. He then took a pen out of his pocket and drew three circles on the napkin.

"Here's where the hurricane is right now." He pointed to a circle a distance away from the other two. "This circle is Cayman. The big circle above it is Cuba." He then drew a line. Presumably, the path of the hurricane. It seemed like it was headed right toward Cuba based on the line.

Stormy continued. "Right now, it looks like the hurricane is going to miss the Caymans all together. They'll get some wind and rain, but it won't be that bad."

"This line is where I think it will go," he said.

The line extended up to the eastern edge of Cuba and then northward. It didn't take a sharp turn until well past Cuba. It looked like it would miss the US, but the Bahamas lay right in its track.

Josh turned to Jamie. "Why are you so dead set on getting into Cuba? Is that where the missing girl is?"

"You're going to take all this risk for one girl?" Monica interjected before Jamie had a chance to answer.

She didn't mind Monica's negativity. It didn't seem mean spirited in the least. She was only stating her opinions. Jamie appreciated a strong woman who stood up for her principles, even if they might not suit Jamie's ends. Even then, she felt the need to defend herself.

"It's not just one girl," Jamie replied, "It's five. Five American girls were kidnapped on their senior high trips. We believe they're in Cuba. Our intel has found their exact location. And yes. I would go there even if it was only one girl. That's my job."

That seemed to satisfy Monica because she went back to eating.

"The Dominican Republic and Haiti are going to get hit first," Stormy continued. He seemed to be enjoying the opportunity to display his skills. "It almost certainly is going to hit Cuba. Here's the problem. I think the eye will hug the north coastline. It's not going to be a direct hit. That doesn't mean it won't be bad; it just means it won't be as bad as it could've been. Of course, these are just projected tracks. It could turn and go out into the Atlantic and not hit anything."

"What is the probability it follows that line?" Josh asked.

"The hurricane hasn't moved off track at all. So far, it's doing everything I've predicted it would do. That doesn't mean things will stay that way. It has a mind of its own. We'll know more tomorrow when we go up. Here's your problem, Mandy. If it takes this path, the eye is going to be off the coast of Cuba. Not by much. But a little. If the eye doesn't pass over land, then you're screwed."

"Could I land in the water and swim in?" Jamie asked.

"Not a chance," Stormy said. "While the winds aren't bad in the eye, the waves are still 12-15 feet at the surface. You'd never survive landing in the water."

"Let's assume for the sake of discussion that the eye goes over land. Is it possible to parachute out of your plane and survive?" Jamie asked.

"No!" Monica said.

"I disagree," Josh retorted. He looked right at Jamie. "Just so you know, I was a paratrooper in a past life. My job in the war was to parachute behind enemy lines. My commanders didn't care what the conditions were. If the fighting on the ground dictated a jump, then we went, rain, sleet, or snow. I've jumped in every condition imaginable."

"Like the postman," A-Rad quipped.

"Have you ever jumped in a hurricane?" Monica asked, ignoring A-Rad who seemed to be the jokester of the group.

"Well... no," Josh admitted.

"Has anyone ever tried it?" Monica asked.

"I doubt it. I've never heard of it until now."

"First time for everything," Jamie said.

Josh took the napkin from Stormy and grabbed the pen out of his hand.

He drew another big circle and then a small one right in the center. Jamie assumed that was the hurricane and the eye.

Then he drew another big circle. "This is the eye," he said. "I want to make it bigger so I can show y'all how this would work."

"We fly the plane into the eye like this," Josh drew a small plane and then a path through the outer edge of the hurricane, into the eye and then through it, all the way to the edge. "The hurricane is moving this way. How fast would you say it's going, Stormy?"

"Eleven to twelve miles per hour."

"Assuming the eye is fifteen miles wide, that still gives Mandy over an hour to find shelter. And believe me, you're going to need it. This is the biggest storm I've ever seen."

Stormy nodded in agreement.

"Are y'all forgetting something?" Monica asked.

"What's that?" Josh answered.

"It's freakin' Cuba. We don't have permission to fly into their airspace."

"I thought about that," A-Rad replied. "We're going to be coming in from the back side of the hurricane. We'll still be in international waters when it hits Cuba. Once we enter the storm, their radar won't pick up our plane. Even if it does, it'll look like a debris field. We'll get in and out before they even know we're there."

"Worst case scenario is they spot us," Josh added. "We just say we ventured into their airspace by accident. Got disoriented in the storm. No harm no foul."

Jamie could hardly contain her excitement. She didn't have to convince them of anything. They were making the arguments for her. Better than she could even.

"So, will you do it?" Jamie asked.

"We have to ask our boss," Josh said.

"Do you think he'll say yes?"

In unison they all said, "No way."

"Not in a million years," Josh said.

"There's no way he'll let us fly our bird over Cuba," A-Rad said, shaking his head violently back and forth for emphasis. "Interesting discussion though. I'd love to try it."

Jamie's heart sunk.

"You have to convince him," Jamie pleaded. "Five American teenage girl's lives depend on it. I've got to get into Cuba somehow. Let me talk to him."

"We'll ask. But I'm not promising anything."

"What's his name? And contact information. I'll have my boss call him."

Josh wrote it on the edge of the napkin.

"Here's my number." Jamie wrote her name and number on the napkin and tore off that section and gave it to Josh. "I'm going to speak with my boss. He's the director of field operations for the sex-trafficking division of the CIA. He has the ear of the director and can get the ear of the president himself. If you guys are willing to do it, I can get it approved with my boss."

"I'm willing," Josh said.

"Me too," A-Rad chimed in.

That was encouraging. Although not that much. The truth was... Brad wouldn't approve this mission in a million years. Well... Brad might, but his bosses wouldn't. The sadness returned with a vengeance. A lot of good ideas in the field never got off the napkin they were drawn on.

Jamie made herself tamp down the depression. Maybe they would approve it. Until they didn't, she'd hold out hope. Otherwise, this had all been a waste of time. Except it was good to know the hurricane wasn't going to hit the Caymans. That would make her movements easier if the mission weren't approved. She could regroup and think of another plan.

Maybe she could find a boat to take her to Cuba. If the radar was down, the sonar might be too.

Jamie stood from her chair. "Nice meeting ya," she said as she started to walk away.

"Nice meeting you too," Josh said. "We'll be in touch."

"One last question," Jamie said. "When will the storm make landfall in Cuba?"

"That's a Stormy question," Josh said.

"With its current path and trajectory, it'll make landfall in about thirty-four to thirty-six -hours," he said.

"Thank you."

Jamie shuddered as she walked away. Now she wondered if she even wanted the mission to be approved. If it were, she'd have to parachute into Cuba in the dark!

36

Jamie took a deep breath and dialed Brad's number, feeling a lot of trepidation. Yet, determined to do everything in her power to convince him to let her parachute into Cuba. Brad had already said she could go if she could find a way to get in undetected. The plane would work. The hurricane trackers said so themselves. The plan was dangerous and risky, and the hurricane might not even go over Cuba, but right now, it was the only option she had.

Whatever it took to convince him. Throw whatever tantrum was necessary. Threaten to resign if he said no. She halfway meant it. They sent her to do a job. Having her hands tied at every turn, and having to ask permission to do what she thought was best was getting frustrating.

Brad answered before she had all her thoughts together. "I thought you were on a flight home," he said, in his traditional non greeting, greeting.

"I'm still in Cayman. I came up with an idea."

"This better be good."

"It is. I'm going to parachute into Cuba."

No comment.

"On a hurricane tracker plane," she continued. "I've already talked to the crew. It's an Air Force plane, so we aren't putting civilians in harm's way."

Still no comment. Nothing but dead silence.

"The plan is for them to fly me into the eye of the hurricane. I'll parachute into Cuba, find the girls, and get them out."

Brad still didn't say anything. She didn't know if he was patronizing her or if they had lost connection. So, she said, "Are you still there?"

"I'm here."

More silence.

"The beauty of the plan is that Cuba will never know I was there. Their radar systems won't detect the plane in the hurricane. Besides, they tell me this storm is so big their radar system will be down for a while anyway."

The silence on the other end of the phone made Jamie want to scream. She returned the favor and decided not to say another word until he responded.

After several more agonizing seconds Brad said, "Sounds like a good plan. Let's do it."

Jamie almost dropped the phone.

"Just like that? You're giving me permission without even talking to your bosses or asking one question? That's not like you."

"I did talk to my bosses. Got out of a meeting with them a few minutes ago. The kidnappings are all over the news. Sara Morgan's father has caused quite a stir in the media and that's all they're talking about. I'm getting a lot of pressure to solve this case. Especially since we know where the girls are."

"I would imagine the brass is pretty upset knowing Cuba is behind it."

"Some people think it's an act of war. They're ready to send the troops in if necessary. This seems like a better plan."

"So, you like my idea?"

"Why wouldn't I? I'm not the idiot who's going to jump out of a plane into a hurricane. If you're crazy enough to do it, I'm crazy enough to let you."

Up to now, Jamie hadn't given a place to the fear. If she were honest with herself, she didn't believe they'd let her do it. So, she never allowed herself to fully consider the consequences. Now that she had permission, she was coming face to face with the dread of it.

Jamie tamped it down and moved on to the last obstacle. "The only problem might be the hurricane tracker's boss. We need his permission."

"Do you have his name and number?"

Jamie recited it to him.

"What else do you need from me?" Brad asked.

"An exit plan. A way to get the girl's out."

"What if the eye of the hurricane doesn't go over Cuba?"

"Then we go to Plan B."

"What's Plan B?"

"I have no idea."

***

After the call was concluded, Jamie rushed back to the restaurant. The crew was still there. They'd finished eating and were posing for pictures with tourists and signing autographs.

Jamie got Josh's attention. "I got permission from my boss," she said excitedly.

"So did we!" Josh said. The second time in ten minutes she'd been shocked.

"Why didn't you call me?" Jamie said.

"I didn't get the chance. I was occupied with all my adoring fans."

"So, what's the next step?"

"We're going to fly back to our base in Mississippi. You're coming with us. We need parachutes. Supplies. Weapons."

"Sounds good." Jamie had wondered where she was going to get what she needed. Problem solved.

"We'll take a side trip over to the hurricane and fly through it a few times to get you acclimated. That way you'll know what it feels like. We can also go over procedures for the jump."

"Okay," she said nervously as her heart suddenly started racing at the thought of flying into the hurricane.

"When was the last time you jumped?" Josh asked.

"About six months ago."

"You may be a little rusty then. We'll take you up and do a few practice jumps. We're going to need to get you trained on jumping by coordinates."

"I've practiced that, but it's been a while. Why do I need to jump with coordinates?" That meant she'd have to jump by following a small handheld device rather than by sight.

"One thing Monica thought of was that everything's going to be pitch black. All the electricity will be out in Cuba."

"I hadn't thought of that."

"That's why we need to go back to Mississippi and do some planning. There may be a dozen more things we haven't thought about that could get us killed."

"Us?"

"Yeah! I'm jumping with you." Josh raised his chin and grinned.

"Oh no! I work alone."

"That's the deal. Take it or leave it. My boss said we could do it, but only if I jump with you."

"I'll be fine. There's no reason for you to risk your life. Besides, you have no experience in covert operations. You'll slow me down. No offense."

"How many times have you jumped?"

"A couple hundred. Maybe four hundred."

"I've taken thousands of jumps. In all kinds of scenarios. Anything can happen while you're up there. The wind could shift. The parachute could be torn by the winds. You could lose your bearings in the dark and drift off course. You need me. I'm experienced and can help you. We'll wear a radio and will be able to communicate with each other. I'll guide you down."

"There may be a firefight when we find the girls. I don't know what kind of hornet's nest I'm walking into."

"Sister, I've killed more bad guys in one day than you will in your entire career. I was in the special forces in Afghanistan, Syria, and Iraq. I'm not afraid of a few Cubans."

Jamie tried to think of another excuse as to why he shouldn't come but nothing came to mind. The more she thought about it, the more it sounded like a good idea. He was right. The thought of jumping out of the plane in total darkness, not able to see the ground below terrified her. Having a second experienced gun at the house might also come in handy.

Look at the positive side of things, and pick your battles, were two things Curly drilled into her. Sounded like Josh wasn't going to take no for an answer anyway. He controlled her ride. She had no other option but to say yes.

"Okay," she said reluctantly, but only for his benefit. "But... I'm in charge once we get on the ground. Are you okay with that?"

Josh stood at attention and formally saluted.

"Sir. Yes sir," he said jokingly. "Colonel Josh Richardson reporting for duty."

"I didn't know you were a colonel!" Jamie's cheeks suddenly felt hot.

"Retired colonel. Our squadron is made up of reserves. We've all been out of action for a while. Truthfully, we're kinda excited to get back in the fray."

"Let's hope and pray there's not a fray," Jamie said.

***

Sandy Beach Hotel

Carolyn and Sean were in their hotel room having a heated discussion. Sean had informed her that he got the loan for the ransom, but he had to sign a personal guarantee to do it.

"First thing tomorrow morning, I'm going to set up an account at a Cayman bank and have the money transferred in," Sean said. "When the kidnappers call, I'll get wiring instructions and arrange a location to pick up Sara."

"I still think we should go to the police," Carolyn said, emphatically.

"We already discussed this. No police."

"The CIA lady said we were making a mistake."

"I'm not making a mistake. I know what I'm doing."

"She said it could be a scam. I tend to agree with her."

"How do the kidnappers know my phone number?"

"I asked the lady that very question. A cell phone number is not that hard to get. They might get it off your letterhead, website, or business card."

"It's not on my letterhead or website."

"Is it on your business card?"

"Yes. But how would the kidnappers have one of my cards."

"I don't know."

"Exactly. You're not making sense, Carolyn. Quit listening to that CIA person. What has she done to find Sara? Nothing! What has anyone done? I'm the only one doing anything."

"I've been doing stuff," she said defensively. "I organized the searches. We put up more than a thousand flyers today. You're not the only one doing something."

Carolyn realized getting in an argument about who had done more was counterproductive and taking the focus off the real problem. They had no proof the kidnappers actually had Sara. She wished more than anything in the world that they did, and that the ransom would bring her back home to them. Why didn't she have more faith?

Sean wasn't making it easier by belittling her efforts. "Those are a waste of time," he said. "I have an arrangement with the kidnappers. All we have to do is transfer the money and Sara can come home."

His phone rang interrupting their argument.

"I have the money," Sean said after a short greeting. He frantically motioned for Carolyn to get him something. She didn't understand at first.

"Hold on," he said to the person on the phone. "Get me a pen and paper."

She grabbed the one on the desk and handed it to him.

"I'm ready," Sean said with the phone at his ear in one hand and his other ready to write. Carolyn held the pad so it wouldn't move when he started writing.

After he'd written the set of numbers, Sean said, "Let me repeat them to you to make sure they're right."

Apparently, they were because he said, "Okay. Got it. The money will be in my account tomorrow. I'll wire it to you as soon as I get it. Call me and we'll arrange the transfer."

"Ask him to let you talk to Sara?" Carolyn said, with as much urgency as she could muster.

Sean ignored her.

"I can assure you that the police know nothing about our arrangement," he said, turning his back to her.

"Ask him about Sara? Is she okay?"

Sean hung up the phone.

"Why didn't you ask him? Make him prove he actually has her."

"They do have her."

"What if they don't? If we pay out the twenty million dollars and it's all a scam, then what do we do? Would the insurance company even reimburse you? We could lose everything. Our house. Your business." Tears began to run down her cheeks.

"Calm down," Sean said. He put both hands on her shoulders and stared into her eyes. "We're this close to getting Sara back. Be patient. One or two more days, and you'll have your daughter back."

"I hope you're right."

"I know I am."

Carolyn went into the bathroom where she started sobbing. Her feelings were all over the emotional map. Optimism that this was going to work, but a nagging feeling that the CIA agent was right, and it was a scam. How could she possibly know? Was it worth a twenty-million-dollar risk? Of course, Sara's life was worth whatever it cost. If she knew these people had Sara and would return her, she'd pay the money in a heartbeat.

She started to cry again. Sean seemed so sure. Still, he didn't have to be so mean about it.

Carolyn didn't know whether to be happy or sad.

37

Somewhere off the coast of Cuba
The next day

Hurricane Delilah, as she was named, wasn't being cooperative. As expected, she was hugging the north coastline of Cuba. Sometimes the eye was over the land but most of the time, over water. Barely. Agonizingly close enough to where they could jump, but far enough away from the coast that a jump was impossible.

As Stormy described, Delilah wobbled like a six-hundred-pound man with bad knees. Half of it was over land and half over sea. That made it extremely unstable. Just when they thought a window had opened for Jamie and Josh to jump, it closed, and they had to sit back down and wait.

Like the Samson in the Bible, Jamie may have met her match with Delilah.

She pounded her fist against the side of the metal wall. Then stood back up. Alternating between pacing and sitting. Ironically, her seat belt wasn't necessary. Even though the most powerful storm in years was right outside the window, the ride inside was as smooth as a canoe on still waters.

The plane flew around in circles inside the eye, biding time. Before the sun set and total darkness enveloped them, one would've thought they were out for an afternoon plane ride. The constant roar of the four turbo prop engines was the only sound disturbing the calm and peaceful eye of the hurricane. If not for the fact that her teeth and jaw hurt from the violent shaking of the plane as it went through the outer bands of the hurricane to get to the eye, she would think she was flying in a luxury commercial jet.

That thought caused her to laugh. The accommodations were anything but luxurious. The back was like a gutted war plane that hauled cargo. Everything was bolted down. She was surrounded by metal.

Jamie looked out the windows. All she could see were the wings of the plane and the lights strobing. She sat back down. Nothing infuriated her more than circumstances beyond her control. To be so close to being able to save the girls, and yet they might as well be back in Mississippi. All that training for nothing.

Jamie was thankful for the extra day of preparation and had a growing appreciation for the crew of the 53rd Weather Reconnaissance Squadron. Especially Josh and A-Rad. Professional in every way, the planning had grown into a full-scale logistical operation involving several branches of government and more than a hundred people.

Josh made Jamie execute more than a dozen parachute jumps at various altitudes and simulate several different stress exercises to be prepared for every contingency. For each jump, she carried more than thirty pounds of equipment. At first, the plan was to parachute in the supplies. That was quickly scrapped. They had a limited amount of time to find shelter before the eye of the hurricane passed over them and they'd be faced with a hundred and fifty mile an hour winds with gusts up to two hundred miles per hour. Searching for the supplies would waste valuable time.

They even spent time in a wind tunnel simulating the wind speeds they'd face once they were on the ground. When Jamie lost her feet and cut her hand on a metal rod on the floor, that training was scrapped. No use getting injured and putting themselves through that. The short time in the tunnel at least gave her an idea of what she might encounter. At forty miles an hour, the wind moved her slightly. At sixty miles per hour, she could barely stay on her feet. At a hundred and twenty miles per hour, she thought she was going to die, even with the harness holding her in place.

She couldn't imagine what a hundred and fifty plus miles per hour felt like and, while she was an adrenaline junkie, that was one thing she wanted to avoid. Finding shelter was a key to survival. One twig flying through the air at that speed was like a dart and could penetrate her skin like a speeding bullet.

Finding shelter and getting out of the wind was imperative. According to the plan, they expected to have little time to accomplish that feat.

A moot point. It didn't seem like a jump was going to happen.

Stormy monitored the storm from his position in the back of the plane. A row of seats with orange shoulder straps lined her side of the plane. From her vantage point, she had a good view of what he was seeing.

"It's turning," Stormy said through the headphones they were all wearing.

"Which way?" she heard Josh say.

"Out to sea," Stormy answered.

Stormy had predicted that at some point the hurricane would turn. Right now, it was headed northwest. Eventually, Delilah would make a sharp ninety degree turn and start churning northeast having left a path of destruction behind. Thankfully, the projected path took it out into the Atlantic, and the US mainland would be spared.

Jamie had no idea how such a monstrosity could turn on a dime with the flexibility of an Olympic gymnast.

"Look at this," Stormy said excitedly.

Jamie and Josh bolted from their seats. Delilah was wobbling again. Apparently, it wasn't making the turn as easily as Stormy had predicted. The eye was going back and forth. Shifting positions almost serpentining like Jamie had many times when she was being shot at. The upper body and lower body weren't moving together. The bands were moving counterclockwise. The hurricane was turning into itself. Almost like a kite flying against the wind.

One minute the eye was over land. The next minute it was several miles over sea.

"What's it going to do?" Josh asked.

"It's going to turn back over land one more time," Stormy predicted.

"How far?"

"Just far enough that there might be a small window."

"How far?" Josh shouted.

"I don't know. All I know is that this is your last chance to jump. After this last wobble, I think it'll turn completely away from Cuba."

"We have to jump," Jamie said.

"You can't jump now," Stormy said. "We're still over water."

"Can I get to the land with a freefall dive?"

"You'd have to go headfirst for more than eight thousand feet. You can't glide down normally. You'll have to wait until the last second to open your chute."

"But can I do it?"

"If Delilah turns at all, the winds will blow you back into the sea. You're as good as dead."

"Can I do it, Stormy?"

"Even if you do manage to make it to land, the eastern wall of the hurricane will be on you as soon as it turns." Stormy was pointing at his screen. The eastern wall of the eye was right on the coastline. "You won't have time to find shelter. You'll have several minutes. If that."

"This is the third time I've asked this question. Can I make it to land?"

"Yes," Stormy said. "Maybe. But you have to go right now. You have less than five minutes to decide. After that, the window will close."

Jamie looked at Josh. He stared back. His eyes gave away his indecision. But his clenched jaw told her he wanted to do it. His narrow eyebrows and furrowed brow told her he wasn't sure.

"I'll go alone, Josh. It's too risky for you."

"I won't let you go alone."

"This is my job. You have a wife and kids. I have to take the risk. You don't. Thanks for everything." Jamie kissed him on the cheek. Then she hugged Stormy's neck from behind him. Jamie began adjusting her gear. Actually, buying time to drum up the courage.

"There's not enough time to enter the coordinates," Josh said. "You'll be flying blind."

"I have the night vision goggles."

In the planning, they determined that the coordinates would be a backup. They could wear the goggles. It illuminated the light sky like it was daytime.

"You're going to be over water," Josh explained. "You won't even be able to see the land until you're right over it. It would be easy for you to become disoriented. You need the coordinates to make sure you're headed in the right direction."

"A-Rad, can you hear me," Jamie said.

"I got you."

"Can you get closer to the shore and line up the door, so when I jump, I'm facing toward Cuba?"

"Roger that. It's your rodeo."

She felt the plane lurch as A-Rad began moving the plane into position.

"Tell me when you're ready for me to jump," Jamie said to him.

"You have to hurry!" Stormy said. "The hurricane has started to turn."

Jamie opened the door after latching herself to the safety harness. A swoosh of air burst into the cargo hold. If not for the harness she might've tumbled out.

"Be careful!" Josh said.

"Don't say that!" Jamie retorted. "That's bad luck."

"What?" Josh replied.

"Never mind. I'll tell you later."

"You're good to go," A-Rad said.

"You can still make it," Stormy added.

That's all the encouragement she needed.

Jamie unhooked the safety harness, took one look at Josh, and went running out the door. The last thing she heard before being hit by the night air was Josh saying in her headset, "I'm coming with you."

38

Jamie flew out of the plane like a high-speed race car. Zero to sixty in two seconds. Rather than assuming the normal spread-eagle position, arms forward up and back, head up, and legs at a forty-five-degree angle, Jamie went into a full freefall. Hands by her side, body rigid, legs together. She only used her hands to secure the night vision goggles into place. Her body was perfectly straight, like a luge racer at the Olympics. Only she was not on her back but propelled headfirst through space at an incredibly high rate of speed.

So fast, she barely had time to process all the information needed to make it out of this predicament alive.

To complicate things, it took a moment for her eyes to adjust to the green glow of the goggles. When she could see her surroundings, the only thing visible was the churning of the ocean below which was getting closer by the second. Alarm bells went off in her head when she didn't immediately see land.

The calculations in her mind were spinning like a computer which was hard to do and still maintain focus on the landing. If there was a landing. If she ended up in water, was it still considered a *landing*? The dumbest questions entered her mind at the most inopportune times. Other more pressing matters need to override those thoughts.

When do I pull the chute?
Where should I land?
How far is it before I'm over land?
Is Josh above me?

Is this how I'm going to die?

A-Rad said the plane would be at an altitude of about ten thousand feet when they jumped. Could she count on that? Any variation could be deadly. She'd be traveling about one hundred fifty-to-two hundred miles per hour in her current position. Ideally, she would deploy her chute at about 2,000 feet and glide down. She didn't have that luxury. Without seeing the land, she had to stay in the form of a missile for as long as possible.

Landing in the ocean was a death sentence.

They had considered wearing inflatable life preservers. That plan was nixed. Landing in the water was not an option. Even with a life preserver, the ocean would eat them alive. So, they wouldn't even consider jumping unless they were over land. So much for that plan. Why did Jamie always end up in such precarious positions? Murphy's Law seemed to be the only law she didn't regularly break when on a mission.

The clock in her head said it was time to pull the chute. Jamie waited an extra ten seconds. She relaxed her neck and shoulders to prepare for the violent jerk of her body when the chute deployed at that speed.

The jolt of pulling the ripcord almost took her breath away.

When she got her bearings, she looked for land.

It has to be there.

Lightning illuminated the sky. A mixed blessing. That helped her to see, but that meant the walls of the hurricane were closing in. In addition, the sudden flash of light blinded her. She reached up and jerked off her goggles. It helped her to see better.

Then she spotted it.

Land!

Just ahead.

Jamie could make out the beach and the trees.

She was coming in too fast.

Jamie put her feet out and arms back to create drag with the toggles of the chute. If she slowed down too much, she'd land in the water.

Not enough, and she'd crash into the land. Likely breaking her legs. Or worse. She could get splattered against the trees. Actually... not worse. Worse would be getting stuck in the trees and then the hurricane winds would batter the life out of her. It gave her no consolation that she could pick which way she died.

By land or by sea?

Once again, stupid thoughts were clouding the issue, even if they were humorous.

An idea popped into her head, pushing everything else out. If she could land on the beach, the sand would break her fall.

At this speed how could she land with such precision? The beach was no more than fifty paces wide.

This is crazy!

Self -incrimination was not productive at that moment. She was speeding toward the earth like a gannet diving for a fish. Her muscles were crying out in pain as she strained to slow her descent. Her heart was beating out of her chest, and she wasn't sure when she took her last breath.

Jamie strained even harder against the forces working against her.

Speed. Lift. Drag. Centrifugal force.

A few miles per hour might mean the difference between life and death, paralysis or walking away sore. At some point, luck or fate would take over. Until then, she'd use every ounce of her strength to determine the outcome.

I have to do it.

For the girls.

I have to save Sara.

In stressful situations, Jamie's senses came alive. Curly said she could react on the spur of the moment better than anyone he'd ever trained. It would take every ounce of Jamie's innate ability to come out of this alive.

And God's help.

She said a quick prayer.

Very quick.

That helped. Somehow, she felt calm even though her heart was racing. Fear was no longer in the equation.

The land was coming at her in a blur.

She cleared the ocean.

Barely.

Jamie lifted her legs to keep them out of the water. The spray of the surf splashed her face in confirming how close she was to disaster. The salt water burned her eyes.

Jamie landed on the beach and rolled, relaxing her body and letting it go where momentum took her. The lines of the chute wrapped around her, pinning her arms. The breath was knocked out of her.

A quick assessment confirmed nothing was broken. Jamie had the presence of mind, to roll back in the same direction to free her from the lines of the parachute.

I'm going to be sore.

I have to hurry.

Not until I thank God first.

Jamie said another quick prayer of thanksgiving and bolted to her feet. She could feel the winds from the hurricane as the eye wall was closing in. Maybe, she should've waited a little longer to thank God. She wasn't safe yet.

It wouldn't hurt to thank him twice. A dozen times, if necessary.

When she got to her feet, a gust of wind filled the parachute and started pulling her toward the ocean. It took all of her strength to win the tug of war battle.

When the gust subsided, Jamie quickly unhooked the harness. She was just a few feet away from the water and the waves which were now taller than her. Free of the harness, she threw the chute to the ground. A gust of wind took it out into the ocean out of her sight in seconds. The gust almost blew her off her feet.

When she stabilized, Jamie allowed herself a few seconds to search the sky for Josh. No sign of him.

I need shelter.

She looked both ways. What she saw didn't give her hope. The only options appeared to be three piers. One to the east and two to the west. The one to the east was closer, but if Josh did jump, he'd land to the west. He would've jumped a few seconds later than she, so he would have to land in that direction.

I hope he didn't jump.

She took off running west, just in case. Her wobbly legs took a few seconds to respond. Running in the sand made things harder.

Also, the hurricane winds were moving counterclockwise, so she was running right into the wind. Before she was thankful for the direction of the winds. That direction was probably what carried her to the land. Without it she would've landed in the water. Now they were working against her.

Jamie somehow made it to the first pier. The end was constructed in concrete for extra reinforcement. Probably to withstand a hurricane. Also, concrete would last longer in the elements. Underneath the foundation was shelter. It would have to do. The pier had large, wooden posts that held it up. They would hold her. The only problem was the tide. The tide would likely make it all the way to her position.

While she'd survive it, the last thing she wanted was to be buffeted for four to six hours by one wave after another.

Actually, the last thing she wanted was to be without shelter. Dealing with the waves was better than dealing with the winds.

There must be a better alternative.

The other pier, further down the beach was higher on the land. She decided to chance sprinting to it. The hurricane east wall was to her left. She could see and hear the sounds of it as it tore through everything in its path.

At a later time, she'd take time to marvel at the wonder of an eye wall. Things were still fairly calm in her position. Several hundred yards away, maybe a mile, the destructive winds of the hurricane were destroying structures and trees like they were toothpicks.

Jamie made it to the other pier. Fortunately, Delilah seemed to be frozen in place and wasn't coming upon her as fast as she expected.

While this location wasn't ideal, it was better. The water wouldn't get all the way to her location. The biggest problem would be the wind. She wasn't completely out of the elements even under the pier.

It had started to rain. The droplets stung as the increased winds sent them sideways through the air. A strange sight to behold.

In the center of the pier was one large pole. Same as the other pier. Jamie took a band out of her supply pack. A thick, leather strap, designed especially for this purpose.

Josh's idea.

Where was he?

Adjustable, and heavy duty, Jamie wrapped it around herself and then around the pole. Once secured, Jamie wrapped her legs around the pole and then tightened the strap securing her snugly against it.

While the position was uncomfortable, she'd be safe. As long as the pier held. If the pole stayed in place, she would too. The walkway on the pier might get blown away. In fact, Jamie expected it. Especially the part that extended out into the ocean. The concrete barrier and the basic foundation should hold. Probably. Jamie was counting on the structure withstanding the winds. If not, they'd find her dead body still attached to the pole.

The Cuban government would likely never know what a young American girl was doing in Cuba, armed, and with military supplies no less. In a hurricane.

As she pondered that thought, something caught her attention out of the corner of her eye.

What's that?

A parachute.

Josh!

He was headed straight for the beach, just west of her. The location she had expected, although she'd given up hope of seeing him. He was in the same predicament she'd been in moments before. Trying to land on the head of a needle. His situation was more dire. He had to battle the winds. Josh was struggling to keep the chute at an angle so he wouldn't be blown out into the sea.

Jamie saw immediately how much more experienced he was. She wasn't sure she could do the same thing. A casual observer might think he didn't know what he was doing. Jamie knew that was the farthest thing from the truth. Few people could maneuver the chute in those conditions and live to tell about it.

Josh somehow did it. But he came down hard.

Rolled.

Jamie let out a scream, but he was too far away to hear her. Jamie unbuckled the band. By the sound of the roaring train, Delilah was upon them.

Jamie was sprinting again.

Josh didn't move right away. Probably stunned from the fall.

He was at least fifty yards away.

She struggled to fight the wind and keep her pace. When she was halfway there, Josh rose to his feet, but he was looking the other way. Probably for shelter. Maybe for her.

Finally, he turned toward her. He started flailing his arms. The body motion was telling her to go back. He unhooked his harness and started running toward her. She turned back. If he was unhurt, there was no reason to run toward him. She motioned for him to follow her and started sprinting back to where she had come.

Jamie didn't look back. Didn't need to. He caught up with her before she got to the shelter. The winds had increased considerably. The eye was moving offshore. Debris was flying around. Jamie had to dodge flying trees and limbs.

She felt the winds start to lift her off her feet. She dropped to the ground to get lower. She might have to crawl the rest of the way. Only twenty yards or so to go. She could do it. Josh came behind her and lifted her to her feet. Together, the added weight gave them more strength to withstand the winds.

Two are better than one. When one falls, the other is there to pick them up.

Jamie remembered the Bible verse.

They made it under the shelter just in time.

Jamie took a position against the pole. Josh settled in behind her. He was talking, but she couldn't hear what he was saying from the roar of Delilah who had unleashed her ungodly attack on them.

A woman's scorn.

They scooted closer together and Jamie wrapped her arms around the pole. As she reached for the band, a gust of wind caught it, picked it up, and blew it away. Just out of her reach.

Jamie let out a swear word.

Sorry, God.

Josh wrapped his legs around her and squeezed to lock her in. Then put his arms around her waist. In any other situation, she would've felt uncomfortable with the closeness.

Sorry, Alex.

She tightened her grip around the pole. He tightened his grip around her waist.

Then... they held on for dear life.

39

The next morning

Hurricane Delilah pounded their position under the pier relentlessly the entire night. By far, the worst night of Jamie's life. Several times, she thought she was going to die. Just as many times, she wished she were dead.

Somehow Josh managed to get his band out of his supply pack and secure it around them.

When a tornado, spawned by the hurricane, barreled through, the band was the only thing that saved them. The entire pier was destroyed except for the posts that remained standing and, mercifully, the section of the foundation right above them. The only thing protecting them from the brutal onslaught.

"Let's never do this again," Josh said, sometime in the middle of the night. Occasionally, the hurricane's fury subsided for short periods of time. The rest of the time, the roar from the winds were so loud they couldn't hear themselves speak.

"I told you not to jump," Jamie said, defiant to the end. "I would've been fine if I hadn't had to go save your ass."

She said it in such a way that he would know she was kidding. Truthfully, she was glad he was there. His arms wrapped around her didn't add any protection from the elements, but they did provide her with a sense of security. Comfort. The two had a bond now. There's something special that forms when you face death with someone. Soldiers know it.

CIA operatives feel it. It's not romantic or sexual. It's primal. An intrinsic feeling that you've experienced something together that few people understand.

Whether it's in a fox hole, or strapped to a pole in a hurricane, when you figuratively go to hell and back with someone, you can't help but feel differently about someone who has helped you to survive.

With Alex, she had both. They'd faced death together on more than one occasion. And they had a romantic bond. Not sexual. She was saving herself for marriage. The long night gave her a lot of time to think. They needed to set a wedding date. If she survived this, that would be one of the first things they discussed when she saw him.

When the last dangerous outer bands of the hurricane passed, Josh released the belt and they attempted to stand. The entire night the muscles in their arms and legs had no respite as they clutched the pole and each other. Jamie stood like a ninety-year-old woman getting up from a wheelchair. Her legs were wobbly, and every muscle in her body ached. Several minutes of stretches and jogging in place got her feet under her.

Once she did, she took out her satellite phone and called Brad.

"I figured you were dead," he answered.

"Thanks for the show of confidence in your best operative."

"So, you're the best now?"

"I'm the first person in the world to jump out of a plane into a hurricane. All for a mission you sent me on. I think that qualifies as your best agent."

"I agree."

Jamie almost fell over. That was the closest Brad would probably ever get to giving her a compliment.

"I guess you'll never be able to doubt my commitment to a mission again," Jamie said.

"Hang tight," he responded without acknowledging her remark. "I have someone on their way to bring you the motorcycles."

The satellite phone had a tracker. Brad could obviously see their location.

SAVING SARA

In the planning, they figured the roads would be nearly impassable. They had to have a way to get to the girls' location. Once the hurricane passed, a man in Cuba would bring them two motorcycles and some supplies including weapons.

"Where do we meet him?" she asked.

"Don't go east. There's a big five-star resort just around the corner from you. Fairly new. Probably built to withstand a hurricane. Backup generators and the like. There'll be a lot of activity there. I'm surprised you didn't go there for shelter."

That realization hit her almost as hard as the hurricane had.

"Go just up the hill and to the west," Brad continued. "You'll find a clearing. He'll find you there."

Jamie hung up the phone.

"What did he say?" Josh asked.

She didn't have the heart to tell him that they were only a few hundred yards away from a five-star resort.

If they'd only known.

***

The house where the girls were presumed to be held was owned by a Cuban oligarch named Rico Mirabal. More of a compound than a house. It took four hours to make the two-hour drive. They had parachuted in near the city of Nuevitas on the north shore, and the compound was outside Santa Cruz del Sur on the south shore.

They wouldn't have made it through the impassable roads at all, if not for the bikes.

The ride was heartbreaking. The devastation incomprehensible. The people they encountered didn't even give them a second look. Most were walking around in a daze. They saw homes destroyed. Buildings collapsed. People searching for loved ones. Animals roaming aimlessly without a home. Bodies being pulled out of the rubble. Looks of anguish and disbelief were on everyone's faces.

Too many times to count, Jamie wanted to stop and help the people. She couldn't. She had a singular focus. Get to the house and find the girls. If they were there. Something they were surer about now than ever before.

Alex had hacked into the financial records of Rico and found a five-million-dollar transfer to one of El Mata's accounts in Mexico. Proof positive the two conspired to kidnap the five girls. One million dollars each. The one kidnapping went bad and El Mata had already been paid. That's why there was a sixth girl, Jamie presumed. Why they went all the way to the Cayman Islands to snatch another girl was anyone's guess. Probably because the heat was too hot in Mexico to risk another kidnapping.

Whatever.

They'd know more when they found Sara. She might provide them with some answers. If Lars and Jake Fossey were involved, hopefully Sara would be able to confirm it.

Josh and Jamie didn't rush right into the compound. The further south they traveled, the less damage they had encountered. In this area, the only sign that a hurricane came through were a few downed trees and power lines. The house still had power. Probably from a generator, considering the downed lines. Everything around the house looked like business as usual, and Jamie wasn't anxious to storm in without gathering some intel.

Curly had drilled that into her. Josh agreed. He'd planned and executed hundreds of missions and was a stickler for operational details as well. A chemistry was developing between them. With each passing moment, Jamie was happier he was there.

They formed a plan.

Alex sent a layout of the house to her satellite phone. She didn't know how he did it, but it didn't seem like there was anything he couldn't hack into. In one of Rico's bank accounts, he found a payment to an architect. He hacked into the architect's files and found the designs for the house. Even found pictures of the completed project. Jamie and Josh knew every ingress and egress and every room in the house. They even had a good idea where the girls would be held.

They were there. Jamie could feel it. She had a sixth sense about these things.

The plan was for them to split up. A two-pronged assault. Josh was wearing green fatigues. He also was carrying an AS Val—an older model Russian assault rifle with a silencer.

Jamie went around to the back.

Once she was in position, Josh rode right up to the main guard gate. Wearing the helmet, they would have no idea he wasn't one of their men or a government soldier.

When the men left their posts and approached, Josh opened fire and gunned down the three guards. The silencer muted the sound so it wouldn't alert anyone in the house. He moved the men off the road and opened the gate at the guard tower.

From Jamie's vantage point, she could see everything. In their reconnaissance they noticed that the back of the house wasn't guarded. Why would it be? The house was in Cuba. The most lock-downed country in the western hemisphere. The last thing Rico would ever expect would be an assault on his personal residence. The guards at the gate were probably mostly for show. To make him feel important.

More than likely he wasn't even there. Alex tracked his yacht to an island in the south Caribbean Sea. Jamie hoped and prayed he hadn't taken the girls with him. Given the heavy armed presence at the gate, she presumed he hadn't.

"You're hot!" Josh said. "Go! Go! Go!"

Her cue to move. Jamie sprinted from her position to the back door of the house. Her legs cried out at the sudden exertion. She was still trying to get her sea legs, so to speak.

When she got to the door, she listened for any sounds coming from inside the house. From the plans, she knew the back door opened into the kitchen. Inside was some activity but no voices. Probably one person eating.

Jamie tried the handle. The door was unlocked. She burst through it. As she suspected, one man was sitting at a table eating a bowl of cereal.

"Te muevas mueres," Jamie said to the man quietly but firmly with her Sig pointed at him. "You move, you die."

He sat his spoon down on the table. Slowly.

"How many men are in the house?" she asked roughly.

He didn't answer right away.

Jamie moved closer and waved the gun like she was about to fire it.

"Cinco."

Five.

"Where are the girls?"

Reading his eyes told her all she needed to know. The girls were there.

Jamie rushed around the table and pushed the gun into his nose causing his head to lean backward. His eyes widened in terror.

"Where are the girls?" she said barely above a whisper but with enough force to scare the wits out of him.

He pointed to a door off the kitchen that Jamie knew led to the basement. That's what she had expected but needed confirmation.

She heard two taps come from the front entrance.

"Two more down," Josh said in her ear.

He had eliminated two more threats. Jamie raised the gun and slammed the butt of it into the back of the man's head. He slumped in the chair.

"One down in the kitchen. Two more somewhere," Jamie warned Josh.

"Do you want me to find them?"

"The girls are in the basement. Come to the kitchen and cover me. I'm going down."

She'd rather have Josh guarding her exit. Jamie didn't want to be stuck in the basement and have to shoot her way out. Rico's men would have the high ground.

When he appeared, she nodded at him and turned the doorknob. Locked. She could shoot it open, but the bullets would go through the door. Without knowing what was on the other side, she couldn't take the chance. The girls could've heard the commotion and come up the stairs to see what it was all about.

Kicking the door down would make too much noise. Picking the lock would take too much time.

Jamie started going through the kitchen drawers until she found the silverware. She took a butterknife and went back to the door. She slid the knife between the door and the door frame. Starting about three inches above the latch, she slid the knife down until she hit the bolt. From there, she began sweeping the end of the knife inward until the latch moved.

It popped open.

"That's a handy trick. You'll have to teach me that someday," Josh said.

Jamie merely nodded and rushed down the stairs with her gun drawn. At the bottom of the stairs, she swept the gun to the left and right. It wasn't so much a basement as it was a luxury suite. The girls probably considered it a prison. As far as conditions went, this was as good as it got for girls in slavery.

She pushed open a door.

A bedroom.

A girl let out a scream.

Five beds.

They had been asleep.

One bed was empty.

Groggily. the girls sat up and looked at her in stunned disbelief.

Jamie recognized them from the pictures.

Four of them.

Not five.

Sara wasn't there.

40

"Get dressed," Jamie said to the girls. "I've come to take you home."

Their faces lit up as they jumped out of bed and went to the closet and started packing.

"Hurry!" Jamie said as they were taking longer than she'd like.

So far, she hadn't heard any gunshots at the top of the stairs. The other two guards must not know they were there since they hadn't engaged Josh. How long that would last was anyone's guess.

"Leave everything," Jamie instructed. "Just put on some clothes and your shoes." She hated to be harsh with the girls considering everything they'd been through, but she needed for them to know she was serious. They had no idea how much danger they were in.

When they were all dressed, she instructed them to follow behind her. Jamie led the way with her gun drawn.

"We're coming out," Jamie said.

"Clear," Josh responded.

Jamie opened the door and led the girls out of the kitchen and toward the garage. Obviously, they couldn't take the girls out on the motorcycles. They had a different plan. Rico was a collector of cars. His garage was as big as his house. The plan was for them to drive the girls out in one of his cars. Hopefully, without getting shot at.

"You go on ahead with the girls," Josh said. "I've got your back."

"You're coming with us," Jamie said.

"I'll be right behind you. Let me know when you've got everybody safe in the car."

Turned out that the closest car was a Rolls Royce. With darkened windows.

Perfect.

The keys were in it. *Even better.* She wasn't sure if she could hot wire a Rolls Royce.

Jamie hit the garage door opener remote, and the massive door began to rise, making a loud racket. If the two guards didn't know they were there before, they did now and would come to see what the commotion was about.

"We're ready," Jamie radioed Josh.

Gunshots erupted in her earpiece.

"Josh!"

"Go! I'll be fine. Get the girls to the drop off point. I'll meet you there."

His voice was excited. He was breathing hard. Jamie could hear the gunshots in her headset. Every part of her wanted to go back and help him. She couldn't. The girls were the priority.

Jamie sped out of the garage, down the driveway, and onto the street. Fortunately, she was heading west where the hurricane had not done any real damage, so the roads should be clear. She took out her phone and locked onto her destination. While she had the escape route memorized, the phone would serve as a backup.

She ripped off the headset and threw it on the floor when she could no longer hear Josh's voice. She pounded her fist on the steering wheel and then realized she was scaring the girls.

Calmly, after taking in a deep breath, she said, "Hi girls, my name is Mandy."

Each girl introduced themselves. Jamie had already matched the names by the pictures. When on a mission, the girl's images were etched in her mind.

"Was there another girl?" Jamie asked. "A girl named Sara."

They all shook their heads no.

She was so sure Sara would be there.

Where is she?

Grand Cayman

Carolyn paced the hotel room nervously. Today was the day Sean was to meet the kidnappers. In a couple hours to be exact. Her emotions were seesawing back and forth between hope and optimism and doom and gloom. She didn't know if she could take much more of this.

"Everything's going to be fine," Sean said to her.

He was in front of the mirror, straightening his shirt and jacket.

"I'm worried sick," she said.

Sean had wired the kidnappers the money first thing that morning. Twenty-million dollars. Carolyn couldn't help but think the worst. What if they were scammers and the CIA lady was right? Where would they get the money for a real reward if somebody did come forward with information?

Sean seemed so sure he was right. She admitted to herself that she didn't fully trust him.

The transfer was to be at eleven. Sean wouldn't tell her the location. He took out his phone and dialed a number.

"I want my airplane fueled and on the tarmac, ready to go at noon," Sean said to the person on the other end.

As soon as he picked up Sara, they were leaving. Going back to Dallas. Carolyn wanted so much to believe that was true.

Sean dialed another number.

"Be at the airport at eleven thirty," Sean said. "Where the private jets land and take off." He mouthed to Carolyn that he was talking to the reporter. Sean had promised the television station an exclusive as soon as Sara was found. That buoyed Carolyn's spirits further. Sean wouldn't be calling the reporter unless he was sure.

"Bring your TV crew," Sean added. "You can't tell anyone else though. If you do, you won't get the exclusive."

He didn't say anything for a good thirty seconds.

"I can't tell you what's happening," Sean finally said, "but it'll be big. I promise that."

Sean hung up the phone and walked over to where Carolyn was standing. Her hands were shaking. The anxiety was so strong, she thought her heart was going to burst out of her chest.

"I'm going to go get Sara," Sean said reassuringly. "I've arranged a car to pick you up from the hotel at eleven thirty. He'll take you to the airport. Right to the plane. With our bags. And Sara's bags."

They still had her luggage from when she went missing.

She'll need her things.

Carolyn shuddered at the thought of where Sara might've been and what might've happened to her. Truthfully, she had never let her mind go there. Would she still have the same daughter when she got home? Sean had already lined up a counselor for Sara. That seemed like a good idea.

Her mind was in a battle.

Were these the real kidnappers?

Was it all a scam?

Are we about to lose twenty million dollars?

At this point, nothing could be gained by expressing any of those concerns. She'd tried to talk Sean out of this until she was blue in the face. The money was already wired. All she could do was hope for the best and trust God.

And Sean.

He seems so sure.

***

Santa Cruz del Sur, Cuba

Jamie pulled into the rendezvous point without incident.

She went straight to the port. Brad had arranged for a humanitarian boat to arrive with supplies in Santa Cruz del Sur as soon as the hurricane had passed. A brilliant extraction plan.

She called ahead to let them know the packages were on the way.

Four of them.

The authorities had already left after inspecting the boat leaving behind one man to make sure nothing fishy was going on. Now the crew, made up of CIA employees, were unloading the supplies. They kept the one Cuban in charge of monitoring the activities busy. Fortunately, it was only one guy and he was inexperienced. The island had much bigger issues to deal with, Jamie presumed, than worrying about anything suspicious happening with a humanitarian ship.

Jamie parked the Rolls Royce in the parking lot and the girls got out and walked right onto the boat. No one stopped to ask them any questions. Rico parked his yacht there, so they were probably used to seeing his car parked in the lot.

Jamie spotted Alex immediately. She sprinted down the pier and into his arms and kissed him profusely.

"Seems like you're happy to see me," he said.

"You have no idea."

"Let me get back to work and we can talk later," Alex said. "I want to finish unloading as fast as possible and get out of here."

Jamie introduced him to the girls. He already knew Sara wasn't with them since she had called ahead. Another operative, a woman, whisked the girls off, and they disappeared below deck in the flash of an eye. They'd stay out of sight until they were ready to leave.

"We can't go yet," Jamie said to Alex. "Josh isn't here."

"What happened?"

"He got in a gunfight protecting our backs. So we could get out of there. He said to go without him, and he'd meet me at the rendezvous point."

Jamie felt the emotions of it welling inside of her like a volcano about to erupt. She hated it when operational priorities made her choose between two agonizing options.

"I had to leave him," Jamie said, not allowing tears to well up in her eyes, even though they wanted to. "The girls were more important," she explained, trying to convince herself as much as justify her actions to Alex. If anybody would understand, it would be him.

"Good call," Alex said. "Josh knew the risk."

While Alex had never met Josh, he knew of him from the planning.

"No man left behind," Jamie said.

"Sometimes the mission overrides the code."

"If he doesn't show up, you can leave without me."

"We don't even know if he's alive."

"We can't just leave him here. If it were anywhere else but Cuba, I'd say he could fend for himself. With the hurricane and everything, there's no other way for him to get off the island. We certainly can't come back for him."

"There'll be another hurricane sometime soon. You can parachute in."

Alex's attempt at being funny.

"I'll never do that again."

Jamie braced for more pushback and was prepared to make her argument. While she didn't want to get angry with Alex, leaving Josh wasn't an option for her. This was her mission. Alex couldn't make her leave.

"I understand," Alex said. "If he's not back, I'll go with you. But this boat is leaving as soon as the supplies are off. We have to get into international waters as soon as possible and get these girls home."

As if she couldn't love him more.

"Thank you," she said.

***

The car to pick up Carolyn from the hotel at eleven thirty arrived early. She was already downstairs in the lobby waiting with her bags. Pacing around the hotel room was driving her crazy.

The drive to the airport took less than fifteen minutes.

Emotions were churning inside of her like an eddy.

The driver pulled up next to the plane and she got out. Sean had told her to wait outside. The reporter and cameraman were waiting as well. He started filming as she got out of the car.

No more than five minutes later another car pulled up. Sean got out. Carolyn watched with anticipation. It's all she could do to not run right over there.

Right after that... Sara emerged from the car. Her blonde hair glistened in the sunshine.

Jubilation exploded inside of Carolyn like a Fourth of July fireworks finale.

She couldn't believe her eyes.

Sara was alive!

Carolyn ran to her and Sara started crying the second she saw her mother. Carolyn was already bawling. She took Sara in her arms and squeezed her as hard as she could.

"Honey, did they hurt you?" Carolyn said.

"I'm fine, Mom. I just want to go home."

Sean was beaming. Carolyn would've hugged him, but she wasn't going to let Sara out of her arms.

Sean had been right. She had worried needlessly. Should've trusted her husband more.

"Let's go Carolyn," Sean said. "We need to leave."

Sean was right about that as well. They needed to get out of there as soon as possible.

First, they had to talk to the reporters. Sean did the talking. He stood at the microphone, and Carolyn and Sara stood next to him, still in the shot, but to the side. Carolyn had her arm around Sara.

"I got a call this morning from an anonymous source telling me where Sara was," Sean said. "I went to the location a few minutes ago and found her there alone. No one else was around. I'm thankful to have her back alive."

Sean made no mention of the ransom.

"What emotions are you feeling?" the reporter asked Carolyn.

"I'm thrilled. This is the happiest day of my life. I'm just ready to go home so the healing can begin."

"Where did they take you Sara?" the reporter asked.

"On a boat."

"Did you recognize the kidnappers?"

Sean cut her off. "Sara will have no more comments. I want to thank everyone who volunteered. Those who helped search and put out flyers. We're thankful to everyone in the Caymans and we're grateful to be going home."

With that, Sean ushered Carolyn and Sara toward the plane. They got in, took off, and left.

Carolyn was relieved that the nightmare was finally over.

***

Police Headquarters

The investigative team was meeting in the conference room, discussing the status of the Sara Morgan case. It had been four days since she went missing, and they were no closer to finding her than they were on day one.

Commissioner Hughes had followed up on all the leads. They'd searched every square inch of the island. Dive teams had been in every lake on the island. Searches had been conducted in the ocean in each direction. Even the smaller islands, Little Cayman and Cayman Brac, were searched.

Fortunately, the hurricane had missed the island, and the searches weren't hampered in any way. Tremendous pressure was being put on the commissioner from the governor and from the media to find the girl. The father's nonstop appearances on television were fueling the flames that his department was not doing enough to find Sara. Some were even calling for his resignation.

He needed to fill the team in on his most promising lead. Present in the room were his detectives and Roy Jones, the FBI agent assigned to the case. All his leads had ended in dead ends as well.

"I got a call from a field operator with the CIA. You remember the young woman who was here a couple of days ago? Mandy Nobles?"

Everyone shook their heads yes.

"Apparently, the CIA believes that Sara was taken to Cuba. They think they even know her exact location. Mandy Nobles is there right now looking for Sara and the other four missing girls."

"How is she going to Cuba?" Roz asked. "Everything is shut down. Cuba got smashed by the hurricane. Worst storm in a century."

"I know that. But apparently that doesn't matter. She's going in anyway. They're supposed to let me know when they know something."

A knock on the door interrupted the conversation. Hughes was finished anyway.

"They found Sara," his assistant said as she stuck her head around the door.

It took the commissioner a moment to process that information.

"Who did?" Hughes asked as his heart started racing and blood pressure soaring.

"Turn on the news. Sara is with her father at the airport."

Hughes grabbed the remote and turned on the television. The camera was fixed on a plane taxiing on the runway. Seconds later it took off.

The banner on the bottom of the screen said *Missing Girl Found Alive*.

"What the. . . " Hughes said the last part of the sentence under his breath.

41

Six weeks later

When Sara went missing six weeks ago that was the worst time in Carolyn Morgan's life. The time since her daughter returned home safely had been the best of her life.

Sitting in the *Milk & Honey Day Spa* having an all-day outing with her daughter brought a huge smile to her face as she glanced across the room at Sara getting her nails done. Bubbling with life. It had taken a while, but the old Sara was returning.

"How's Sara doing?" Valerie, the spa owner and good friend asked. The woman was working on her hair as she'd done for more than twelve years.

"She's doing much better, thank you."

"I bet it was quite an ordeal."

"She won't really talk about it," Carolyn said with a twinge of hurt and anger at what the kidnappers did to her daughter. All she knew was that Sara wasn't sexually abused, and they treated her pretty well, considering. As well as could be hoped, anyway. Sara had spent several hours at the FBI office being questioned which was an ordeal in and of itself.

"It's a miracle she came back alive," Valerie said. "We were praying for y'all and for Sara."

"The kidnappers didn't hurt her physically. Just emotionally. They kept her locked up in a boat. She wasn't allowed to go on deck, and she couldn't see their faces. They brought her food and water. It could've been a lot worse."

"Did they ever catch them? Must not have. I never heard anything on the news."

"Never did. I don't think they even have any leads."

"The main thing is that she's safe. She looks beautiful."

They both looked over at her. Sara was chatting away, as was her nature. In that way, she was more like her dad. Outgoing. Carolyn was more reserved. At first, Sara had gone into a shell. It didn't take long for her to snap out of it, though. Carolyn wasn't sure if she had just suppressed the emotions, or if she really was doing better.

"The best thing is that she's going to SMU and staying home for college. I'm thrilled!" Carolyn said. "Before the kidnapping, Sara considered going to Texas Tech. I wanted her to stay closer to home."

"That's good," Valerie said. "SMU's a wonderful school. Is she going to live at home?"

"For the first year, at least," Carolyn responded. "We'll see how it goes from there. Sean doesn't want Sara to live in fear. You know. Be afraid to go out in the world. What happened, happened. Sara survived it. We all did. I sort of understand Sean's point. But I still worry about her."

The good thing was that they weren't fighting about it. Things with Sean had never been better. The kidnapping in some weird way brought them closer. She would be eternally grateful for what Sean did for Sara. Even though she wasn't his biological daughter, the fact that he was willing to pay out twenty million dollars to get her back was amazing. Thankfully, the insurance company reimbursed them the money.

Sean seemed happier as well. His business was thriving. Ironically, the notoriety from the kidnapping made Sean a celebrity in the Dallas business scene. His championing of Sara's cause on local and national television endeared him in the hearts and minds of the locals.

People saw him as a fighter. A man who loved his family. Trustworthy. An important quality to have when you ran an investment firm. People didn't turn over control of their money to just anyone. Sean's reputation was growing, and he'd even had calls about a possible book deal for Sara and him. He was thinking about hiring an agent.

The big sale he was working on when Sara went missing closed, made Sean millions, and eased his financial pressure. Since that deal was finalized, the money and new clients had been pouring in.

In every way, she felt like they were on top of the world.

Sara came bouncing over to show Carolyn her nails. "Look Mom. I'm trying a new color. What do you think?" Sara asked.

"I love it," Carolyn responded.

"It's beautiful," Valerie said.

"What's next?" Sara asked.

"A pedicure," Valerie responded. "As soon as I'm done with your mother's hair. Then you both get a facial. On the house. My treat."

Sara bounded away, obviously excited. The spa day was good for her. Good for both of them. It felt like old times. Every four weeks since Sara was six, they'd been coming to this spa together. For a time, she wondered if they'd ever have the opportunity again.

Carolyn was kicking herself for having those thoughts. For whatever reason, she couldn't get the kidnapping out of her mind. Sean was much better at it. He seemed to have moved on. Sara, as well. The counselor said Sara was doing well. Sean had suggested maybe Carolyn needed to see someone.

It's going to take time, she decided. Eventually, the kidnapping would be a distant memory and the feelings of anxiety would go away. They always do when bad things happen. For whatever reason, every-thing reminded her of those horrible days. She'd even had nightmares about it. Woke up in a cold sweat on more than one occasion.

At any rate, she wasn't going to let it ruin the time they were hav-ing today. When they were done, the plan was to go shopping for new clothes.

Carolyn wasn't sure if lavishing gifts on Sara was for her benefit or for Sara's. Either way, they could afford it. Sean said their net worth had doubled since the kidnapping.

Valerie swung her around in the chair, so she was facing the mirror. "How's that, beautiful?"

"Amazing! As always. You're a miracle worker. How do you make me look so good?"

"I have a lot to work with."

Carolyn waved her hand dismissively. "Look at my wrinkles," she said, leaning forward in the chair toward the mirror. "I find a new one every day. If you didn't color my hair, I think I'd find new gray hair every day."

"Tell me about it," Valerie said. She patted herself on the stomach and thighs. "I lost my figure years ago. That's what kids will do to you. We're getting older, honey. We're just going to have to accept it."

"I'm going to enjoy my figure as long as I can," Carolyn said. "It's only a matter of time."

She was considering Botox and plastic surgery. Now that things were getting back to normal, she would give it more thought. A quick air kiss toward Valerie's cheek and Carolyn was off to find Sara.

For the next few hours, they were pampered like a queen and a princess. Pedicure. Facial. Seaweed wrap. If Carolyn hadn't just had her hair done, they would've gotten a massage. Instead, they had their makeup reapplied and finally prepared to leave.

Valerie was with another customer. Sara and Carolyn went over and said goodbye anyway. They both gave her a hug and thanked her profusely.

"I feel like a new person," Carolyn said.

"My whole body is tingling," Sara said.

"It's so good to see you two," Valerie said. "Come back and see us again, soon."

Carolyn paid and they exited the back of the building where the VIP customers parked along with the owner. Sean bought Carolyn a new Mercedes a couple of weeks ago. Surprised her with it. A sport's model. Carolyn had always driven bigger cars. This one was taking some time for her to get used to.

"Where do you want to go for lunch?" Carolyn asked Sara, talking across the roof as she fumbled to figure out how to open the car door. She was used to a fob. This one was opened by her fingerprint.

Before Sara could answer, a car pulled into the parking lot at a high rate of speed and came to a stop right behind Carolyn's car.

"Hey!" Carolyn said. "I was just leaving. You're blocking my path."

Two men got out of the car. Wearing ski masks and brandishing guns.

Sara let out a scream. Carolyn tried to, but nothing came out.

"Stay right there," one of them said. One man came to Carolyn's side of the car. The other man went to Sara. He grabbed her arm. She screamed again.

"Shut up!" the one nearest Carolyn said. He pointed the gun right at Carolyn's head. "One more sound out of you, Sara, and I'll blow your mother's brains out."

How does he know Sara's name?

Are these the same men who kidnapped Sara before?

"I know you," Sara said. "I recognize your voice. You're the ones who kidnapped me in Cayman." Sara's words confirmed what Carolyn already suspected.

"You have your money," Carolyn said. "Leave us alone."

"Not enough money," the one man said roughly. "We want more. Turns out your daughter is a gold mine. You tell that husband of yours we want twenty million dollars! If he doesn't pay up, Sara will die!"

"No!" Sara cried out. The man dragged Sara toward the car. Sara was a big girl. An athlete. He couldn't make her go without force.

"Leave my daughter alone!" Carolyn shouted.

The spa was at the front of the building. They were too far away for anyone inside to hear them. Also, the inside was noisy. Music playing. Hair dryers blowing. They couldn't hear them. At least no one came to help them.

"Sara, do you want your mother to die?" the man asked roughly.

Sara's face filled with sheer terror and her eyes glazed over with a frozen stare on her face. Clearly unsure what to do.

"Don't go with him," Carolyn cried.

"I have to Mother," Sara said. "They'll kill you. I'll be alright."

"The girl has more sense than her mother," the man said roughly. "She's right. Pay the money, and we won't hurt her. Twenty million. Tell your husband, we'll be in touch. And no police or the girl dies."

The driver got back in the car that was still running. Sara got in the back seat with the other man. His gun was on her. The terror on Sara's face had turned to a look of resignation. Her face was against the window looking at her mother as they drove away.

Old familiar feelings returned. She was living the nightmare all over again. Carolyn couldn't believe this was happening.

As the men drove away, she started to run after them. Then she had the presence of mind to stop and get in her car.

She started it and sped away after them.

42

Arlington, Virginia

Jamie and Alex sat down for a meal at one of their favorite local restaurants. Earlier than usual. A late lunch or early dinner, depending upon how one looked at it. They'd just finished an intense workout at Luke's MMA gym, and they were both famished. Jamie's body had not fully recovered from her eight-hour MMA fight with Delilah in Cuba, and she never seemed to get enough to eat or drink.

She also never seemed to have enough time with Alex. For the first time in six weeks, they were actually alone together. While Jamie was clinging to the pole being plummeted by hurricane Delilah, all she could think about was Alex. Determined that if she survived it, one of the first things she was going to talk to him about was setting a wedding date.

Turns out it wasn't the first thing. Every time she tried to broach the subject, something came up. The best laid plans were for naught. The entire trip back from Cuba was spent interviewing the girls trying to gain intel on what they knew about their abductors. Once they delivered the girls to their parents in Miami, Alex and Jamie caught a quick flight home.

Upon arrival, Alex was immediately sent on a mission.

When he returned three weeks later, Jamie was already gone to El Salvador.

Some girls there were lured to a photoshoot, promised money and a possible career as a model. When they disappeared, the local authorities had no clue how to find them. Jamie was sent in to find the ring and rescue the missing girls. By chance, Jamie was approached in a local diner and offered the same promises. She pretended to let them dupe her and take her back to where they had enslaved the other girls.

In the still of the night, Jamie and the girls sneaked away. She saved them with only a minor gunfight—if there were such a thing. The best kind of mission. Jamie preferred the gunfight to the hurricane, oddly enough.

Her backside was still sore from the night in Cuba and when she moved the wrong way in the chair from sitting too long, she felt it. So, she changed positions, once again trying to get comfortable. The waitress filled their waters for the fourth or fifth time. Jamie had lost count.

"We have a drinking problem," Jamie quipped when they had summoned the waitress over once again for refills.

She didn't answer but dutifully filled their glasses. This time setting the pitcher on the table.

"Thank you for being so understanding in Cuba about going after Josh," Jamie said to Alex.

"No problem. No man left behind. Like you said. I couldn't leave you in Cuba alone."

"Alone with *him*?" she asked, somewhat jokingly. Was he being chivalrous or jealous? She'd been dying to ask.

"Isn't he married? With kids?" Alex asked.

"Yes. But some guys might still be jealous."

"He's too old for you. And not your type."

"What exactly is my type?"

"Me!"

"Arrogant and full of himself?"

"Exactly. That's your type. Me." He pointed at his chest when he said it. "Besides, unlike you, I'm not the jealous type."

"Let's not go there." Jamie was afraid he'd bring that up. A few months before, Alex had gone off-mission and infiltrated a cyber lab in North Korea. Jamie went to find him. When she learned he had a girl with him, she became beside herself with jealousy. Almost obsessively. Turned out the girl was thirteen-years old. Alex had rescued her from a prison. She hadn't heard the end of it from him.

"I won't go there," Alex said with a laugh. "I think I've milked that for all it's worth. Sooner or later, you'll do something else for me to rag you about. Anyway... about Josh, I trust you. After seeing him, I knew I didn't have anything to worry about."

Just as they were about to leave the rendezvous point in Cuba to go find Josh, he showed up on his motorcycle. No worse for the wear. It took him a while to extract himself from Rico's house, but eventually he sent the two guards to meet their maker.

Jamie couldn't help but laugh at the banter with Alex. This was what she was missing in her life. Quality time with him.

"You don't have anything to worry about anyway," Jamie said. "I love you."

"Back at you," Alex said.

"How romantic! You have such a way with words. You really know how to put a girl in the mood."

"Mood for what?"

"A proposal," she blurted out.

There... she said it. The topic had been broached.

"What kind of a proposal?" he asked.

"Marriage."

"I already proposed to you. In South Korea. You accepted. You're stuck with me."

"I know. I think we should do something about it. You know... get permanently stuck."

"What did you have in mind?"

"Come on, Alex. You're not that slow. Let's get married and make it official."

"Okay. Why now?"

"I feel sorry for you."

"Why do you feel sorry for me?"

"I've made you wait a long time to have sex with me. You've been a very good boy. Patient too."

"You want to marry me out of pity?" his smile was bigger than she had ever seen it. She thought she noticed his cheeks turning red.

"Sure, why not. Everybody has a reason for getting married. That's mine."

"I don't mind waiting. Good things come to those who wait, the saying goes."

"Why wait any longer?"

Alex didn't say anything right away. His eyes narrowed and his lips pursed as he seemed to be deep in thought. "Sounds good to me. When do you want to do it?"

"What do you think?"

"How about tomorrow?"

"That's a little quick for me. I have to prepare. Who's going to do the wedding?"

It actually wasn't that quick. They weren't going to have a big wedding. Alex's parents were killed in a car crash when he was a teenager. Jamie's mother died of cancer when she was seventeen. Her father was an astronaut who she only met once. He's on a one-way mission to the ends of the universe. They had no friends due to the nature of their jobs. A one-day turnaround wedding wasn't that hard to pull off.

"How about Curly?"

"Curly? He can't marry us."

"Yes, he can. Years ago, he went on a mission disguised as a missionary. He liked it so much, when he got back, he sent off for a license through an internet company. He can officially perform weddings."

"I had no idea."

"Ask him. He'll tell you. He's a minister of the gospel." Alex lowered his voice into a rich bass sound as he said it. His attempt at trying to sound like a preacher.

"Not tomorrow, but soon," Jamie said.

"If we don't set a date, we won't do it. Something will come up."

"What could come up to keep us from getting married?"

As she said it, Jamie's phone rang. She almost didn't answer it, but it rang so infrequently, it had to be something urgent.

"Hello," she said.

"Is this Mandy?" The woman sounded distressed.

"You have the wrong number."

"Do you know a Mandy Nobles? This is the number I have for her."

Jamie suddenly remembered her cover ID in Cayman. The voice sounded familiar as well. Before she answered, it came to her. "Mrs. Morgan. This is Mandy. I'm sorry. I didn't recognize you."

"You said I could call you if I needed something."

"Of course. What's going on?"

"Sara has been kidnapped again!"

"What happened?"

"We were coming out of the spa, and two men trapped us in. They were wearing ski masks and had guns. They took Sara."

"You should call the police."

"They said they'd kill Sara if I did."

"How can I help you?"

"I need you to find Sara."

"This is a matter for local law enforcement. I'm not allowed to operate inside the United States."

"It's the same men who kidnapped Sara before. Doesn't that make it the same case?"

"How do you know it's the same men?"

"Sara recognized their voices. And they asked for the same amount of ransom. Twenty million dollars."

"Twenty million dollars!"

Alex looked as startled as Jamie felt.

"That's how much Sean paid to get Sara back."

"Oh, Carolyn! I told you paying a ransom was a bad idea. I thought the kidnappers released her on their own. I had no idea you paid a ransom."

"I told Sean what you said. But he insisted. It worked. We paid the money and they let Sara go. Now they want another twenty million."

"How did you pay the first amount? That's a lot of money."

"Sean took out an insurance policy. It covered up to twenty million dollars. The insurance company has already paid us back."

"Maybe they'll pay a second time. That's the easiest solution."

"I don't know. This time seems different. Sean is really worried."

"I would be too. Even if you pay the twenty again, how do you know they won't keep doing it?"

"That's why I need your help. You said you could find Sara the first time."

"I wouldn't know where to begin."

"I have a partial license plate number. It's a Florida plate with an X on it. I chased the car. They went down Prestonwood to Parker road. I lost them when they got on the Dallas Tollway."

An idea suddenly popped into Jamie's head. "How do you pay tolls in Dallas?" Jamie asked.

"What do you mean?"

"Is it a toll booth or electronically?"

"We have a car tag. We drive through, they take a picture of our license plate and we pay later."

"Hold on just a second."

Jamie put the call on mute. "Can you hack into the video footage on the tollway in Dallas?" she asked Alex.

"Yes, but I would be breaking the law."

Jamie unmuted the phone and began talking again to Carolyn. "What time of day was it?"

"Around four o'clock."

Jamie repeated it for Alex's benefit.

"Which direction were they headed?"

"South."

"They got on at Parker road?"

"Right."

"What color car?"

"White SUV. Ford Escape."

Jamie put her hand over the microphone. "It's a white SUV."

"Great!" Alex said. "There's probably a thousand of them on the Dallas Parkway at four o'clock in the afternoon," he said sarcastically.

Jamie ignored the comment. She knew he'd help her if she pressed the issue.

"Anything else you can tell me about the kidnappers?" Jamie asked Carolyn.

"I have their bank account number. The one we wired the money to the first time."

"Give me that."

Jamie pulled out a pen and wrote down the numbers as she called them out. "Perfect. I'll see what I can do."

"Thank you so much. I can't believe this has happened again."

Carolyn started to sob.

Jamie wasn't sure how to reassure her. The first time, Jamie had promised Carolyn she'd have Sara back to her within forty-eight hours. Everything turned out okay, but not because of Jamie's considerable efforts.

"I'll call you as soon as I know something," Jamie said. "Let me know if Sean hears from the kidnappers."

Jamie hung up the phone.

"The girl from Caymans has been kidnapped again," Jamie explained to Alex.

"I figured as much based on what I heard. Unbelievable."

"She doesn't want to go to the police. Do you think we should try and find her?"

"I don't know, Jamie. Brad would have a fit if he knew we were operating on US soil."

"I can't ask him. He'd never say yes. Can you at least look at the footage and can you do so without anyone knowing you were there?"

"I can try. What am I looking for?"

"A white SUV. Ford Escape. Florida license plate. One of the letters is an X. Headed south on Dallas Tollway. It got on at Parker road. It couldn't get off without the video capturing the license plate. Once you know the plate number, then we can track the car."

Alex took a deep breath and exhaled noticeably.

"Wait a minute," Jamie said. "Never mind. I have something better. Something not illegal."

"I like the sound of that."

Jamie handed him the paper she had written on.

"What's this?"

"They paid a twenty-million-dollar ransom to get Sara back. This is the bank account where the money was wired. Routing number and account number. Find the owner of that account and you find our kidnappers."

"I can do that."

A better plan. Jamie could justify this to Brad. She'd just say that she was following up on a lead from the previous mission.

They finished their meal in what seemed like record time. Talk about a wedding date would have to wait.

***

Back at Alex's condo, he went to his home office, and Jamie went in the living room to devise a plan. Even if Alex did find the men, she had to think about how she could justify going after them.

She could hear Alex furiously typing away on his keyboard. When Alex was in work mode, she knew not to bother him. After three hours, he emerged from the office. She still had no justification for getting involved. Because there wasn't one.

"I found the account," Alex said.

Jamie's heart started beating faster. "What you got?"

She got off the couch and moved over to the kitchen table. He sat down, and she looked over his shoulder.

Alex began. "It's a Cayman account. I know that from the routing number. Two brothers were signers on it. Gil and Federico Orasco. They own the account. Twenty million dollars was wired in. Just like you said. Eighteen million was wired out to another account and one million was withdrawn, and one million sent to a third account."

"Okay. That's good information. How do I find Gil and Freddie?"

"I also looked at the Dallas Tollway footage."

"Oh... Alex. You shouldn't have done that," Jamie said, even though she knew he would.

"Oh well. What's done is done," he said. "I'll spare you the details. Bottom line. The two men own a boat in Florida."

"Sara was taken on a boat."

"The boat is moored in Miami."

"Would they have taken her all the way to Miami?"

"That's the best place to start. I don't think they'd stay in Dallas."

"Do you have an address?"

Alex looked at her incredulously, like 'why would you ask me such a question?'. "Of course," he said. He handed her a piece of paper. "Marina and stall number. You're welcome."

"You *are* amazing! Have I told you that I love you?" Jamie planted a big kiss on his lips.

"Do you want me to trace the money?" he asked, not taking advantage of the kiss. Once Alex was in work mode, she had a hard time getting him out of it. Jamie was often the same way. Getting the two of them on the same page was never easy.

"What's the point?" Jamie said. "We know where the money came from. It came from Sara's father's account. We know the two men who received it. What they did with it afterward doesn't really matter. They were probably just trying to make it untraceable."

"What's your next move?" Alex asked.

"I guess I'm going to Miami."

43

Somewhere North of Dallas, Texas
The next day

Jamie didn't go to Miami. She went to Dallas and found herself in a difficult dilemma.

She was certain Sara was being held by the two kidnappers in a cabin in the woods less than a hundred yards from her location in a remote location north of Dallas. In front of the cabin was a white Ford Escape—Florida license plate XBY 039.

It had been a good move not to go to Miami after all. When Alex discovered the two kidnappers owned a boat in Miami, Jamie's first instinct was to go there immediately. After more consideration, she realized Sara wouldn't be there. How would they transport a young and athletic eighteen-year-old girl twenty hours in an SUV? In Cayman, they managed to get her on a boat by drugging her. Once the drugs wore off, it wasn't hard to hold her captive on a boat in the middle of the sea.

They wouldn't have that same success in this scenario. Jamie assumed they were holding her somewhere in Dallas. Besides, once the ransom demand was met, they wouldn't want to turn around and drive back from Miami with a hostage in the car.

After further digging, Alex found a transaction on one of the men's credit cards. A cabin rental on Lake Ray Roberts, a couple hours north of Dallas in a secluded location. Jamie caught the first flight to Dallas and found the cabin with no trouble at all.

The dilemma was not a moral one. She had no problem storming the cabin, killing the two bad guys, dumping their bodies in the lake, and never losing a second's sleep over it. The two men had broken the two greatest commandments: Love God with all your heart, soul, and mind, and love your neighbor as yourself.

The laws she tried to live by.

But then there were man's laws. The CIA charter established by Congress in 1947 prohibited the CIA from operating on US soil. The agency was designed to investigate and monitor *foreign* threats to the security of the United States. The FBI, Homeland Security, ICE, and a dozen or more other organizations were tasked with domestic threats. The two men inside were US citizens who had rights under the Constitution. Due Process. Unlawful search and seizure. Miranda rights. Privacy. Innocent until proven guilty. Jamie swore an oath to uphold the Constitution.

By just being at the cabin, Jamie was precariously close to violating federal law. No judge or jury would convict Jamie if she went into that cabin to save Sara. In this instance, Brad was her judge and jury. He'd decide if she acted properly. Overseas, nobody cared what laws she broke as long as she didn't get caught and her actions were "righteous." Done for the right reasons. Ultimately, Brad was the one who made that determination. Jamie knew the line and never crossed it. While Brad didn't always agree with her actions for "CYA" reasons, so far, he had never questioned her motives.

He wouldn't now either. A young girl was in trouble. She just had to not cross the line which was a lot more defined in the states than overseas. Technically, if Jamie could prove that Sara's life was in imminent danger, she would be justified going in as a US citizen.

Unless something went wrong.

God forbid, Sara got caught up in the crossfire. For example, Jamie killed the men and some technicality said it was unnecessary force. Manslaughter. Murder even. Obstruction of justice and perjury if she didn't tell all the facts about why she was there to begin with. At this point, she hadn't crossed the line.

The right call for Jamie was to notify the FBI or local law enforcement and let them handle it. She'd already called Roy Jones and tipped him off about the boat. Jones was the FBI agent from Dallas who was at the meeting in Cayman.

He thanked her profusely. They were out of leads. Jamie felt certain they'd find Sara's DNA on the boat. Jones would go through the proper channels. Establish probable cause. Get a search warrant. Search the boat. Build his case against the kidnappers.

Jamie and Alex had no jeopardy when it came to that lead. Alex established it by hacking the kidnappers bank account in the Cayman Islands. Jamie was investigating a kidnapping of an American on foreign soil. She was perfectly within her rights to pursue every lead. Even the lead to the cabin was established through that account. Jamie was still on solid footing.

Her mind kept going back to Alex. He had broken a few laws to get her this far. If she called the FBI, the entire case could be thrown out by a shifty defense lawyer.

How did the FBI know about the cabin? By evidence obtained illegally.

A dilemma.

Then there was Brad. Her mind kept going there. While she would never implicate Alex, it wouldn't be hard for Brad to connect the dots. She had no explanation for how she found the cabin or tracked the car. If she killed the men, that created an entire new set of problems.

She could always claim self-defense. That was her best argument.

The decision was made. She was going in and hoping for the best. Not storm in with guns blazing. She'd walk up to the door and pretend to be a neighbor wanting to borrow a cup of sugar. At that point, she was a US citizen. Perfectly within her rights. She had a concealed carry permit, so she could have the gun on her.

She'd force a confrontation. Texas has a stand-your-ground law. Self-defense was her right as well. Ironically, the stand-your-ground law benefitted the kidnappers in this situation. This was their property. She was the threat.

Complicated.

Probably why Congress prohibited CIA operatives from conducting operations on US soil. Too messy.

Jamie got out of the car and prepared to move.

Then hesitated.

Do the right thing.

After more internal infighting, she took her phone out of her pocket and dialed a number.

"Agent Jones," the man answered.

"Mandy Nobles here. I have another lead for you. Sara's kidnappers are in Dallas. I've tracked them to a location. I'm outside the house now."

She gave him the location.

A sense of relief came over her.

"There's another development you should know about."

"What's that?" Jones said.

"Sara's in the cabin. The same guys kidnapped her again."

Jamie explained about the spa and the Ford Escape. She had promised Carolyn she wouldn't involve the police. Another moral dilemma. Breaking a promise. One she never should've made. The only thing important was to save Sara. And protect her career, if possible.

"The mom should've called us," he said.

"She was afraid. The kidnappers said they'd kill Sara if they didn't pay the ransom."

Jamie explained about the first twenty million dollars and the insurance. Full disclosure. At this point, she was all in on going through the proper channels and letting the chips fall where they may. The only thing she withheld was Alex's involvement. Fortunately, Jones didn't even ask how she knew where the kidnappers were. He seemed happy she was involving him.

"Hang tight. We're on our way."

Jamie knew that Jones didn't need a search warrant with that information. He had reason to believe a girl's life was in danger, so he could go in and be perfectly justified. Use force if necessary. Jamie was off the hook as well. She'd followed procedure. Brad would be happy that she'd contacted Jones. He'd overlook any other minor offenses. A girl's life was saved after all.

Then a blood curdling scream penetrated the otherwise serene setting.

Coming from the cabin.

Jamie sprung into action. Instinctively.

Without any conscious thought.

Within thirty seconds she was at the door of the cabin. She could hear shouting inside.

A girl was crying. Pleading. It had to be Sara.

"You're hurting me," she said.

A window in the cabin was open so she could hear perfectly.

"Your old man refuses to pay the ransom," a man said roughly, confirming what Jamie already knew.

The man's words were filled with rage. Fury.

Jamie heard the sound of an open hand slapped against a cheek. Then the sound of Sara sobbing.

The door was locked. Jamie stepped back. With a swift kick, powered by surging adrenaline, she shattered the lock, loosening it from the jamb. It swung open.

She bolted through the door with her gun drawn. Within seconds she was at the opened door of the bedroom at the back of the house where the sounds had come from. Jamie rounded the corner cautiously, letting them see the gun before they saw her.

Two men were standing in front of a bed that was against the wall. Jamie entered with the gun pointed directly at them. Sara was on the bed, behind them. Holding her cheek that had a red welt on it.

The men didn't appear to be armed, but she couldn't see the back of their pants, where most idiots kept their guns.

'Move away from her," Jamie shouted.

The one man had a sly grin on his face. He was missing a couple of teeth making his smile almost sinister looking.

"I said to move away from the girl," Jamie shouted.

"Stay where you are," the toothless guy said to the other man. Presumably his brother. His hand was to his side. A knife was in it.

Jamie couldn't fire. Sara was behind them. Jamie was a good enough shot that from that close a range, she wouldn't miss. But the bullets were high velocity. She'd seen them go right through a body. They could hit Sara.

Too risky.

The men looked ready for a fight.

"Drop the gun or I'll cut the girl," toothless said.

"Give it up. It's over. The FBI is on its way. We found the boat. In Miami."

His eyes widened in surprise.

"So far, you're just in it for kidnapping. Don't add assault to it. Or worse. Don't make me kill you."

Jamie wanted to pull the trigger so bad, based on the horror they'd put the family through. At the same time, she didn't mind if they spent the rest of their lives in jail.

It needs to be in self-defense.

Righteous.

A knife qualified, but the lines were blurred. Force could only be used as a last resort.

Jamie needed to diffuse the situation. She put the gun in her front pocket. Her pants were specially designed for concealing a weapon. That would make them turn their focus away from Sara and on her.

"You just made a big mistake," toothless said.

Two against one. Not a fair fight at all. For them. Curly always said that Jamie should never lose a fight against two guys. No matter how big, strong, fast, or capable they were. Not if he did his job right and trained her properly.

The angle was wrong, though. The configuration was a triangle. In a two-against-one fight, she needed to get them in line with each other. In a triangle formation, if both attacked at the same time, that made it harder to take them out. Not for her. But in a normal fight.

The bigger consideration was getting them away from the bed. Away from Sara.

Jamie circled to her left. When she did, the second guy was behind the first. In a line. Just like Curly taught her. Now it was one against one. He had a knife. She had superior training and skill.

And the element of surprise.

Before he could blink an eye, Jamie hit him in the midsection with a side kick, sending him sprawling into his brother. All of the man's air came rushing out at once in a loud swoosh.

The brother had a gun!

He must've had it in the back of his pants. Taken it out while he was hidden from her view, behind his brother.

Sara let out a scream.

The brother raised his arm to fire. Jamie reached for her gun. He was slightly ahead of her. She dropped to the floor, rolled, and fired two shots into his chest before he could fire one. He fell to the side. Toothless had recovered enough to raise the knife like he was going to throw it at Jamie.

She put a bullet between his eyes. A pink mist sprayed onto the wall behind him.

Jamie was quickly on the bed to shield Sara's eyes from the carnage.

No need to check the men. They were dead.

The only regret was not being able to question them. Jamie didn't know the whole story.

Who hired them?

Was it El Mata?

Were the Fossey's involved?

Commissioner Hughes had a working theory that Lars Fossey provided them with a boat. Jake Fossey, the son, drugged Sara and took her to the boat. Now she knew the brother's already had a boat. Maybe the Fossey's were innocent after all.

But who drugged Sara at the bar?

Who got her to the boat?

Now. . . they might never know.

44

It took five hours before Jamie and Sara could leave FBI headquarters. Six, including the hour spent at the house waiting for Roy Jones and his men to arrive.

Jamie and Sara were in an interrogation room together. Considering the circumstances, the time spent was pleasant. Jamie was impressed with Sara. Surprisingly resilient, Sara was already feeling better by the time her parents arrived at the building.

Carolyn and Sean were ushered in almost immediately. Carolyn went straight for Sara. As one would expect, they both burst into tears when they saw each other. Sean was stoic, almost in shock. He expressed several times how thankful he was that Jamie killed those men and brought Sara back to them.

"I'm glad they got what they deserved," Sean said.

The parents were allowed to stay in the room until Roy Jones got there to question them.

After a couple hours of fairly light interrogation, Roy Jones said they could leave.

"Hang around for a couple of days," he said to Jamie. "In case we have any more questions."

Jamie wasn't sure what they needed her for, but she had to do what he said. What happened was fairly straightforward. Jamie and Sara both related the events truthfully.

Agent Jones told Jamie a forensic team had gone through the boat. They found blonde hairs and a lot of DNA. They already had Sara's DNA on file from the first kidnapping. He expected them to match. Sara gave him a description of where she was confined in the boat, and it matched the description of the boat in Miami.

The results of the DNA would take a couple of months. No hurry now. The two men were dead. Their secrets went to the grave with them.

"Can we take you to dinner tomorrow night?" Sean asked Jamie in the parking lot as they all prepared to leave.

"Yes!" Sara chimed in. "Please say yes."

"We want to thank you for all you've done for us," Carolyn said.

"It's not necessary. It's my job. I'm glad Sara's safe."

"Please. It's our treat," Sean said. "It's the least we can do."

Jamie reluctantly agreed. She was going to be in town for a couple days anyway. Spending more time with Sara actually appealed to her. While she still didn't like Sean, he was becoming more tolerable.

When she pulled out of the parking lot, Jamie called Brad and filled him in on what happened. Jones had already called him, so he knew about most of it.

All he said was, "I'm glad the girl's okay." She had expected all kinds of pushback and was prepared to defend her actions. The time spent preparing her arguments was not necessary.

Brad was stoic, almost sober about the whole thing, and he certainly didn't offer her any compliments. From her perspective, five girls were rescued. A very successful mission in her eyes. It'd be nice if he just acknowledged it for once.

Alex called while she was on the phone to Brad. She decided to wait until she got to the hotel to call him back. Telling the details a third time didn't appeal to her at that moment. The stress in her neck and shoulders told her she needed to unwind first.

When she arrived at the hotel, Jamie got right in the shower. After a shootout, a hot shower was the only thing that really calmed her nerves. It's like she needed to wash the memory of the event off of her. Like somehow the pink mist had gotten on her and not the wall. After the shower, she'd go to the fitness center and run for a full hour. Even though she had just taken a shower. Sweating got the rest out of her.

Brad thought it was a strange ritual. Curly said that everyone processes getting over a gunfight in different ways. Whatever kept your sanity intact for the next mission was all that mattered.

When she got back to the room, she took another shower. When she got out, she had two messages from Alex. She listened to her voicemails and then called him back.

"How ya doing?" he asked.

"The kidnappers are dead. Sara's safe."

"Awesome! Proud of you."

Since their handlers never paid them compliments, they both tried to be as affirming as possible to each other.

Jamie explained everything to him. The cabin. The scream. Toothless man with the knife. His brother pulled a gun. The gunshots.

"It was a righteous kill," Alex said.

She already knew that, but it felt good hearing him say it. Some operatives beat themselves up about even good kills. Some hated the term "righteous" arguing killing a man was only the lesser of two evils. Necessary kill was what they preferred. Jamie preferred righteous. Meaning it was right. In God's eyes anyway. The most important thing to her. That she could justify what she did to God.

In this instance, she could. The fact that the FBI, Brad, and Alex put their stamp of approval on it was a bonus.

"In your message, you said you had some news," Jamie said to Alex.

"I did some more investigation on the money trail," Alex said.

"Hardly matters now. The men are dead."

Then she rethought that statement. "That's actually a good idea. Maybe the FBI can recover the money for the insurance company."

"Let me finish."

Alex must've found something to be that short with her.

"One million dollars went into an account owned by Lars Fossey."

"The bar owner! I knew he was lying. So that SOB was involved after all. Commissioner Hughes will be glad to hear that."

"Looks like it."

"What about the rest of the money? Where did it go?"

"I'm getting to that. Has anyone ever told you that you're very impatient?"

"You tell me that all the time. Did anyone ever tell you that you take a long time getting to the point?"

Alex didn't respond. Instead, he said, "Finding the money trail was not easy to do. It took me all night."

"Why did you go to all that trouble then?"

"I was bored. It was fun, actually. Are you sitting down?"

"No. I'm standing." She was in front of the mirror combing out her hair.

"Sit down."

"Just tell me what you found."

He told her.

Jamie immediately sat down in stunned disbelief.

***

The Jonathan Club
The next night

The Morgan's were members of an exclusive club on the top floor of a high rise building in the Galleria area of Dallas. Members paid upwards of a hundred thousand dollars a year to be members of the club. Sean explained this to Jamie over dinner.

"Many a business deal has been closed in this room," he said in a bragging way.

"I can imagine," Jamie replied. She was genuinely impressed. The upscale ambience was luxurious. The food was prepared by a five-star Michelin chef who had amassed eight stars over his career. Another fact Sean was quick to point out in a smug way.

Jamie didn't remember ever eating a meal as good as that one.

The conversation was pleasant as well. Sara was the bright light of the evening. Bubbly. As personable as she was pretty. In her own way.

Sean took the liberty of ordering a special dessert. A lemon Whirligig soaked in raspberry sauce. The four of them shared it. The dessert was so rich, they only finished three quarters of it.

"I'm stuffed," Jamie said.

"Me too," Sara replied.

"I'm glad you enjoyed it," Sean said in a tone that signified he was pleased with himself. He obviously enjoyed impressing people with his wealth and prestige.

"Daddy has something for you," Sara said to Jamie out of the blue.

"For me?" Jamie asked. Curious and totally surprised.

Sean pulled an envelope out of his suit jacket and handed it to Jamie.

"What's this?" she asked.

"Open it," Sara said.

Jamie tore the edge and pulled out what was a check.

One million dollars.

The name was blank.

"What's this for?" Jamie asked.

"It's for you," Sara said, excitedly.

"I left the name blank," Sean explained. "I assume Mandy Nobles is not your real name. Being a CIA agent and all. Just fill in your real name and deposit it in your account. It's a cashier's check, so you don't have to worry about it clearing."

Jamie put the check back in the envelope and set it on the table in front of Sean who was sitting right across from her.

Then she said, "I can't accept that."

"It's the reward money," Sean replied. "There was a million-dollar reward offered for Sara's safe return. You deserve it. You brought Sara home to us."

"It was my idea," Sara said. "I want you to have it."

"I was just doing my job. I'm not allowed to accept money. I'd get fired."

"With that kind of money, you'll never have to work again," Sean said.

"I love my job. I don't do it for the money." Jamie took Sara's hand. "Thank you, but there are more girls like Sara out there who need rescuing."

"Give it to charity then," Carolyn blurted out.

Jamie suddenly had an idea.

"There's a charity I work with called *Save The Girls*. It's a Christian organization. They always need donations. They rescue girls all across the world. I'll give it to them if that's okay."

"Do whatever you want with it," Sean replied. "Keep it. Give it to charity."

"I'll give it to *Save The Girls*."

"It's settled then," Sean said as he adjusted the sleeves on his expensive suit.

"I have to go to the bathroom," Sara said, hugging Jamie's neck from behind as she stood.

"I'll go with you," Carolyn said.

When they were out of earshot, Jamie leaned across the table. Sean leaned forward as well.

"I have a question," Jamie said to him in a lowered voice. "How did the kidnappers know that your insurance payout was exactly twenty million dollars?"

Sean sat back in his chair and wiped his lips with his napkin. "Just a coincidence, I guess," he replied.

"At first, that's what I thought. After all, what kind of man would kidnap his own stepdaughter for money?"

"I have no idea what you're talking about."

She noticed a slight tic in one eye as he said it. A sign he was lying.

"Did you know that Sarotte means Sara in France?"

His eyes widened. A sign he was panicking inside.

"Of course, you did," Jamie added.

"What do you want?" Sean asked.

"Tell me about *Sarotte Investment Group*."

"I don't know what you're talking about," Sean said angrily.

"Sarotte Investment Group is a French company. Owned by you. One of dozens of foreign companies you own. How did eighteen million dollars of the ransom end up in a checking account owned by your corporation?"

Sean's jaw clenched. His eyes formed into a steely stare.

"I suggest you leave, right now, before I have you thrown out of here."

Carolyn and Sara walked up right as he said it.

"Sean Morgan. Why are you being rude to Mandy?" Carolyn said sternly.

"Do you want to tell her, Sean, or should I?" Jamie met his stare with her own.

"Tell me what?" Carolyn asked, looking at Jamie then back at Sean. Neither of them took their eyes off the other.

Sean ignored Carolyn. His eyes stayed fixed on Jamie's. If his look were daggers, she'd be dead, ten times over. It reminded her of the way Frankie the Assassin looked at her at the start of their sparring session.

"Sean! What's going on?" Carolyn said, with more urgency.

He obviously wasn't going to tell them.

"I hate to be the one to tell you this," Jamie began. "I'm really sorry. But Sean is the one behind Sara's kidnapping."

"What?" Carolyn said.

Sara let out a loud groan.

"That's ridiculous," Sean said.

"Is it true?" Sara said, as tears welled up in her eyes.

Sean didn't answer.

"Daddy. What's she talking about?"

"Sean?" Carolyn said roughly. "Answer your daughter. Why won't you look at us?"

Still dead silence. He fidgeted in his chair. Leaned back. Then forward. Pulled on his sleeves. Like he was about to bolt the room. Or at least wanted to.

"Oh, my word!" Carolyn said. "Tell me it's not true and I'll believe you."

Sara already knew it was true because she said, "Daddy, how could you? Do you know the hell you put me through?"

"Your life was never in danger," Sean retorted. "The men were given strict instructions not to hurt you."

"Are you kidding me? They had a knife and gun. They held me against my will. They drugged me! Dragged me onto a boat like I was a rag doll. They would've killed Mandy if she hadn't killed them first."

"That wasn't supposed to happen," he replied, in a sociopathic calm. "I'm sorry."

"You're sorry?" Sara blurted. "You think an apology means anything to me? I hate you!"

"You don't understand. You're just a child," Sean said.

People in the restaurant were starting to stare.

"Agent Jones is by the elevators, waiting," Jamie said. "Do you want to go with him voluntarily or do you want him to come into your club and handcuff you in front of all these people and drag you out of here like the dog you really are?"

Sean looked at Carolyn and then at Sara and then back at Jamie.

"Your choice!" Jamie said more roughly.

Sean stood to his feet. "I did it for us," Sean said. "We were going to lose everything. I really am sorry."

Carolyn burst into tears. Surprisingly, Sara had successfully fought hers back.

"I hope you rot in hell," she shouted at her father. "You disgust me!"

Sean stood and walked out of the restaurant. "You're a horrible man!" Sara shouted across the room at him.

Jamie reached out and took Sara's hand. What could she possibly say in a moment like this to make it better? Nothing. So, she kept quiet. Prepared to put her arm around Sara if she collapsed into her.

"I can't believe my Dad would do this to me," Sara said angrily.

Carolyn sat in her chair in stunned belief. Her eyes followed her husband out the door. She was obviously still in shock. In one moment, her whole world had come crashing down on her. Jamie felt bad that they had to find out this way. Really, there was no good way to learn that your husband was a liar and a thief.

"He planned the whole thing," Jamie said. "He paid the Fossey's a million bucks to drug you in the bar. Jake Fossey took you to Rum Point and put you on that boat. The Orasco brothers got a million dollars as well."

"Why did they kidnap me again? Was daddy in on that?" Sara asked.

"I don't think so. The Orasco brothers got greedy. When they learned that Sean kept the other eighteen million, I guess that ticked them off. They didn't think he deserved it, since they did all the work. That's why they were trying to blackmail him for the rest of it. They're dead though. So, I'm just speculating."

"I can't believe it," Carolyn said. "I didn't think my husband was capable of such a thing."

"People will do a lot of things for money."

"Yeah well, no decent father would do that to his daughter," Carolyn retorted.

"I agree with you," Jamie said.

"I'm so embarrassed," she said. "You risked your life to save my daughter, and my own husband was involved. He could've stopped it at any time but didn't. He let you put your life on the line for Sara."

You have no idea, Jamie wanted to say. The thought of hurricane Delilah entered her mind. Instead, she replied soberly, "I'm sorry you had to learn about it this way."

"Don't be. I can't thank you enough."

"The FBI is going to have questions for both of you," Jamie said.

"Why would they want to question us?" Carolyn asked.

"Probably to find out if you knew anything about it."

"I didn't," Carolyn said.

She looked straight at her daughter. "I had no idea. I swear to you."

"I know Mom. You're a victim too."

Jamie couldn't help but admire Sara and her fortitude.

They stood to leave.

"If you don't mind, I'd like to stay here for a few more minutes," Jamie said.

"Stay as long as you want. The bill's already paid. Have a drink if you want."

Jamie stood and gave them each a reassuring hug. When they walked out, Jamie sat down and began eating the rest of the dessert that remained on the table.

Each bite was more satisfying than the one before it especially since Sean had paid for it.

I never liked that father.

45

CIA headquarters
Langley, Virginia

Brad summoned Jamie and Alex to CIA headquarters. Presumably, to be given a mission. They were sitting in his office, waiting for him to get out of another meeting.

"We can't go on a mission," Jamie said to Alex. "We're getting married tomorrow."

"The wedding can be put off," Alex said.

"The mission can be put off!" Jamie retorted. "There's nothing *that* important happening in the world that won't be there a week from now."

"I agree. I was just joking."

She wasn't sure if he was.

"Are you getting cold feet?" Jamie asked.

"My feet are very warm. Hot in fact."

"Good, because if you don't marry me tomorrow, I'll hunt you down and kill you."

Alex put his head back and laughed out loud.

Jamie continued in her most serious tone. "Besides, Curly's already lined up to do the ceremony. He'll kill you if you don't show up just for wasting his time."

"Curly doesn't believe in marriage," Alex replied. "He thinks men are crazy to get tied to a ball and chain for life. Field operatives should not have any romantic ties. According to Curly."

"Yeah. I know all about his views on marriage."

Jamie tried to mimic Curly's voice. "Romantic ties will get you killed. Have all the sex you want. Just don't get married." She smiled at her success in sounding like him. "Curly's a typical man."

"Not all men are like Curly," Alex said defensively. "I agreed to marry you, didn't I?"

Jamie rolled her eyes. "Anyway. Back me up on this. I'm going to tell Brad we can't go. If he tries to make us, I'll threaten to quit."

Fortunately, Brad walked in the door after she had finished that sentence. If he heard her, he didn't let on.

"Let me get right to the point," Brad said as he sat down behind his desk. Jamie prepared her arguments.

"You're both fired!" Brad blurted out.

"What?" Jamie said. The words came out before she had even processed his words in her brain.

"Both of us?" Alex said. "What did I do?"

Jamie glared at Alex then at Brad. In the back of her mind, she had considered the possibility that the meeting was about Dallas and the Sara Morgan kidnapping. A couple weeks had passed, and she thought the subject was never going to be brought up. She thought everyone was satisfied by the outcome.

Brad answered. "For starters. . . going into North Korea without authority."

"I went there because I found Pok. Do I need to remind you that I found the nuclear codes? A couple US cities might not be around today if not for me."

"How about conducting an investigation on US soil," Brad retorted. "Not only is that against the CIA code of conduct in our charter, it's against federal law. You're lucky you aren't getting arrested."

"We found a missing girl," Alex argued. "That should count for something. And why is Jamie getting fired? I did that on my own. She didn't even know about it. Fire me. But she doesn't deserve it."

A sudden warmth filled Jamie's heart overriding the rage building inside of her. Alex was sticking up for her. Another reason why she was so in love with him. Even if they were fired, as long as they had each other, she could find a way to be happy. At the moment, though, she was going to fight for her job with every ounce of her being.

"Thank you, Alex," Jamie said, trying to maintain a softer tone. "But I did know about it. I'm the one who asked Alex to look up the license plate information. If anyone should be fired it should be me. But I don't think either of us deserve it."

Alex looked at her and flashed a smile. As far as Jamie was concerned, they were one ship. They'd both sink together.

"Exactly," Brad said. "You can't conduct operations on US soil. Even if it turns out for the best."

"I gave you four good years of my life," Jamie said, her voice cracking and tears trying to escape her eyes. "I risked my life for this country. Alex and I are two of your best operatives. America will be less safe because of you."

"Save the dramatics. I need both of your badges and guns," Brad said.

Any minute now, Jamie expected MP's to show up at the door and escort them out of the building. The reality hit her like a cement truck. More like a rollover accident with no seat belt around her waist to protect her. She felt like her emotions were about to be ejected from the safety of the car. This CIA building had been her home for all these years. She'd never considered a life apart from it.

And there was nothing she could do about it. Arguing wouldn't do any good. It'd make them look weak. She wasn't weak. This was an injustice, but she wouldn't beg Brad for her job back.

Jamie stood and pulled her gun out of the holster. As she sat it on the table, she pointed it right at Brad. He jumped. Then she slammed her CIA badge on the desk.

Alex did the same thing. Except for pointing his gun at them.

"Been nice knowing you," Jamie said, as she turned to leave. "By the way, you aren't invited to my wedding tomorrow."

He wasn't invited anyway. The only people who were going to be there were Curly, her best friend Emily, and Alex's best man, Luke, the owner of the MMA gym.

"Sit down," Brad said. "I'm not done with you."

"You can't tell me what to do," Jamie said. "You fired me, remember. I don't work for you anymore."

Brad pulled some papers out of his desk. "I need you to sign these."

"What are they?" Alex said, as he took them in his hands and began reading.

"Incorporation papers. Organizational minutes."

"For what?" Jamie asked.

"For your new corporation."

Alex looked up from reading. They were both still standing. "What's the AJAX corporation?" Alex asked.

Jamie snatched the papers from his hand.

"If you'll sit down, I'll explain it to you," Brad said.

They both sat.

"AJAX is a corporation, duly formed in the state of Delaware, that is owned equally by the two of you. AJAX stands for Alex and Jamie. Get it. AX and JA in the middle. Good idea, don't you think?"

Neither of them responded. Alex's jaw was still clenched. He didn't seem in the mood for small talk. Or games.

Neither was Jamie. Brad needed to start making sense, and fast. The gun was still within reach. The thought made Jamie laugh on the inside though she tried to maintain a stern and serious demeanor on the outside.

"Anyway," Brad continued, "you'll conduct your operations out of that corporation."

"Does this mean we're not fired?" Jamie asked, not understanding what he meant.

"You're definitely fired. I meant what I said. The two of you go off the reservation far too often. I can't control you."

They had no comeback.

"I'm tired of wondering what you might do next," Brad continued. "You play hard and fast with the rules, and the end justifies the means for you two. It's only a matter of time before it blows up in your faces. Our faces."

'I don't understand," Alex said. "You're firing us, and you don't want us to conduct operations for you because we are 'too hard to control.'" Alex made two quotation marks in the air with his hands. "Yet you want us to run operations out of a corporation called AJAX."

"You do understand," Brad said.

"Someone, please explain it to me then," Jamie said. "Cause I don't have a clue."

"AJAX is off the books," he said. "It has no ties to the CIA at all. You work independently of us. The CIA is not funding this. Do whatever you want to do. You can operate inside the United States or outside. Go after Pok if you want, Alex. Jamie you can work with *Save The Girls* with no restrictions. I will feed you missions that are top priority for the CIA, but we can't handle or won't handle for whatever reason."

"That sounds good and all," Jamie said, "but if the CIA isn't funding it, where will we get the money? Operations cost dollars, as you know. We've got to travel. We'll need weapons. You made me give you back my gun."

"Do you remember the two billion dollars you stole from Omar Asaf?" Brad said.

Jamie had a mission where she went to Belarus to rescue girls sold into slavery through a mail order bride business owned by Asaf. Through a series of shrewd maneuvers, Jamie and Alex confiscated all the money out of his bank accounts and commandeered his airplane.

"Of course," Jamie said.

"And the airplane," Brad said.

"A bombardier Global 7000," Alex chimed in. "A sweet ride."

Jamie could feel the tension leaving the room.

"What about them?" Jamie asked.

"AJAX owns them now."

"You're giving us two billion dollars!" Jamie said.

"Not exactly," Brad said. "AJAX owns the money and the plane. They're at your disposal. But... you obviously don't need two billion dollars. But you do need working capital. You'll need to rent offices.

Hire employees. Get computers. Desks. Supplies. Those kinds of things. Alex, you need to get Kryptonite back online."

Kryptonite was a software Alex developed to combat cyber terrorism and destroy other networks. A lethal computer virus. The CIA was afraid to use it. Something that frustrated Alex.

"You need to build safeguards to Kryptonite so what happened in North Korea doesn't happen again," Brad said.

"I got you," Alex responded, his head down, deep in thought.

"Omar's money is a problem for us anyway," Brad said. "We have no way of putting it on our books. Same with the plane. As far as the world knows, Asaf just disappeared. They don't know that we have him down in Git-Mo. We'd just as soon keep it that way. The world thinks he's hiding with all his money and his plane. We'd rather not have to explain to Congress how we got the money. Besides, they'd just spend it on one of their programs. You can use it to go after more terrorists."

"How will that work?" Jamie asked.

"You can operate off the interest," Brad said. "Once a year, you'll submit a budget. The council will approve it."

"How much is that a year?" Alex asked.

Jamie could almost see the wheels churning in his eyes. This was right in Alex's wheelhouse.

"Two hundred million dollars a year. That'll be your budget to start with for the foreseeable future. If you need more, we can draw off the two billion. Otherwise, you can keep going for as long as you want."

"We can do a lot of good with that money," Jamie said.

"I know you can. That's why I trust you with it. The idea came to me when you told me about the one million dollars from Sean Morgan. You didn't have to tell me about it."

"It was the right thing to do," Jamie said.

"That's what I mean. I know I can trust the two of you explicitly. You're not in it for the money. You gave the million to *Save The Girls*."

"What's this council you mentioned?" Alex asked. "Who's on it?"

"Need to know basis. Classified information. The council will oversee your actions. Set your parameters. All you need to know is that for the most part, you're on your own. If you get caught, we will disavow any ties to you. If you get thrown into prison in North Korea, don't expect us to come bail you out. No official diplomatic efforts will be used on your behalf."

"Will we have access to any CIA assets? Safe houses. Computer systems. Databases. Face recognition software," Alex asked.

Brad answered. "On a limited basis. As you need them. I can assure you, I'll do everything I can to help you with your missions. We want you to succeed."

"Did you have to be so dramatic with all the 'you're fired' nonsense?" Jamie asked. "You're lucky I didn't pull the trigger when I pointed the gun at you."

"I admit it. I wanted to make you squirm a little. I thought it would be funny," Brad said.

"It wasn't," Jamie said roughly.

"When do we start?" Alex said.

"Right now. I have a mission for you."

"We'll start a week from Monday," Jamie said as she stood from her seat. "I'm getting married tomorrow. Then I'm going on a honeymoon."

Jamie stood and pulled Alex out of his chair and toward the door.

As they were exiting the room, Jamie looked back and said with a grin, "You're still not invited to my wedding."

"Have fun! See you when you get back," Brad said.

Jamie let out a squeal as they practically ran down the hall and out of the building to the start of a whole new adventure.

"That meeting didn't go anything like how I expected it to!" she said.

"Me either," Alex replied.

Jamie felt like the luckiest girl in the world.

A new corporation.

AJAX.

She loved the sound of that.

A marriage.

To the man of her dreams.

She could hardly wait to see what God had in store for them next.

Thank you for purchasing this novel from best-selling author, Terry Toler. As an additional thank you, Terry wants to give you a free gift.

Sign up for:
Updates
New Releases
Announcements
At terrytoler.com

We'll send you a copy of *The Book Club*, a Cliff Hangers mystery, free of charge.

READ MORE BOOKS FROM TERRY TOLER

Jamie Austen Thrillers

Read all the Jamie Austen Thrillers. They must be good.
They've been number one on Amazon in ten different countries.
Click on the link below.

THE JAMIE AUSTEN THRILLERS (12 book series)
Kindle Edition (amazon.com)

https://amzn.to/3vmPUy7

Cliff Hangers Mystery Series

Who wants to read a good mystery? We've got you covered! Read the Cliff Hangers where homicide detective, Cliff Ford, solves crimes in Chicago, with help from his wife Julia. These books have everything Terry Toler is known for. Page turning suspense, a hint of romance, and an ending you won't see coming.

The Cliff Hangers Mystery Series (4 book series)
Kindle Edition (amazon.com)

https://amzn.to/36WX3go

About Terry

Terry Toler is an Amazon international # 1 best-selling and award-winning author. He writes clean fiction with a message and life-changing nonfiction. He's a public speaker, entrepreneur, and has authored more than forty books.

Sign up for his newsletter where you'll get free stuff, exclusive content, and news of releases and promotions. He can be followed at terrytoler.com.

If you like his books, please take a few minutes to leave a review on Amazon. We really appreciate it. It helps draw more readers to his books. Thanks!

Made in the USA
Monee, IL
01 April 2024

56154105R10185